This is what ***supposed to***

Steve stood in the lengthening shadows on the front porch. Through the screen door, he watched Taylor and her boys. Suddenly he felt a sense of isolation like none he'd ever encountered.

Far more than a screen door separated him from this family. Past hurts, imagined and real, rooted him to the wooden slats outside. And while the temperature remained at something just under one hundred degrees, he felt chilled. And alone.

He watched as Taylor shooed the triplets toward the kitchen. Then she walked across the room and opened the screen door. And let out a little shriek when she ran right into him.

"It's only me," he said.

"It's…you." And for a moment Taylor allowed herself to forget that Steve was a Texas Ranger, a man with a badge—and her sons' choice for a father.

Dear Reader,

Any month with a new Nora Roberts book *has* to be special, and this month is *extra* special, because this book is the first of a wonderful new trilogy. *Hidden Star* begins THE STARS OF MITHRA, three stories about strong heroines, wonderful heroes—and three gems destined to bring them together. The adventure begins for Bailey James with the loss of her memory—and the entrance of coolheaded (well, until he sees *her*) private eye Cade Parris into her life. He wants to believe in her—not to mention love her—but what is she doing with a sackful of cash and a diamond the size of a baby's fist?

It's a month for miniseries, with Marilyn Pappano revisiting her popular SOUTHERN KNIGHTS with *Convincing Jamey*, and Alicia Scott continuing MAXIMILLIAN'S CHILDREN with *MacNamara's Woman*. Not to mention the final installment of Beverly Bird's THE WEDDING RING, *Saving Susannah*, and the second book of Marilyn Tracy's ALMOST, TEXAS miniseries, *Almost a Family*.

Finally, welcome Intimate Moments' newest author, Maggie Price. She's part of our WOMEN TO WATCH cross-line promotion, with each line introducing a brand-new author to you. In *Prime Suspect*, Maggie spins an irresistible tale about a by-the-book detective falling for a suspect, a beautiful criminal profiler who just may be in over her head. As an aside, you might like to know that Maggie herself once worked as a crime analyst for the Oklahoma City police department.

So enjoy all these novels—and then be sure to come back next month for more of the best romance reading around, right here in Silhouette Intimate Moments.

Yours,

Senior Editor and Editorial Coordinator

Please address questions and book requests to:
Silhouette Reader Service
U.S.: 3010 Walden Ave., P.O. Box 1325, Buffalo, NY 14269
Canadian: P.O. Box 609, Fort Erie, Ont. L2A 5X3

ALMOST A FAMILY

MARILYN TRACY

Silhouette®
INTIMATE™MOMENTS®

Published by Silhouette Books
America's Publisher of Contemporary Romance

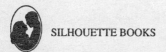 SILHOUETTE BOOKS

ISBN 0-373-07815-3

ALMOST A FAMILY

Books by Marilyn Tracy

Silhouette Intimate Moments

Magic in the Air #311
Blue Ice #362
Echoes of the Garden #387
Too Good To Forget #399
No Place To Run #427
The Fundamental Things Apply #479
Extreme Justice #532
Code Name: Daddy #736
*Almost Perfect #766
*Almost a Family #815

Silhouette Shadows

Sharing the Darkness #34
Memory's Lamp #41
Something Beautiful #51

*Almost, Texas

MARILYN TRACY

lives in Portales, New Mexico, in a ramshackle, turn-of-the-century house with her son, two dogs, three cats and a poltergeist. Between remodeling the house to its original Victorian-cum-Deco state, writing full-time and finishing a forty-foot cement dragon in the back-yard, Marilyn composes full soundtracks to go with each of her novels.

After having lived in both Tel Aviv and Moscow in conjunction with the U.S. State Department, Marilyn enjoys writing about the cultures she's explored and the people she's grown to love. She likes to hear from people who enjoy her books, and always has a pot of coffee on or a glass of wine ready for anyone dropping by, especially if they don't mind chaos and know how to wield a paintbrush.

For Chris

Author Note

Some of the messages posted on Sammie Jo's Mini-mart's bulletin board are curled with age while others appear crisp and new. Unlike most community message boards, a few business cards have been tacked to the one in Almost, Texas, and in many cases the messages don't carry phone numbers but only the author's first name.

Here's a few of the notes to be found on the board:

"Looking for recreational horse for tall man. Must be at least sixteen hands. Call Carolyn and Pete at the ranch."

"One pair of ballet slippers, size seven, needed for upcoming school play. Call Alva Lu."

"Almost Methodist Church Social (canceled last February due to storm) rescheduled for August 20. Sign up below and tell us what you'll be bringing."

"Found: one pair of boy's sneakers. Come by Homer Chalmers's to collect. If you dare."

"Jason, Jonah and Josh are available for two weeks of community service. Call Taylor anytime."

"Missing: One sow hog, answers to Itchy. Call Franklin. Reward of piglet if returned."

"Found, plastic bag containing money. Call Tom Adams, FBI, Lubbock, Texas, (905)555-2121 if you know anything about it."

"Nominations are due for the new officers of the Almost Over-Sixty Club by the end of August. Don't forget to submit your choice and pick up your ballots. Sammie Jo."

"Four mixed collie pups, two males and two females, ready for good homes. Come from Charlie Hampton's cross. Call Doc."

"Need a place to stay while in Almost? Martha Thompson takes boarders. Ask Sammie Jo for directions."

And at the top of the board can be found a faded "Welcome to Almost, Texas" bumper sticker. Beneath those words someone had penned, "Where everyone knows Almost everyone."

Enjoy your stay!

Chapter 1

"You spelled 'killer' wrong."

"Did not."

"Did too. You have *kilker*."

A third voice piped up. "You did! *Kilker*. Ha! That's funny."

"You think it's so funny...you write the letter."

The letter in question was tossed into the air, hung there for a moment as if hesitating, then floated to the West Texas bedroom floor. All three brothers, Jason, Jonah and Joshua, each age eleven and as alike as the proverbial peas in a pod, glared at one another for a good half a minute before abandoning the potential argument in favor of continuing their endeavor.

Jonah picked up the paper, blew on it and handed it back to the original author, Jason. "Read what we got so far," he commanded.

Jason cleared his throat theatrically. "Dear Ranger Steve Kessler—"

"That sounds dorky," Josh interrupted.

"Shut up," Jason and Jonah said simultaneously, causing the three to trade another round of glares.

"Just read it," Josh demanded of Jason.

"Okay. Here goes. 'We're writing this letter to inform you that something bad is happening in Almost.'"

Jonah leaned forward and snatched the letter from Jason's hands. "I didn't agree to this. We shouldn't start with a lie."

"Who says we're lying?" Josh protested. "Something bad's bound to be happening. You know, like somewhere."

"Josh...that's not what I meant."

"I know, but I don't think Texas Ranger Steve Kessler is going to come roaring in here with his flashers going because Aunt Sammie Jo has corns on her toes."

Jason nipped the letter back from Jonah's fingers. "*Anyway...*

It's very dangerous and we can't write about it in this letter in case the wrong people find this and hurt us or something. We're pretty sure there's a *killer* loose. We think you better come down here right away. You can stay at our house while you investigate."

Jonah flopped off the edge of the bed, resting his elbows on the mattress and cupping his chin with his hands. "That's pretty good. But...isn't he going to wonder why we don't just ask Uncle Pete for help?"

"Nah. He only met him once," Josh said. "Besides, Uncle Pete's not with the FBI anymore. He quit, remember? All he does now is teach school."

All three boys fell silent in contemplation of this abject

betrayal on their new uncle's part. Anyone who would rather teach school than be with the FBI had to have a real problem.

"He's still gonna wonder," Jonah said finally.

Jason shook his head. "You worry about everything, I swear. Don't you remember? Texas Ranger Steve Kessler knew Dad."

Josh raised his hand, as if still in school. "I vote we vote."

The other two nodded solemnly.

Josh intoned, "I vote we send this important letter. All in favor say hey." He gave his own shout of affirmation at the same time his brothers did. "The heys have it. We'll mail it this afternoon."

"He's not gonna believe we saw a killer."

"He sure won't if we leave it spelled *kilker!* Cross it out and spell it right this time."

"Think we ought to tell Mom that a Texas Ranger might be staying with us?" Jonah asked to the chorused scorn of his brothers.

"Are you crazy? She'd kill us."

"Yeah, for lying, number one—"

"I told you so—"

"And number two for us saying he could stay here without even asking her first."

"He can have *my* bed."

Jonah looked worried for a moment, his brows drawn into a frown. Then his face cleared. "You know what? I'll bet Texas Ranger Steve Kessler won't even pay attention to this letter." He grinned while his brothers stared at him as if he'd just suggested the sun wouldn't rise in the morning.

Josh scoffed, "After what happened out at Aunt Carolyn's? No way. Drugs and stuff, bad guys, Uncle Pete

beating up Bubba Wannamacher? The police taking him
away? Bubba, I mean, not Uncle Pete.''

Jason added excitedly, ''Yeah, Josh is right. The Texas
Rangers'll come, all right. 'Specially Steve Kessler. He's
the Man! The thing is, we just gotta plant some clues and
junk so he'll have something to investigate once he gets
here.''

''How are we gonna do that around Almost? Everybody
knows *everything* everybody's doing.''

The three boys pondered this minor problem for a few
minutes, all of them staring at the ceiling as if for divine
inspiration. Jason, as usual, was the first to look down.
''Not everything.''

His identical brothers looked at him in question.

Jason shrugged. ''It's like this. Oh, sure, everybody
knows what grades we're making in school and stuff, but
nobody pays attention to *kids*. You know, like, if we're
just playing. That's what kids are supposed to do, right?''
He waved his hand. ''Like, we're just out playing ball,
riding bikes. That's us. Just kids. Hunting lizards, painting
porches. Stuff, just regular stuff. Nobody's going to think
anything about that.''

Jonah and Josh exchanged glances.

''Right? You know I'm right. Nobody's gonna notice
us doing *nothing*.''

Jonah and Josh allowed this to be a strong possibility.

''But what kind of clues are we going to plant?'' Jonah
asked.

For the next fifteen minutes or so, the triplets tossed
around ideas, throwing out the more outrageous sugges-
tions such as leading Steve Kessler to think Aunt Sammie
Jo was really a murderer who had been hiding out in
Almost, Texas, for nearly forty years.

''We don't want to get anybody innocent in trouble,''

Jonah said, still resting his elbows on the bed but sliding his knees apart so that he also sat on the floor. "'Specially like Aunt Sammie Jo. We *like* her."

Josh flipped to his stomach to lie diagonally across his bed. "Besides, Texas Ranger Steve Kessler won't care about old murders. There's some kind of law of limits or something that lets you get off scot-free if they don't catch you right away."

Jason backed him up. "Yeah, I saw that on TV the other night. It's called a statue of limits. It's, like, two months or something."

Jonah, ever the collective conscience of the trio, continued to look doubtful. "But what if—"

"You're the one who wanted to write the letter," Josh interrupted.

"Yeah. This whole thing was all your idea," Jason added.

"It was not," Jonah protested hotly. "We all voted that he would be the perfect dad for us."

"And for Mom."

"Yeah, but a husband to her, not a dad."

All three of them dissolved into giggles. Several minutes of exaggerated gagging noises and stomach clutching passed before they remembered the matter at hand.

Jason said, "But he'll need some clues and stuff. You know, like a mystery."

"Yeah, like a treasure hunt."

"Exactly! That's what Dad said being a cop was like."

This last comment cast a definite pall on their hilarity. All three boys suddenly couldn't look at one another.

Josh said in a small voice, "But in treasure hunts you don't get killed."

No eyes met on that one. Then Jonah brightened. "But

we're not planning for anybody to really get killed. Just for Texas Ranger Steve Kessler to *think* somebody has so he'll come here.''

"Yeah, like, and fall in love with Mom," Josh said.

The three brothers met one another's eyes now. All three nodded as if sealing a vow.

Jonah said, "So how long can falling in love take, anyway?"

"Couple of days," Jason said knowledgeably. When Jonah looked at him skeptically, he shrugged. "I saw it on TV. You did, too. You were there, Mr. Know-Everything-about-Everything. Couple of days, max. All he has to do is kiss Mom one time and, *blowie,* he's gone."

Josh nodded. "Two days tops. Heck, heroes fall in love in an hour on TV. And that's the true kind of stuff. In comic books, all they have to do is look at each other. Besides, Mom's awful pretty."

It was Jason who looked doubtful now. "I dunno. Lindsay Ackerman—"

His brothers fell back as if electrified by the bedspreads of their respective beds. "Not Lindsay Ackerman again!" they yelled in unison. "Lindsay Ackerman says, Lindsay says…"

"Quit it, guys," Jason said.

His brothers fell silent. They were both a little in awe of the fact that Jason, the eldest of the three, was the first to have a real live girlfriend, even if all Jason did with her was talk.

Jonah sat up. "Hey, I know. What about filling up a baggie with some baking soda—"

"And putting it in the shed behind the school?"

"Yeah and we can mix up some fake blood—"

"With our chemistry set, like we did for Mrs. Drexler's class?"

"And we can dribble it outside the shed."

"And we can wear some of Dad's shoes so we can leave big old footprints in the dirt."

"Cool."

"Yeah, way cool."

"I think we should put in the letter that we found a grave or something."

"That's good, Jason. Should we dig one?"

"Sure. All we have to do is leave another clue there."

"I know, a piece of paper that leads him somewhere else."

"On the other side of Mr. Hampton's barn."

"He's not gonna get the letter for a few days. We'll have time to think up other stuff in the meantime."

The three boys looked at one another, grinning broadly. Nothing had been decided but a total agreement had been reached.

"We're really going to do this?" Jonah asked.

"Sure. Why not?" Jason asked back.

"We could get in *big* trouble," Jonah suggested.

Josh shook his head. "As Dad used to say, what's the worst that could happen?"

None of them seemed to want to state the obvious.

Jonah began to outline several possible options, most of which landed them in Boys Ranch. Jason and Josh exchanged long-suffering glances before pouncing on Jonah with war whoops. All three boys dissolved into eleven-year-old giggles, hollering, wrestling and finally rolling off the various beds with considerable clamor.

The bedroom door opened. "All right. Who's being killed?"

* * *

Taylor Leary-Smithton, wise in the ways of eleven-year-old boys, and wiser in the ways of triplets, didn't blink an eye when all three of her sons shrieked with laughter at her question then dived for some papers on Jason's bed and promptly looked as guilty as drug runners caught in the act of accepting a payoff.

Nor did she find it at all unusual when all three boys, with identical expressions of total and wholly unwarranted innocence, asked, "What? We're not doing anything."

She flicked a glance at the hurriedly hidden—and now thoroughly crushed—papers, then studied each of her beautiful, adored and obviously neck-deep-in-something sons.

"Okay, guys, what's going on?"

"Nothing," came the chorused—and utterly expected—answer.

"Mmm-hmm. Right. What's with the papers?"

"What papers?"

Taylor bit the inside of her cheek to keep from smiling. "The papers that Jonah's sitting on and Jason's trying to hide behind his back."

"Homework," Josh offered.

The other two looked so awed by his quick response that Taylor had to fight to withhold an outright chuckle. The fact that school had been out for the summer for some four weeks had apparently escaped their collective attention.

Emboldened by his apparent success, Josh asked, "What's for dinner?"

Jason followed this lead. "Yeah...are we having spaghetti? We *love* your spaghetti."

She glanced at Jonah. He looked decidedly uncomfortable. The worst liar of the three, he was nonetheless a tried-and-true Leary-Smithton. He gave her a sickly, half-hopeful smile. "With garlic bread?"

"Whatever you're up to, it better not be illegal," she said, starting to pull the door shut behind her.

"Us?" came three voices of unrelenting principle.

"You," she replied sternly, pulling the door closed and pausing for a moment to smile broadly before moving down the narrow hallway to the kitchen.

Her not-so-little angels were up to something. She hadn't needed their furtive leaps to cover the papers on the bed to know they were involved in some scheme or another. She'd been aware of something underfoot for at least a week. Covert glances, the legendary mobile Leary eyebrows in full swing—her genetic gift to the trio—and whispered conversations that broke off abruptly the second she walked into a room. But triggering her inner alarm system beyond any of these overt signs had been a seemingly innocuous conversation with her sons not a week before.

"Mom?"

"Yes, Josh?"

"Do you think we're...unruly?"

The use of the unusual word had actually made her stop cooking and turn and stare at one of her three sons. "Do you even know what 'unruly' means?" she'd asked.

A trio of voices answered her.

"Out of control," Jason replied.

Josh added, "Yeah, like we're bad guys."

Jonah, the bridge linking them all, offered, "Like we cause you lots of trouble. Disobedient. Naughty. *Unruly.*"

She hadn't known how to reply for a moment. Of course they were *unruly.* That was the nature of boys. And three of them, all the same age, best friends, ferocious enemies, Learys all three and Smithtons, too, so like their father in temperament, so identical in looks that even she had trouble distinguishing them sometimes, were *unruly* exponentially personified.

"I don't know where you guys came up with that, but I don't think I'm having too much trouble with you." Two years ago she would have said "we" aren't having trouble. She turned to Jonah. "Is this just a new word game?"

"No. We really wanna know."

"Well, I haven't murdered you yet. I suppose that's a good clue that you're all right in my book."

Three young, wholly male faces grinned up at her so guilelessly that she'd frowned down at them. "Is there something I should know about?"

"No," all three had said swiftly. Then they'd touched her, patting her, leaning into her in that instinctively male gesture of reassurance that invariably only serves to alert a female that something underhanded is definitely going on within the household.

And each of her three sons had worn a face of flawless naiveté, an expression she wanted to believe they'd all been born with but suspected had taken years of practice to hone to such incredible perfection.

That's when her alarm bells had begun to ring. And each day since, the timpani had grown a bit stronger, more intense. And add to that the number of times they'd cozened her into making spaghetti. They'd devoured her cheap version of Italian food four times in the past six days. She sighed. At least they always ate well on spaghetti nights, even to the point of polishing off their salads.

What were they up to? And why had her question about somebody being killed caused each of them to look so guilty—and so gleeful?

As she once again fried the ground beef and added the seven spices she normally used for spaghetti sauce, she found she couldn't really bring herself to be overly worried. Whatever they were doing involved writing. That, in and of itself, was practically a miracle. Not for Jonah, maybe, who as self-proclaimed family mediator always tried to make good grades, but for Josh and Jason, anything involving pencil and paper—even if it proved they were drafting the nastiest, filthiest story imaginable—was still a step in the right direction.

She hoped.

As she set the thick noodles the boys loved into boiling water and added a dollop of olive oil, she grinned again, hearing the boys laughing in their large bedroom. In a couple of years their voices would be changing, deepening. But now the high pitches still carried that mischievous angelic quality.

How Doug would have enjoyed this little mystery, she thought.

Normally, thinking about Doug made her feel a little sad, more than a little wistful. Often it made her cry. Tonight, his missing out on the boys' shenanigans made her mildly angry with him. He'd promised he'd be there for her. For *them.* Promised he'd never leave. Promised that having triplets would never prove a trial. *"After all, babe, there's two of us, and for most of the time they'll be with us, we'll be bigger than they are."*

But no, Doug had to go and get himself killed.

And wasn't that the most unfair and horrible thought? However true.

"Boys!" she called, shoving her unaccustomed peevishness to the back of her mind. "Soup's on. Wash up and come set the table!"

A stampeding herd of antelope would have been quieter

than her three boys making a halfhearted pass through the bathroom, then pelting down the hallway to skid into place. Since they were followed by three dogs of varying sizes, three equally curious cats and at least a half ton of West Texas dust, it was several minutes before she felt able to set the food on the table.

"Josh, will you say grace tonight?"

All three of her cherubs folded their hands and thoughtfully bowed their just dampened and combed heads.

Josh flicked a glance at his two brothers, then lowered his eyes piously while clearing his throat. "Grace," he said.

All three boys dissolved into giggles.

Steve Kessler assumed a frown.

Doris Ledbetter, head secretary and administrative assistant in the high-rise Texas Ranger offices in Houston, Texas, stuck her head through the narrow opening leading into his office.

Despite his furrowed brow and upraised hand, she grinned and pushed his door open wider.

"No way," he said before she could speak. "I'm not doing another McUnbelievable the Crime Armadillo deal at some elementary school."

Doris chuckled and crossed the carpeted floor to his desk. "You love it and you know it."

The fact that she was right and he did enjoy the Kids versus Crime gig didn't loosen his frown one iota. It was a game the two of them played: he supposedly hated anything to do with kids, families and anticrime programs, and she purportedly believed otherwise and teased him about it.

"Don't even think you're going to hand me that stack

of callbacks,'' he grumbled, waving a large hand at the sheaf of pink papers in her left hand.

In one hand, she held a collection of phone messages, in the other she carried a single sheet of inexpertly folded notebook paper.

"You've had twenty-three calls in one afternoon," she said, waving the pink papers.

"It's love-a-crime-creature month," he said sourly, but reached for the messages anyway.

She held them back. "Whatever you want to call it," Doris said, "it's working. Admit it, Steve."

"Not a chance. You're telling me that's why I went through Ranger training...so I could pal around with an oversize armadillo?"

He managed to grab the callbacks from her hand and started sifting through them. Patently ignoring her.

Doris chuckled. "You can't pretend I'm not here. Your mama raised you too well."

Steve looked up, trying not to grin.

Doris held the single letter to her chest.

Steve thought Doris was a fine-looking woman. And she was decent, to boot. Nice, even. And she knew about cops. That was important. Very important. She combined just enough cynicism with motherly fussing to keep her team of Rangers in line.

Steve knew he was her favorite and tried never to abuse the position, even if it meant suffering through one of her matchmaking dinners. Since she'd long ago decided that he didn't know what he wanted in a woman—citing his two failed marriages as a surefire indicator of a man who was into commitment just not very hot at selection—she went out of her way to introduce him to a wide variety.

His mother, had she still been alive, would have wholeheartedly approved of Doris's matchmaking. When she died, Steve had found all his baby things still carefully packed away for "someday."

Tom Adams, one of his college roommates and frequent visitor to the Houston Texas Ranger offices, constantly teased him about Doris's dinner nights. Tom, who probably knew him better than any man on the face of the earth, often warned him against asking any of the women out a second time. "Beneath that hard exterior of yours is a heart of pure butter. I'm not telling you that you shouldn't trust a woman, Steve. I'm saying you should trust yourself. Your instincts can spot a criminal at three hundred yards...but you'd put all your money on the wrong woman every time. It's a knack, pal. And you've got it honed to a science."

Tom was right. Deep in Steve's heart he was still childishly convinced that every single human being—the criminal and the law-abiding citizen, the sadist and the victim—possessed a special quality, a unique trait that could make them rise to a form of glory.

Maybe that's why he'd fallen for his former wives. Maybe that's why he still felt something for them, despite his depleted checkbook, his empty condo and a pervasive echo of recriminations, accusations and tears. And maybe that's why he still bought into Doris's matchmaking dinners...because some bruised and battered part of him persisted in believing love, some bizarre fantasy notion of true love, remained possible.

But he knew better now than to gaze into a pair of beautiful eyes and take the quantum leap into a future. Any future.

Doris called him her gullible cynic. "You're the kind of man who falls for a woman in the blink of an eye, and then you blame yourself when they're so clumsy that they fall off the pedestal you made for them."

Doris said now, "And so you won't see anything of them."

"What?" Steve asked. Remarkable as she was, he didn't think Doris possessed psychic abilities.

"The kids who want you to call back," she said, looking down at the thick stack of messages slipping from his fingers.

"Oh. Those."

Doris chuckled then waved the paper she'd held to her chest. "I think you ought to read this letter."

"Why bother? I can dictate it verbatim." Steve hazarded a guess. "'Thanks for coming to talk to our school. What kind of weird animal was that with you?'"

"Not even close," Doris said, dropping it on his desk. "Really, Steve," she said. "It's sweet. It's cute. *And* it's from Almost."

"Where?" he asked, leaning forward and taking the paper by the upper right-hand corner.

Almost, Texas, home of an ongoing drug investigation, home to survivors of a once booming town. And home to Taylor Smithton, widow of Doug Smithton, an old college friend, a fellow law officer, a man who symbolized the great potentials and the terrible pitfalls in life.

"Just a kid—or kids, plural—trying to get your attention, I'd say. But then again, there might be something to it."

Steve scarcely noticed the moment Doris left the room and softly closed the door behind her; his entire being focused on the letter in his hands.

He read it once, then again, and finally, he sighed and tossed the grammatically imperfect and atrociously spelled letter to his desk.

He tried not to hope that some clue to wrapping up a partially unresolved case might come from this letter.

What would kids know about an international drug-running operation? Still, the first real breakthrough to the case had happened in Almost just this past spring.

But he didn't think the answer lay between the lines of this particular missive. These three kids, Jason, Jonah and Joshua Leary-Smithton, claimed a killer—the word had been reprinted after the writer had crossed out "kilker"—was on the loose in their little town.

He didn't believe their story for a single second and probably would have tossed the letter into the wastebasket but for two reasons: one, the kids were writing from Almost, and strange things had been happening in Almost; and two, they claimed to be the sons of a fallen peace officer, his and Tom's old college roommate, Doug Smithton.

While being from Almost and the sons of a fallen officer—a man with whom he'd once shared a thousand pizzas and stood on the stoop outside the dormitory at the break of dawn, staring into the sunrise because staying up all night together would somehow grant their wishes—didn't automatically mean they were trustworthy, it did mean that he couldn't simply discount their unbelievable tale. And it meant that he must, at least, acknowledge their jumbled warning.

Doug's *kids*. He recalled Doug sauntering into his and Tom's dorm room that first afternoon. *"You'd better like beer and Motown."*

A simple letter should do the trick. A phone call to their mother would do it even faster.

Back in those long-ago days of college life, Steve had seen a photograph of the boys' mother on Doug's nightstand. She hadn't been a mother then. In the photo on the nightstand, in the albums, in the yearbooks, she'd been a pretty girl, a homecoming queen to a class of fifteen. Nice. The girl next door.

Steve stared out the window of his high-rise office, not really seeing Houston's clean, city skyline, picturing instead the dusty, dry Texas Panhandle and the even dustier and drier section of land surrounding the little town of Almost.

He'd been there for a couple of days earlier this spring. It had rained only a few days before his official "visit," ending a five-year drought, and the entire countryside, the grasses still brown and the terrain as flat as the proverbial pancake, had been mired in thick, red clay mud.

The black earth, reportedly the hallmark of West Texas farmland, hadn't been apparent anywhere near Almost. There, the entire terrain appeared tinted with rust. And two days later, the Almost mud had dried to a rough, crusty red surface that curled in shapes that resembled fancy Christmas cookies and shattered beneath his boots as easily as if it had been exactly that.

And he'd been there a year before that. As a pallbearer. That time he'd been in the little town of Almost to see his college buddy to his final rest. Until he met Doug, he hadn't even known what Motown was and had never tasted a beer.

And though he'd felt that he already knew her, he'd met Taylor Leary-Smithton for the first time at Doug's funeral. He'd recognized her the first moment he saw her across a crowded, frost-encrusted funeral home lawn. He'd have known her anywhere from Doug's photographs.

On that cold afternoon, a day that tormented him still, Steve had felt he knew Doug's wife better than anyone else present. He'd heard about her daily for four long years, had joked with her on the phone and had plotted birthday gifts and Christmas presents for her.

He knew her, and yet when he'd stood beside her that dreadful day, he'd simply taken her cold hand into his for a brief second and kissed her reddened cheek before escorting her into the small mortuary chapel. And he'd stood at attention, a white-gloved salute pressing against his forehead as she had placed a farewell rose on her husband's coffin.

"Steve?" she'd asked, looking up at him through a veil of unshed tears. *"Doug's Steve?"*

When the FBI had conscripted him into a case involving Almost last Spring, he hadn't hesitated. He'd marginally assisted in the roundup of some local drug smugglers at that time.

And he'd seen Doug's wife—Doug's *widow*—from a distance. On that occasion, he hadn't spoken to her and knew she'd never seen him; he was merely another undercover agent. And she hadn't seemed to recognize him. He'd been conscious of a profound relief that in the aftermath of the arrest she hadn't picked him out of the crowd at her sister-in-law's home, because he hadn't known what to say to Doug's widow.

And talking to her about Doug had been right up there on his top-ten list of least-favorite things to do.

Surely a simple phone call about her sons' letter would be sufficient. Ask the kids about their so-called town troubles, ask the mom what her sons were up to, chat for a minute, express the department's concern for their general welfare, then hang up.

Duty would be done, goodwill would be felt all around. He'd be the good guy, the man in the white hat. And she'd never know how he'd memorized every nuance of her face, every line of her body. He even reached for the phone, then realized, typical of their father, the authors of the letter had only included a return address, no telephone number. He depressed a button on his state-of-the-art desk phone and asked Doris to find the Almost number for him.

"Wouldn't you rather have the whole number?" she asked saucily.

Steve didn't bother replying. Doris played this game with half the towns in Texas, most of the more amusingly named ones seemingly located in the heart of the Panhandle. Happy, Shallowater, Levelland, Turnaround, Sorrow, Dimmit—which, according to local lore, had one letter substituted for another vowel—Farsee, Whiteface, Purty, Simple, Throughway and Needmore... The list went on and on. Between Almost and Happy, Texas, it was a tossup for the more bizarrely named institutions. The Happy Courthouse, the Almost Volunteer Fire Department. The Happy Baptist Church, the Almost Methodist. The Happy Police Department, the Almost Public School.

Strangely, it seemed Happy, just outside of Canyon, Texas, was exactly what the name implied: a happy little community. By the same token, Almost was a town that didn't seem quite together. The place had some six hundred people or so, but because county lines crossed right through the center of town, the community was rumored to have no cohesive municipal government.

And even though Steve's roots were embedded in the dry, flat Panhandle of Texas, the type of people living in the tiny towns that dotted that achingly poor stretch of ground scared him to death. Tom had told him years before, back when Doug had still been alive, "Stay away from West Texas, Steve. People out there need people, and you're a give-people-what-they-need sort of guy. You'd be fried in a week."

And Tom was right. Again. So, despite his roots, Steve

held to the conviction that he was better suited to the broad avenues and skyscrapers of the big city any day and should leave the smell of the farm and ranch to those who could appreciate it.

Steve smiled, remembering how Doug had described his hometown. It had sounded just like his own. Steve had been raised out on a farm near Pep, Texas, a town of less than thirty-five people. Almost was practically a metropolis by comparison.

But that laid-back atmosphere wasn't his cup of tea anymore. Give him an interesting and lively nightlife, an active sports life and a safety-laden triple-action job. He'd probably die of boredom in an Almost solitary afternoon.

Doris buzzed him back. "I've got the number for you and tried it. There's no answer."

And, Steve thought wryly, no answering machine. What would a person need with a message machine in a town where hollering out the front door would let everyone within five blocks know exactly what you were up to?

"I think you should just go out there," Doris drawled.

"Oh, you do," Steve said, wishing he didn't agree.

"Yes. Your pornography-ring case has slowed down," Doris said. "Besides, it's the 'what if' principle."

The "what if" principle was the informal rule applying to hunches, gut instincts, crank phone calls and letters. What if the caller or writer was onto something? What if there was some element of reality in a nutcase's bizarre reporting?

Steve grimaced at the intercom but said, "All right. Book me a flight to Lubbock."

"Today?"

He flicked open his Day-Timer. He had nothing he couldn't reschedule for the next few days. He thought about Doug Smithton's widow, the mother of his three would-be informants. And he thought about Doug. And he thought about all the long nights he'd spent sleeping in the same room with Doug, envying him, jealous of him, wishing the blue-eyed girl in the photographs gazed at him with the same love she evidenced for Doug.

He said, "Might as well make it today. And arrange a rental car on the other end. And, Doris? Make sure I have a return flight tomorrow."

"What if there's really something to their story?"

"Right. Kilkers on the loose in Almost, Texas. I'm shaking in my boots."

But he was.

Chapter 2

Without the slightest idea that step one of their plan had worked to perfection, Joshua, Jason and Jonah decided the afternoon would be well spent inspecting their various faked evidences of a crime committed in their community.

Their first stop was the shed behind the Almost Public School. The baggies they'd carefully loaded with baking soda were still intact and just visible in the tall brown weeds flanking the back of the shed.

"Good thing we left the dogs at home," Jonah said.

"Yeah, they'd probably eat all our clues!"

They each had a dog, all of them mutts and all named after an animal the canine seemed least like. Jonah's dog, Elephant, was a champagne-colored terrier-Chihuahua cross that liked to crawl on his master's lap and growl at the cats that tormented him. Jason's mutt, a huge collie-Saint Bernard cross called Shrew, would have escorted burglars into the house—had there been any. And Josh's dog, Wolverine—nicknamed Wolfie—was frightened of his own shadow, even after three years of Leary-Smithton camaraderie.

"When Texas Ranger Steve Kessler comes, we'll have to leave the dogs at home. They'd give everything away."

"Too bad all this isn't true. Our dogs would find the killer real fast."

The boys considered their pets' respective strengths. They knew from long experience that comparisons led to arguments and had tacitly agreed they all possessed superior animals.

After a rambling, circuitous route through town, stopping to pitch a few balls with some school friends and swapping the time of day with Mrs. Sanders—who always managed to have fresh baked cookies on a hot summer afternoon when all the other grandmothers in town didn't like to turn on their ovens—and spending at least twenty minutes staring at Lindsay Ackerman's empty front yard, they found themselves at the very edge of town with only a half-grown, uncrowned sorghum field to cross and Mr. Hampton's barn in clear sight.

"What if the fake blood we made didn't turn rusty brown like it was supposed to?" Jonah asked.

"That's what we're checking out, doofus," Jason responded.

"But what'll we do if it didn't?"

Josh shrugged for Jason. "Make some redder stuff, I guess."

"We better get sticks," Jason said, searching around for a likely weapon.

"Yeah. Snakes."

Jonah shuddered. "Ee-yuck." He looked about for a stick and didn't see one. He picked up a likely rock.

"We'll have to use a piece of bamboo from the side of Mr. Hampton's house," Josh suggested.

"There's even more snakes around bamboo. Mom said."

"We'll stay outside the thicket and just pull out three dried old ones."

They approached Mr. Hampton's house with the insouciance of three children who knew everyone in town and had always had complete access to any part of the town they chose. They picked out three perfectly straight, dried bamboo shoots from the large clump against Mr. Hampton's front porch.

"Maybe we should ask—"

"Nah. Remember? He told us he wished we'd take the whole blamed bunch of it right out at the roots."

"Oh, yeah."

"'Sides, we're only taking the dead ones."

Mr. Hampton stepped out the front door and slowly crossed the porch. The boys knew him to be in his late seventies, but he stood straight and tall, and from his position above them on the well-tended porch, the septuagenarian seemed to be eight feet tall and nearly as broad across the shoulders. His shadow was thick enough to shade all three boys from the sun.

"You young'uns want to watch out for snakes."

They backed up five paces before telling him that's what they needed the bamboo for.

"Get you some tough ones," Mr. Hampton recommended. "Slap the ground with them to make sure they won't break on you."

The boys rushed forward, grabbed at dried stalks and leapt back again.

Jonah tested his stick—it didn't break but made a perfect thwacking sound—then asked, "You mind if we cross your sorghum field, Mr. Hampton?"

He earned a quick nudge from Jason and a half glare from Josh.

"You ain't up to mischief, are you, boys?"

"No, sir," said all three in chorus.

All eight feet of Mr. Hampton seemed to shake for a moment. "Long as you don't whack the sorghum with those sticks of yourn, I don't have anything bad to say about it. I'm testing it out instead of maize this year. You knew about that, of course. And mind you stay out of the barn. There's some rotten boards in the loft. I'd hate to have to come fetch you outta there. You hear me?"

The three of them, already running across Mr. Hampton's yard and heading for the sorghum field, ran backward for a while, calling out promises to do as he said. Within seconds they were hip-deep in the stunted-looking cornless cornfield, heading straight for the barn.

"I didn't know Mr. Hampton's barn had a loft," Jason said.

"I didn't, either," Jonah said.

"Way cool," Josh said.

The brothers looked at one another, then, as one, let out a whoop and took off in a sprint down the neat rows of sorghum.

Taylor dried her hands on a tea towel as she elbowed open the screen door leading to her front porch. The screen was so dust-covered and bent from three boys' seeming refusal to use the wood slats protecting the mesh that she couldn't make out much more than that the man standing on her porch was tall.

When she saw him without the dusty filter of the screen door, she checked in the act of asking if she could help him. His eyes were the brownest, warmest eyes she'd ever seen. Framed by thick black eyelashes, those eyes seemed to speak all by themselves. His brown hair, neatly combed back from an off-center part, waved slightly and looked soft to the touch. And the quiet, somewhat understated Western-cut gray suit he wore didn't hide the breadth of his shoulders or the tapered line at his waist. He held a well-crafted straw cowboy hat against his thigh, though his hair didn't have a crease.

Taylor wondered if she was taking all this in just because he was a stranger in Almost, or whether there was some special magic about him that would make all women feel as if they had to memorize him before he got away. If he was selling something, she felt fairly certain most women would buy whatever that might be.

When he smiled, she realized she'd been standing in her half-open doorway simply gawking at him the way a thirteen-year-old at a first sock hop might stare at a real dance partner.

"Taylor Smithton?" he asked, his expression inscrutable.

Surprisingly his voice didn't detract from his attractiveness. She didn't know why, but something in the rich, accented tones reminded her of chocolate.

Because she'd been born and bred in Almost—as they said in reverse in those parts of the country—she found it strange to be called by her husband's last name of Smithton. In Almost, she was a Leary-Smithton, but still considered mostly a Leary.

"Yes. What can I do for you?"

Something about him seemed familiar, as if she should have known him. The feeling was exacerbated by a fleeting look of disappointment that flitted across his face. But he introduced himself and held up a small card case he'd apparently slipped into his right hand before even knocking on her door.

She looked at it and saw the name Steve Kessler. And though she was aware that she'd heard the name somewhere before, it was the badge that held her attention, the badge proclaiming him a Texas Ranger.

Something had happened to the boys. For a moment, her heart seemed to stop beating. She thought she heard a faint whisper of sound from somewhere far away and realized it was only his hat brushing against his trouser leg. If something had happened to her sons, she couldn't possibly be hearing mundane sounds, could she?

Bad things had happened in Almost in the spring. But that couldn't be what brought a Texas Ranger to her door in the middle of summer. She tried reading his expression, gazed into his brown eyes, hoping to understand his reason for knocking on her door.

"It's about your sons…" he started to say.

What had happened to them? A sudden rush of pure fear-inspired adrenaline coursed through her veins, forcing her heart to resume beating or burst. A memory of the day Doug was killed collided with a hitherto undetected, prescient knowledge that something terrible had happened to her children.

"Not again," she said, unaware she was even speaking.

She let the screen door fall back into place and swiftly shut the main door on this harbinger of bad news. Whatever he had to tell her could wait. Forever.

If she didn't hear it, it wouldn't be true.

Steve stared at the closed door for several seconds, thoroughly nonplussed. He looked down at his open badge to see if someone had switched his ID in some bizarre joke, as if Doris might have made up a card reading Steve Kessler, Murderer. But no, the wording was familiar and correct.

However, he'd witnessed the color draining from Taylor Smithton's lovely face. For a second or two he'd thought she would pitch right to the porch in a faint, her tea towel still draped in one hand. But she'd slammed the front door on him instead.

Maybe there really was something going on in Almost. Few people slammed doors on Texas Rangers.

He hesitated, then slipped his badge back into his inside breast pocket before knocking on her door a second time. "Mrs. Smithton?" he called out.

He received no answer but somehow he felt aware of her standing just inside the door. Maybe even leaning back against it.

He started to knock again when he understood. *Not again,* she'd said. And somehow he knew exactly what she meant. He hadn't caught it from any heightened awareness of her or from a psychic connection or any mysterious source. He just suddenly and sadly remembered she was a widow of a cop killed in the line of duty.

On a sunny day, some two years earlier, two uniformed officers, state troopers most likely, must have come to her door to tell her the news that her husband was down. Whoever came that day must have flashed a badge at her after confirming her identity.

She must believe he'd come to tell her something horrible about her sons.

He cursed himself for not just introducing himself and putting her at her ease before shoving the badge in her face. He should have thought it through first, not acted out of a strange nervousness at seeing her again. She didn't know him from the man in the moon; it was only natural she'd leap to the wrong conclusion. Before he could think of something to shout that would reassure her through her closed door, she opened it.

"I'm sorry," she said. "I—"

"It's okay," he said quickly, cutting her explanation off. "I'm not here—"

"It's not the boys, is it?"

It was, but not in the way she thought. "As far as I know, they're fine," he said, meeting her gaze directly. "Honestly."

She closed her eyes for a brief, timeless moment. She sagged against the doorjamb, then after uttering a whispered oath—or prayer—she pushed herself erect and opened her eyes again. She smiled at him, albeit tremulously. "I'm not really crazy," she said. "And I really haven't forgotten who you are either. You were at Doug's funeral, weren't you? His college roommate?"

Surprising him—again—she pushed the screen door open, this time inviting him inside.

As he stepped past her into the cool air of her darkened living room, he thought of the contrasts between city and country people. In the city, a smart woman would never invite a man into her home just on a glimpse of a badge; too many women had been lured into feelings of safety because they'd thought the man they were dealing with was associated with law enforcement. This woman didn't even lock her door. But then, she'd said she remembered him.

Then she closed that same door behind him.

The living room drapes were pulled against the afternoon sun. The floor was hardwood and sported a large, well-used carpet in a shade of either dark green or blue. The matching sofa and love seat were also dark and were marginally lightened by swirls of a contrasting color. Her walls were covered in soothing sea prints and bursts of wildflower stills. The effect was that of standing at the bottom of the sea.

She stepped around him and pulled the cord at the side of the floor-to-ceiling drapes, flooding the room with light. Now, instead of the bottom of the sea, he felt the room exuded the essence of cool, garden-fresh, dappled summer.

Like the woman herself, he thought irrelevantly.

Taylor Leary-Smithton's eyes were blue, the same color as the sky on a July afternoon and as warm and alluring. She'd pulled her thick blond hair back from her neck in a simple ponytail, strengthening the impression of summer heat and of refreshing afternoon breezes.

Naturally, she was older than she'd been in the photographs, but with the years had come a poise, a graceful self-confidence. If anything, she was more beautiful now than she'd been all those years ago. And she'd been remarkable then.

"I'm not usually such an idiot," she said, and smiled again.

The smile took Steve's breath away. A smile in a photograph, that of a young girl on the threshold of life, didn't begin to convey what a full-grown, living, breathing woman could achieve.

"Won't you sit down?" She waved a slender hand at the sofa. "Can I get you something? Iced tea and lemonade are both made." She stepped toward a broad hallway that presumably led to her kitchen.

"No, that's all right," he said, not moving to the sofa. He knew the sooner he got out of here, the better it would be for him. Everything about her, from her beautiful face to her obvious nervousness, set alarms jangling through him. She seemed exactly the kind of woman mothers wanted their sons to bring home, the kind of woman fathers would brag about their sons finding. Doris would have invited her to dinner on one look.

Her pretty eyes widened as he reached into his breast pocket for the letter her boys had written him.

"I came because of this," he said, withdrawing the bizarre correspondence and handing it to her.

He maintained a neutral expression as she took the letter from his hands, and he watched closely as she frowned and carefully unfolded the torn notebook paper. He noted the moment her eyes flickered, then dropped to the triple signatures. And he caught the hint of a sigh as she raised her gaze back to the beginning of the letter.

When she'd finished reading it through for the second time, she looked up at him. "I don't know what to say."

He wanted to smile, to get her to smile, too, but instead he only nodded. "Then this is just a prank?" It was a simple matter of self-preservation for him to hold her at arm's length, to remain the formal officer.

But he rather liked the way her back stiffened a little and her chin lifted. Her lips compressed slightly.

"A bid for attention, maybe?" he asked, and hated himself when she flinched.

"I don't know their reasons for writing you this," she said coolly. He had the fleeting thought that the boys were lucky to have a mom like this on their side. She wasn't giving anything away that might get them deeper in trouble.

"Maybe they could tell me?" he asked.

"They're certainly the only ones who could," she said, her voice dipping into the arctic zone. Not only would she not get them deeper in trouble, but he felt sorry for anyone who might try.

He smiled then, knowing it was time for a grin, hoping it didn't look as practiced as it felt. "Are they home?"

She shook her head, her blue eyes twin ice cubes. "They're out playing."

He couldn't help the glance out the front window at the empty yard.

"In town somewhere," she elaborated, her stance colder than either her voice or her eyes.

Again he was struck by the differences between small town and city living. In a city, a mother generally knew within a park bench or two exactly where her children were; it was a matter of survival. In a small town, kids could roam anywhere with relative impunity.

"Do you think you could call them?" he asked politely. "While seemingly a harmless enough prank, it really could have serious consequences. False reports and alarms can carry felony charges. I'd like to hear the explanation for *that* from them." He held his hand out for the letter.

It seemed to Steve that she looked down at his hand as if he'd shoved it inside a sewer pipe before holding it out to her. She glanced from his broad palm to her sons' epistle with an expression defying classification. She placed the letter in his fingers as if it burned her own.

Without saying another word, she turned her back on him and again opened the front door before stepping outside. He grinned as she called out for her sons in a voice strong enough to stop a train at full running speed.

His mother had called him to supper in just such a voice, tone clear and filled with motherly love. *Stee-eve. Steve Kessler.* He was suddenly taken straight through time to his childhood. Easier times, lazier times. Hot sunny days hung before him like a mirage, memories of romping through lawns that needed mowing and hedges that needed trimming.

Taylor stepped inside and Steve noted that she seemed far too fragile to have such a big voice. Too delicate to have three eleven-year-old boys. Triplets. Involuntarily he glanced at her slender waist, then, as he realized his solecism, jerked his eyes back to her face.

"If they're too far away to have heard me," she said, "someone will spread the word that I'm looking for them." She flipped the tea towel over her shoulder and let it rest there against her cotton blouse. Her legs were slightly parted and she dug her fingers into her jeans pockets. The stance seemed slightly confrontational.

Steve smiled, though he wasn't quite sure at what.

"Would you care for that tea or lemonade now? You could have a wait."

His grin broadened and he was relieved to see one side of her full lips curve upward. "Sounds good." At her look of inquiry, he added, "Lemonade."

It was her turn to look relieved, and he understood she was glad to have something to do to fill the time until her boys showed up.

Completely ignoring Western etiquette, he followed her down the hallway to her kitchen. But Taylor didn't seem to notice or object.

The kitchen felt much larger than it actually was due to its creamy sand-colored walls and equally pale tiled countertops.

The cabinets were all open-faced, with no doors hiding foodstuffs or dishes. A jar of peanut butter was nestled between a crystal goblet and a bottle of soy sauce. A tidy row of antique jars filled with assorted ingredients interrupted a jumble of *Star Wars* action figures.

Steve had a feeling of "what you see is what you get" that both intrigued and disturbed him. He was used to women who masked their private lives. Hell, for all he knew, some of the women he didn't-quite-date didn't even have kitchens, let alone kitchens where everything showed right up front.

He found himself wondering what her bedroom looked like.

"Here you go," she said.

Like her kitchen, her frosty smile didn't hide anything.

The boys raced the last fifteen yards to the Hampton barn, arguing loudly about who actually won. After some discussion and mapping out of footprints, two of the brothers acclaimed Jonah the winner by a shoelace.

Giggling and good-naturedly roughhousing one another, they rounded the Hampton barn at quarter speed and ran into each other in their abrupt halts.

Everything was exactly as they had left it four days before—footprints, fake blood on the walls—but for one glaring difference: a dead guy lay in the dust.

Jonah smashed into Jason, who slammed into Josh. None of them breathed for a long moment, then Jason whispered a swear word.

And the dead guy moaned.

All three boys jumped at least a foot in the air and yiped a little.

The not-quite-dead guy turned his head in their direction. His mouth moved and a trickle of blood snaked down onto his chin.

"Holy moly," Josh breathed.

"Sh. He's trying to talk or something."

"I—I think w-we should go get some h-help," Jonah stammered, turning his body as if to leave. But his feet stayed where they were and his gaze remained riveted on the dying man.

"Cold," the man rasped, then coughed a ghastly chortle.

"He's cold," Jason translated.

"Shut up! He's still talking."

"Cold."

"See...I told you! He's cold. He must be in shock or something. We heard about that in school, remember?"

"Shut up! Listen!"

"Cold...dray...horse."

"What did he say?"

"He said 'cold dray horse.'"

"What's a dray horse?"

"What does that mean?"

"How should I know?"

"I don't see a horse."

The dying man issued a gurgling moan and stared at them fixedly. Hungrily. He stretched out a long, pale hand. All three boys backed up a full step without even being conscious of it.

The man seemed to wave his hand at the barn, and all three boys turned wide, terrified eyes in that direction.

"Cold..."

Their eyes jerked back to the man.

"Cold..."

"Here we go again," Jason muttered, then giggled in a fear-induced hysteria.

"Shut up, Jason," Jonah and Josh both whispered, then Josh asked in a falsetto that would have embarrassed him dreadfully, had he been aware of it, "Are you okay, mister?"

"'Course he ain't okay, doofus. He's bleeding. Like he's been shot or something."

Then the man waved his arm at the sun and they saw what had been hidden moments before: a bloody hole roughly the size of a quarter just above the pocket on the man's shiny shirt. The guy looked as if someone had thrown about a gallon of water at him, darkening the left side of his shirt and sport jacket, but the boys instinctively knew it was blood that created that effect.

"Yeah, he's bleeding, all right."

"You think we should go get Mr. Hampton?"

"M-Mom. I—I think we should get Mom."

Just then the man jerked all his limbs at once and let loose a horrible rattling moan before plopping back onto the ground with a thud hard enough to raise a small cloud of dust. A fly buzzed around his head for a moment and landed on his bloodied chin.

"Gross."

"Is he dead?"

"I dunno. I'm not going to touch him."

"Me, either."

"What do we do?"

The man on the ground moaned then, making the three brothers jump. Jonah let out a squeak, and as if that were a spell breaker, all of them yelled out loud in unison and seemed to turn in a midair leap. They raced back across the sorghum field, all screaming "Mom!" at the top of their lungs.

Steve waited as Taylor hung up the telephone and turned back to her unexpected guest with a frown. "That was Mr. Hampton. He said the boys just ran past his place hell-bent for leather and screaming bloody murder."

Since, in Steve's opinion, all eleven-year-olds made far too much noise, he didn't speculate aloud as to possible reasons for their screaming.

"That's not really like them, you know," she said.

Beyond a letter written with poor grammar and worse spelling, and probably packed with enough lies to fill the Grand Canyon, he didn't feel qualified to comment on what they might be like.

As if reading his mind, she gave him a look that seemed to say, Don't judge a book by its cover. The simple severity of her expression made him chuckle and raise his hands in mock surrender.

He lowered his hands slowly as he watched the obvious struggle on her face. God, but she was a fine-looking woman.

"I'm not saying I'm condoning what they did," she said, looking away from him. "At the same time..."

"At the same time?"

She gave him a quick, nearly anguished—or perhaps it was embarrassed—glance. "I don't know. You see, part of what they said in the letter was true."

"About Doug?"

She nodded, then said with a tinge of what might have been resentment, "You're right up there with Spider-Man and the Power Rangers."

He nodded, too aware of her, too conscious that his coming personally was precisely what he *shouldn't* have done. This woman was just made for a pedestal.

She nodded again, as though he'd said something, then shot him another glance, this one unreadable. "They had a really hard time after Doug was killed."

Steve again didn't say anything. He couldn't. He was cursing himself for not trusting his first instinct and just pitching the letter in the trash can. Or his second instinct and merely calling her on the phone. This was Doug's wife—widow—he was talking to, and Doug's sons they were talking about.

"It's only been in the last few months that they've seemed to get some of their zip back."

He thought of the implications in their letter—murder and mayhem in their hometown—and tried to fit "zip" into that concept. He remembered some of Doug's wilder pranks in college and hid a grin.

Before he could say anything, the dogs outside in the backyard started a cacophony of barking that would have drowned out an orchestra tuning up. There seemed to be at least twenty of the animals all barking and howling at once. And over that boisterous clamor came the sound of three boys yelling their lungs out.

"Mom! Mom!"

Steve followed as Taylor rushed down the hallway to the living room. He stopped just behind her when the front door crashed open and three identical eleven-year-olds burst into the room.

He'd known they were triplets. He'd seen them at Doug's funeral, and this spring, but seeing them now, flushed from the outdoors, smelling of summer dust and sorghum, he was struck utterly speechless at the incredible likenesses.

They all seemed slightly tall for their age—though Steve wasn't any expert. They all sported Taylor's blond hair and blue eyes, though he could easily see Doug's determined chin and wide mouth. And each of their faces was bright red from exertion and shiny with sweat. Each was gasping desperately for breath. And all of them had wide-eyed expressions of terror on their young faces.

"What on earth—" Taylor began.

All three boys spoke at once.

"D-dead guy…"

"Nearly dead…"

"Dying anyway…"

"Mr. Ham—Hampton's barn…"

"C-cold dray horse…"

"Fly on his chin."

"Shot. Blood everywhere."

"Not everywhere. Just on him."

"Yeah, just on him."

"But probably in the dirt, too."

"Yeah, in the dirt."

Taylor held up her hand. "Whoa. Calm down. One at a time."

Steve frowned a little, noting that they hadn't so much as looked his way. If this game was staged for his benefit, they were some actors, these kids. He decided to remain silent awhile longer.

One of the boys bent over and planted his hands on his knees. He dragged at the air like a fish out of water. Taylor went over and dropped her apparently ever present tea towel on the back of his neck. "Don't try so hard, Jonah. Just relax, honey. Breathe shallowly. Slowly. Okay?"

He did as she suggested. "Better?" she asked after a few seconds.

"Y-yeah."

The other two boys had waited patiently and somewhat indifferently at their brother's seeming attack. It was obviously an oft-repeated scenario. When it was equally obvious that their brother was going to be all right, one of them spoke up. "Really, Mom. Honest. You gotta believe us. There's a nearly dead guy out behind Mr. Hampton's barn."

"He's not dead yet. But I'll betcha a billion dollars he's gonna be."

"Yeah. We s-saw him."

"Yeah, and like, he was mumbling and bleeding from his mouth, and then he jerked like this—" one of the boys dropped to the floor, demonstrated the man's apparent death throes, then scrambled to his feet "—and then he didn't move anymore."

"Did you touch him?" Taylor asked. Steve thought her

question had the "you don't know where it's been" in-
tonation and almost laughed aloud.

"Ee-yuck. No way."

The brother who had apparently suffered an asthma attack spied Steve and straightened slowly, suspicion all
over his face.

Steve stepped out of the shadowed hallway into the
light. He expected the boys to recognize him immediately.
After all, they'd written specifically to him, apparently
having been subjected to his McUnbelievable the Crime
Armadillo routine on video. But he *hadn't* anticipated the
boy who spied him to nudge his brothers, and what appeared to be profound relief seemed to cross each of the
three faces staring up at him.

"Wow!"

"How did you know?"

They looked at one another in awe.

"Now everything will be okay."

"Yeah, Texas Ranger Steve Kessler's here."

"Shut up, doofus. He'll think you're a dork."

"*He'll* know what to do about a nearly dead guy."

"Like, *he* sees dead guys all the time."

One of the identical trio spoke to him at last. "The
nearly dead guy is out behind Mr. Hampton's barn."

"Yeah, with flies on him."

"Yeah. Like, he's real gross."

"He's wearing a gold watch."

Steve raised his eyes to meet Taylor's. Her expression
was a combination of defiance and apprehension. She
seemed to have the same uncertainties about this particular story as he did, and that troubled him. She knew her
sons, and if she had doubts...

"Why don't we go have a look?" he asked slowly,

cautiously, not wanting to voice his disbelief outright. Or at least not right away.

"I'm not looking at that guy again. No way."

"No way, José!"

"Too scary."

With the feeling he was walking right into a setup, Steve nonetheless suggested they direct him to the Hampton barn.

"I can do that," Taylor said, her voice devoid of expression.

"Let's go then," Steve said.

"You're not going to leave us here?" one of the triplets asked in a near panicked voice.

"I thought you didn't want to go," Taylor said dryly.

"Not to see the dying guy again, but I'm not going to stay here. What if the killer's around somewhere?"

"Yeah. Somebody shot that guy. What if he followed us home?"

"Holy moly. He might know where we live!"

All three boys pushed a little closer to their mother.

Steve had the feeling he'd stepped in quicksand. "Okay. We'll all go." He raised a hand as the boys all began to talk at once. "And *I'll* have a look at this supposed 'dying guy.'"

The relief on three faces did nothing to soothe him. And the trusting look on Taylor's face only exacerbated his sense of impending doom.

"Don't lock the door," Taylor said, stopping him in the act. "I think we lost the key a couple of years ago."

Steve released the handle, aware the "gullible cynic" was in deep, deep trouble.

Chapter 3

By the time the boys had argued about which one of them got to sit in the window seats of his rental car, how many times the man had said, "Cold dray horse," and who saw the man first, Steve felt prepared to sign an affidavit that he was being had. If they hadn't been Doug's kids, and their mother Doug's widow, he would have acknowledged a good prank, read them a stern lecture and headed back for Houston.

Taylor slid into the passenger's seat in the front and pulled the door behind her without appearing the slightest bit perturbed by her boys' arguments. Beyond an admonition to fasten their seat belts, she looked as if they were embarking on a Sunday afternoon picnic rather than going on a search for a "nearly dead guy."

Though the rental car was a moderate luxury model with a broad, curved dash and seats set far enough apart for a large man to feel comfortable, Steve nonetheless felt confined. He dimly understood the sensation had nothing to do with the size of the car; it was his proximity to Taylor Smithton. As if they really were on that Sunday picnic, her aura of calm good humor seemed to radiate out from her, enveloping all of them in the car, including one Texas Ranger who invariably fell for the wrong women.

"Wow. We're really riding in a car with Texas Ranger Steve Kessler," one of the triplets said.

"Way cool!"

"Aren't you going to put your portable lights on the roof?"

"It's a rental," Steve said.

"Darn."

"Josh..." Taylor murmured warningly.

"Sorry."

Steve admired her equanimity and wished he could steal a measure of it. An hour in the company of these boys would have him joining in their arguments, coming up with wild, improbable schemes, plotting some new mystery as if he were one of them. They had the same incredible magnetism Doug had possessed, and Steve knew himself to be a sucker for a good story.

Of all times to rely on his cynical side, this was the one. He didn't want to explore the reasons why he felt simultaneously ill at ease and completely comfortable around Doug's family; they were many and varied and, at the moment, all vaguely threatening.

Taylor turned her head and her eyebrows lifted slightly. He realized he'd been sitting in the driver's seat, his hand halfway to the ignition, doing nothing more than staring at her.

"Something wrong?" she asked, her contralto voice sending a shiver down his spine.

"What? No. Nothing," he said, lying through his teeth.

She was pretty enough to turn any man's head, and he'd always fancied himself every inch a man, but there was something about her that made him want to know more about her, just listen to her talk.

And that kind of thinking was dangerous. Passion was one thing. Even friendship. But Taylor's fresh-apple-pie smile and just-picked-peaches voice made him acutely uncomfortable. She was too real, too down-home. And he'd been down that aisle a couple of times already.

And even as he turned the engine of the rental, he understood why she made him nervous. She seemed the exact opposite of the women he'd married. As beautiful as they'd been, but in a different way. A quieter, deeper way. And something about that quieter, deeper way made him acutely conscious of how long it had been since he'd been with a family, with a woman.

What was it Doris always said? *Good thinking, Steve. You can't get burned if you're out of the kitchen.*

And Taylor Smithton was the epitome of "kitchen."

"You just go straight and take a left at the big green house on the edge of town," Taylor said softly, West Texas blurring her words, the accent somehow making them a near caress.

Her sons added their instructions.

"The road curves right before Mr. Hampton's place."

"You'll see a gigantic clump of bamboo."

"Yeah, we use that for swords and stuff."

"Mr. Hampton said we could," one added, as if Steve had questioned their right to play with the bamboo.

"Should we have called you from his house, Mom?"

"You did fine, Jonah," Taylor said without turning around to see which of her three sons had asked the question. Steve supposed that in a generation or two he might be able to distinguish the difference between their voices. Not that he'd be there to find out, of course.

"Texas Ranger Steve Kessler?" one of them asked.

"Yes?" he asked back, hiding a grin at the combination of job description and name. And yet, strangely, he found himself straightening his shoulders.

"Who do you suppose the guy is?"

"You've never seen him before?" Steve asked, before he could wonder why he was going along with their gag.

Three chorused negatives came from the back seat, then one of them added, "He didn't look like anybody around here. He had fancy clothes on."

"Yeah, like out of a movie or something."

"And he had funny fingernails."

"Funny fingernails?" Steve asked. He again suffered that feeling of being in quicksand. This was a little more detail than a kid's misguided game should allow.

"They were all shiny. Like he painted them or something. Aunt Carolyn sometimes puts clear gunk on hers, you know, to make them sparkle."

"She's our uncle Craig's wife."

"Widow. But she's married to Uncle Pete now."

"Not sparkle, exactly, but to look *shiny*."

"She's from Dallas," one added, as if that explained her strange behavior.

"It looked real goofy on a guy."

"And his shoes were pointy-toed—"

"But they weren't cowboy boots. They looked like Uncle Cactus's lizard skins. But made into shoes."

"This is where you turn," Taylor said quietly, pointing to the weather-beaten green house on the left-hand side of the highway cutting through Almost. The Hampton place appeared to be the last house in the small town.

Steve signaled and guided the car onto a deeply rutted,

clay-and-gravel dirt road, which forked some thirty yards from the highway. The right fork led to the green house, where an elderly man leaned against the thick pillars of the front porch. The man lifted a hand and Steve returned the courtesy.

"If you stay to the left, you'll go around the back of Mr. Hampton's house and on to the barn. Otherwise you'll have to go all the way around the maize."

"It's sorghum, Mom. Remember?"

"Mr. Hampton's trying sorghum instead of maize."

It was obvious to Steve that the Mr. Hampton in question wanted them to stop and explain why they were on his property. But on the very, very slender chance that the boys were telling anything remotely like the truth, he decided they'd better check the barn before exchanging pleasantries.

It seemed Taylor understood his thinking without his needing to explain anything, for she waved at Mr. Hampton, pointed to the left fork of the road and held her thumb up in question. The older man nodded and waved his hand at the barn.

As Steve took the left bend, he saw the older man carefully step down from his porch and walk slowly to the edge of the house. He shaded his eyes and followed their progress around the back of his home and down the narrow, one-car dirt road leading to the large barn, stained a dark gray by weather and age.

Whether it was because someone else seemed to be taking the boys seriously, or because the boys had fallen preternaturally silent, Steve suddenly didn't want to guide this family around the final bend leading to the barn. He was unexpectedly, inexplicably convinced the boys were telling the truth.

* * *

Taylor's nerves were tightened to a painful jangle. She was inordinately grateful Steve Kessler had shown up that afternoon, of all days. She was aware that he held doubts about her sons' story and didn't blame him. She, on the other hand, was wholly convinced of her sons' encounter with the dying man. Her conviction had come the moment her boys had burst in the front door screaming for her as if they were five again, not eleven.

She'd seen what she knew the Texas Ranger hadn't. Her boys were flushed from exertion and heat, but their lips had been pinched and lined with telltale white, a sure indication of shock.

And once they were in the Texas Ranger's car, she'd been aware of the precise moment the boys had crossed the precipice between hysteric babbling and stunned, frightened silence. They had been talking forty miles to the minute until Steve had turned the car onto the Hampton place. They hadn't made a sound since, except for Jonah's slightly labored breathing. She slipped a hand into her pocket to make sure she'd remembered the ever ready, if seldom used, inhaler. It was there.

She knew without a single doubt that her sons weren't lying about finding a man behind Mr. Hampton's barn. And they weren't lying about his being shot or nearly dead. They'd been raised in West Texas in a small farming and ranching community. They'd seen animals shot and killed.

Before Doug had been shot, they'd been taught the rudiments of gun handling and like most West Texas kids, had gone quail hunting many a time. They'd also been hunting with their Uncle Cactus Jack. Her sons knew what a bullet wound looked like. And if that wasn't enough to convince her, she knew they watched enough television to permanently imprint the knowledge on their brains.

While there might be gaps in her comprehension of what was going on, she knew her sons. She'd known they'd been up to something—well pointed out in the bizarre letter to Steve Kessler—but she was also aware that whatever their motives had been for the letter, whatever their plotting and scheming had hoped to accomplish, her sons hadn't counted on seeing a wounded man out behind Mr. Hampton's barn on this particular afternoon. Taylor would swear to that by everything she held dear.

The Hampton barn was laid out, like many barns in the Panhandle area of West Texas, on what her father had called "annigoglin" lines, or catercorner to the remainder of the usually squared property. The reasons for this unusual diagonal were as varied as winds in the spring, but the most sound suggested that during tornado season— late summer to midautumn—a catercorner barn withstood a tornadic onslaught much better than one presenting a flat side to the high-velocity winds.

To Taylor, the fact that the barn was annigoglin meant only one thing: they couldn't see the very back of the barn from either the main road or the barn road, or from their present location.

"Stop!" Jason yelled.

As if his foot were linked to Jason's voice, Steve stomped on the brake pedal, causing the car to slide a bit in the dust. "What?" he all but yelled.

"H-he's just around the corner of the barn. In the *back* back."

"It's okay, Jason," Taylor said gently, translating for Steve. "Officer Kessler won't make you look at the man again."

On the edge of her peripheral vision she saw Steve's

frown of irritation shift to enlightenment and then to a somewhat rueful expression.

"You guys wait here," he said, putting the car in Park and opening the door.

"Aren't you going to get out your gun?"

"Yeah. What if the guy who shot him is still around?"

Steve reached a hand inside his suit jacket and withdrew his Smith & Wesson .9mm. He couldn't hide his grin this time when all three boys' eyes widened at the awesome weapon.

"Way cool," one of them said.

Before Steve softly shut the door, he heard Taylor say, in her calm contralto, "I'll have your hides for dinner if this is some kind of joke."

He approached the barn with caution, on the very far-off chance that the boys were telling some version of the truth. He hesitated at the corner of the barn, resting his shoulder against the side and glancing back at the car filled with the Smithton family.

Taylor was leaning forward slightly, her eyes on him. She still appeared calm and collected, but something instinctively told him she was anything but. He'd been observed going into a potentially dangerous situation before by bystanders, by fellow officers. But Taylor's regard made him feel different somehow, not heroic necessarily, but taller maybe, or perhaps stronger.

He dragged his gaze from her face, telling himself he was being an idiot.

He studied the dusty ground beyond his safe corner. Because it was midafternoon and the sun hung in the west, his body cast no shadow on this northeastern side of the barn. Nor would a shadow be cast by anyone hiding just around the edge.

Steve drew a deep breath and gripped the gun with both

hands up and slightly to the right of his face. He swung his body around the corner and lowered the gun simultaneously.

And aimed directly at a half-grown sorghum field.

Taylor's breath caught in her throat as Steve Kessler held up his .9mm and then disappeared around the corner of the barn. She didn't realize she'd cocked her head the better to hear the thunderous report of a gun until she heard her own whispered "Don't, don't..."

She wasn't afraid that Steve might shoot someone; she was afraid he would be shot. And killed. The way Doug had been taken from her.

This notion made her frown. Doug had been her husband. Her partner of more than fourteen years. She couldn't lump Steve Kessler and Doug into the same equation. She'd known the Ranger less than an hour.

She told herself the connection was simply that Steve and Doug were both in law enforcement. Peace officers putting themselves on the line for the protection of others. And perhaps because it was her children who had drawn him to Almost, she'd found another, less tenuous correlation between the two men.

She didn't want to consider the more obvious reason she might have inadvertently linked the two men in her mind, the real reason her heart beat a little too rapidly and her hands trembled slightly. From the moment she'd pushed the dust-laden screen door open to see him better, she'd felt as if every nerve ending in her body were shouting an awareness of him to her brain.

And he knew Doug, a voice in her mind whispered. They were connected because of that knowledge.

"He's been gone an awful long time," Jason said.

"Only a couple of minutes or so," Taylor replied.

"What if something happened to him?"

"Yeah, what if the bad guy who shot that dude was lying in wait for him?"

"I don't think that happened," Taylor said, never taking her eyes from the corner of the barn. "Steve Kessler looks pretty capable."

"Yeah, but whoever shot that guy is *capable* of murder. Like killing somebody."

Taylor didn't admit it out loud, but inwardly she acknowledged her son's point.

"Maybe we should go check it out," Josh suggested, fumbling with the door handle.

"Maybe we should just stay exactly where we are. Just like Texas Ranger Steve Kessler told us to do," Taylor said, pointedly looking at her son's grubby hand around the door handle. She waited until he withdrew it before turning her gaze back to the barn.

Another tense minute passed before Steve came back around the edge of the old structure. His gun was out of sight and his expression was grim. He strode to the car with the air of a man barely keeping his temper in check.

He didn't go for the driver's door, reaching instead for the back door. He all but wrenched it open, glaring down at her sons.

"Okay, what kind of game are you three playing?"

The boys stared up at him in seeming shock, then Josh said, "We're not playing any game!"

"No?"

"No way!" Jason said earnestly.

"Was the guy dead?" Jonah asked.

"Let's cut the crap, shall we?" Kessler snapped. "Why don't you tell me what's really going on?"

He held up his left hand for them to see. His fingertips were covered with what seemed to Taylor to be rust.

"What's this?" Steve asked her boys.

To Taylor's horror, her sons exchanged guilty looks, then stared at the floor of the car. She'd been ready to swear in court that her boys were telling the truth. Studying them now, taking in their triplicate expressions of "busted cold," she wanted to throttle them.

"That's what I thought," Steve said. "You guys want to come clean?"

Then Taylor saw a tear snaking down Jonah's cheek.

Whatever they'd done, why ever they might have done it, *she* should be the one to dole out the punishment, the embarrassment. Some tinhorn cop from the big city, old college roommate of Doug's or not, wasn't going to put her sons through anything. They'd been through enough pain and anguish for an army of delinquents.

"What's on your fingers?" she asked Steve coldly.

Steve flicked her a hard glance. "Something from a fifty-dollar chemistry set," he said.

She resisted the urge to flick an equally hard glance in the direction of her errant sons. Instead, she raised her eyes to meet Steve's. "If you knew that, why did you ask?"

His features seemed to melt slightly as his expression shifted from anger to surprise. "What?"

"If they've done something wrong, tell me. I'll take care of it. There's no need to berate them."

"I wasn't berating them—"

"No. You were swearing at them and asking questions you already knew the answers to."

"Swearing? I wasn't—"

She didn't wait for whatever he'd been about to say. She opened the car door and exited his rental as if it were repellent to her. She was relatively certain her inner trembling didn't show as she marched across the expanse of ground leading to the barn. She didn't pause at the corner to raise a weapon, but rounded it with the full intention of discovering whatever he had.

At first she couldn't see anything that might make a grown man angry at three children, cop or not. Then she realized it was precisely what she couldn't see that might have tipped him over the edge. Despite her sons' nearly hysterical account of a man dying back there, no dead or wounded man lay sprawled in the dust. No shiny fingernails, no pointy-toed shoes, no bullet hole in a fancily clothed chest.

"We were telling the truth, Mom!" Jason pleaded.

She hadn't realized her sons had followed her.

"Honest, Mr. Kessler," Jonah asserted.

Taylor wondered if Steve knew he'd been demoted, and risked a glance at him. He was leaning against the edge of the barn near the narrow tack-room door. His expression was anything but inviting. He didn't say anything but looked pointedly at several rust-colored marks halfway up the doorjamb.

Taylor knew her entire family followed his gaze and could tell that at least three Smithtons knew what the stains meant. Jonah, the boys' conscience, nearly tripped over himself as he lunged forward with an explanation.

"We did that. W-we know it was wrong. But we had to get you here. But we didn't know there would be a real nearly dead guy."

Jason, unwilling to let his "younger" brother suffer any consequences alone, stepped into the fray. "You were right. We used our chemistry set to make the fake blood, but we weren't faking about the guy we saw. And his blood was *real!*"

Josh pushed through his brothers. "Yeah, like, there was a guy *dying* right here!" He pointed at the ground.

"He said, 'Cold dray horse,' and then he gagged or something and blood came out of his mouth."

"And a fly landed on him."

"You gotta believe us!"

"Why is that, exactly?" Steve asked, as if they were only having a mildly interesting conversation.

"Well...'cause it's *true!*"

"Yeah. It's a *fact!*"

Taylor literally felt the impact of Steve's gaze when he lifted his eyes to hers. "Do you mind if I ask a few questions now?" he asked her, his sarcasm making her long to swipe his arrogant smirk right from his face.

Whatever he saw in her face was nearly as effective as a slap might have been. His grin faded abruptly and he nodded as if he understood.

He pulled a handkerchief from his pocket and carefully wiped the "blood" from his fingers before looking at the boys again. He folded the handkerchief back to its original square and slid it into his trouser pocket. He then withdrew the letter that had brought him to Almost.

"Which of you would like to explain this?" he asked, holding out the letter.

Taylor watched as her sons exchanged questioning looks. Jason the Brave cleared his throat. "We didn't mean to cause any trouble or anything. We just wanted to get you to Almost."

"And why is that?" Steve asked.

The boys, in unison, looked from Steve to their mom.

Taylor, suddenly and with absolute conviction, didn't want to hear their answer.

"We saw you on TV," Josh said irrelevantly. "At school."

"And?" Steve prompted.

"We really did see a guy dying right here," Jason interjected.

"Let's save old Shiny Fingernails for a minute. I'm still trying to figure out this letter."

"Well, see…"

"It was like this…"

"We were thinking that maybe…"

To Taylor's wonder, Steve Kessler swiftly caught his lower lip between his teeth as if capturing a grin about to get away.

"You were thinking that maybe…?" Steve prompted.

It was Jonah who took a huge gulp of air and let out the whole truth in a breathless whoosh. "We thought that maybe if you came to Almost, you'd see our mom, like, she's real pretty and cool and everything, and you'd like her—"

"And, like, you'd fall in love with her—"

"And you'd marry her—"

"And you'd be our new dad."

Chapter 4

Taylor knew if the ground opened up at her feet she would sink gratefully into oblivion. She fleetingly wished the days of women swooning weren't lost to the past. It would be wonderful to wake up hours later asking where she was. The one thing she *wouldn't* ask was what happened.

Her sons, blood of her blood, flesh of her own, dismissed their duplicity with youthful abandon. Jason pushed past her numb body and pointed at the scuffed ground some three yards from her.

"This is right where the guy was. Right here!"

Jonah followed him and also pointed down. "See? You can tell where he was."

Josh ran to the edge of the sorghum field and slapped a cloud of dust up from the ground between a clump of weeds growing at the flank. "And here's where we were. See? Our bamboo poles are still here."

"I guess we dropped 'em when we ran to get Mom."

"And then a fly landed on the guy's face. It was gross-a-mosso!"

They were telling the truth now, and yet all Taylor could think about was the fact that her boys had written a letter to Steve Kessler spinning a tale of murder and mayhem so that he would come to Almost and fall in love with her. Because they wanted a new dad. Correction: they wanted *him* for a new dad.

She couldn't look at Steve. Every fiber of her being, every synapse in her brain told her this would be a colossal mistake. Even when he cleared his throat, she wouldn't risk a glance in his direction. While the day had seemed hot before, it now seemed aflame.

Over her sons' protestations of honesty, Taylor heard the drone of a car heading toward the highway, footsteps scuffing through the powdered dust, locusts graveling in Mr. Hampton's huge elm trees up by his house, and Steve Kessler's soft voice murmuring something too near her ear for any degree of comfort.

"I don't know them. How much of this should I swallow?"

His words sparked a live wire deep inside of Taylor. She watched her triplets brandishing their bamboo poles over their heads as if they'd fought a dragon and won. But she wouldn't look at Texas Ranger Steve Kessler, would-be new dad to her sons.

"My boys may appear a lot of things to you, *Mr.* Kessler, and maybe for good reason, but take it from me…Smithton boys don't lie."

Steve realized he'd asked her the question just to see her motherly defenses rise to the surface. When her boys had blurted out their plan for her—and his—future, she'd turned deathly pale. And then, almost as swiftly as her color had drained, her whole face had bloomed a bright, painful-looking red.

To tell the truth, his own cheeks were a little on the warm side. The boys' incredible plan seemed to underscore the feelings of unease he'd felt from the moment Taylor opened her door, only to slam it in his face.

"I swear we're telling the truth!" one of the boys asserted. Since they were as alike as one summer day from the next, he couldn't have begun to guess which one it was—except it wasn't the one who seemed to have trouble breathing.

"And what truth is that?" he asked, knowing he was fanning the flames of Taylor's mother anger. He fleetingly apologized to his own mom for all the times she'd had to come to his defense. Unjustifiably.

He hadn't forgotten what it was like to be eleven years old. He wondered if any man ever did. At heart, perhaps all men were one step away from those days when they ran untamed and carefree through tall, dry grasses, hunting mysteries that seemed to be born on a summer's dawn, tracking down elusive signs of Peter Pan, seeking proof that youth was as stable as favorite dinners and television programs that made a child stay awake late into the night questioning the rightness of things.

But one thing he knew for certain about eleven-year-old boys was that they *all* lied. He didn't know if it was a sex-linked chromosome or something that all boys discovered just after learning to speak, but he knew from personal experience that lying was endemic to the male population. And these three boys had admitted to at least one whopper already.

However, too many things about this situation—least of all Taylor Smithton's undeniable attractiveness—didn't add up. He hadn't become a Texas Ranger because there had been a vacancy in the ranks and he'd happened along on the right day. He was one of the elite Rangers because he was good at what he did. And what he often did was simply weigh possibility against probability.

And however improbable it might seem, given the circumstances of three Almost engaging and conniving eleven-year-olds with Doug Smithton's genes floating around in their young bodies, Steve couldn't shake the feeling that at least one element of the boys' story was true. Unless they were the greatest creative geniuses of their time, they'd offered far too much detail about the wounded man *not* to be telling the truth about seeing him.

And, he had to admit, the dropped bamboo sticks, not to mention three perfect sets of sneaker prints that ended right before the strangely scuffed area, an area that sported a very large and very pointy-toed shoe print and darkened muddy spots, tended to add heavy credence to their tale.

But there wasn't enough tea in China or fish in the ocean to make him admit this belief aloud. Especially in front of Taylor, who apparently still couldn't bring herself to look at him. As long as she was angry, she might not think about her sons' bid for him as their new dad. And she might not notice that he half believed her kids. And as long as she didn't know that, she might not consider the notion that a potential killer could be running loose in the peaceful little town of Almost, Texas.

He suggested the boys walk the perimeter of the area and head back to the rental car. He'd spoken reasonably. Calmly. Perhaps patronizingly. He hadn't counted on four sets of Smithton eyes gazing at him in varying degrees of accusation.

"I'll come back and check it out alone," he offered lamely.

"Will you mark it off with crime tape?" one of the

triplets asked. One of the ones without the labored breathing. Jason? Joshua?

"Yeah, like they do on TV? Crime Scene. Do Not Disturb."

"That'd be way cool."

Steve's suspicions almost returned. These boys seemed almost too eager for drama. Then he remembered. All the talk and speculation about the trauma to children was only half-right. Kids could get traumatized, all right, desperately, horribly, and he agreed with all the data spewed out by countless shrinks and talk-show hosts who claimed that hurting a kid was the worst crime possible. At the same time, kids were like rubber balls, bouncing up and leaping toward life, toward second chances and new thought.

These three kids had had a rough time of it; their father had been killed, murdered, and here they were, smack-dab in the middle of a possible mystery while blatantly searching for a new dad. He had to admire their guts. If not their methods.

"You can see right wh-where he was," the one with the rough breathing said, pointing at the scuffed area.

"What's your name, son?"

The boy looked up in surprise, a half-pleased grin—or perhaps a nervous one—creasing his face. "Jonah, sir."

Steve loved West Texas. In Houston, few children ever gave him the courtesy of calling him "sir."

"Well, Jonah, in case your man got up and walked away, we'd better not trample the area, don't you think?"

The look of vast relief that crossed the boy's face set Steve's inner alarm bells jangling again. Whatever they'd lied about before, whatever schemes they'd dreamed up, that look of relief told him there *had* been a wounded, possibly dying man lying right there in the dusty center of the barnyard. He'd have staked his entire reputation as a Ranger on that particular gut feeling.

The three boys joined him at the "crime scene."

"I told you he was the best."

"Yeah, but I don't think he believes us. Not about everything, anyway."

"Well, we did lie in the letter. I told you we shouldn't."

"Mom's gonna kill us."

"I wish Dad was here."

"Doofus. If Dad was here, we wouldn't have written the letter."

"Who're you calling a doofus?"

"Still mad at me?" Steve asked Taylor, hoping she hadn't heard the boys' conversation as they rounded out of sight.

His question sparked her first glance in his direction since the boys had dropped their bombshell. Whatever she glimpsed on his face seemed to capture her attention and made her issue a chagrined smile.

"Did I come off like Mama Bear?"

Her smile reminded him of a summer evening, soft and quiet, filled with promise. The boys were right; she was, *like*, real pretty and cool and everything. "A little," he said.

She cocked an eyebrow at him. "If it was only a little, I wasn't doing my job."

He held up both hands in surrender. "Okay. A lot. You had me shaking. In fact, I think it's safe to say, you literally had me tongue-tied. I haven't felt that way since my own mom yelled at me in the sixth grade."

"If she didn't yell at you after that, you had her thoroughly snowed," she said.

He chuckled, and when she joined him, he momentarily forgot his vow to hold her at arm's length.

Plunging her hands into tepid dishwater, Taylor smiled anew as she remembered the moment when Steve chuckled with her. One minute he'd made her mad enough to drop a wasp's nest on his head and the next he'd made her laugh.

Only four people in the world had ever had that unique ability with her, and of those, only three were still living.

The smile slowly faded from her lips. Steve Kessler wasn't Doug.

But like Steve, Doug would have enjoyed what the boys had done—not condoned, perhaps, but he would have laughed over it. With her. Late at night, spooned together in their bed, he would have recounted the story, his warm chest rumbling against her back. And she would have laughed with him, savoring the feel of his muscled arms around her, holding her close.

Steve Kessler wasn't a bit like Doug. Steve was taller, for one thing. He was darker complected, not much, but some. He had brown eyes. And he had a distance in him that Doug had never seemed to manage. Of course, she'd met Doug in grade school, when both of them had been mere babies, younger than the triplets were now.

And Steve was a grown man.

Her hands stilled on the pot she wasn't scrubbing. What on earth was she thinking? She didn't want another relationship in her life. She had Doug's three sons to raise. That was handful enough. Steve lived in Houston, for heaven's sake. And capping everything, the man was a Texas Ranger, a law enforcement official who might as well wear a target on his chest and back marking the exact spot where bad guys could shoot him dead.

She was only thinking about him because her sons had tapped him as a new father. It was only natural she think about him once they'd planted the thought in her mind.

Taylor resumed her pot scrubbing, scraping the pan with a fervor usually lacking in her dish washing. She rinsed the pan with scalding hot water and swore under her breath as her fingers felt the bite. She all but slammed the pan onto the counter, then stilled as the sound of Joshua's delighted laughter rose even above the sound of running water.

She turned the hot water handle, stemming the flow, only to hear Steve's answering chuckle. She turned toward the laughter as a plant swayed toward the sun.

In the half hour since they'd left the Hampton place, Steve had been talking to the boys separately, taking them one at a time in the living room, hearing their stories on an individual basis, something almost impossible for her triplets to accomplish.

She'd been half-inclined to take umbrage at the implied insult, but her sons had been only too eager to comply. Not just because it was SOP—standard operating procedure when investigating a possible crime, they'd informed her importantly—but, she suspected, because they wanted to be close to Steve Kessler, hero Texas Ranger, the man they had selected out of the hundreds of thousands of men on the planet to be their new dad.

Staring at the closed door separating the kitchen from the hall leading to the living room, Taylor fought the urge to lean her ear against it to hear what was causing Josh to laugh so unaffectedly, so openly with a total stranger.

She remembered a long-ago new-wives orientation she'd endured at the Texas Highway Patrol office in Lubbock. Some unctuous, patronizing psychologist had stood up before the group of brides of all ages and sizes and

told them, "When you marry a cop, you don't just marry
the man, you marry the badge, you marry the uniform,
you marry the scuzzbag on the street who wants to take
down your man. And, girls, you marry control."

That weaselly little psychologist had been as wrong as
the sun shining at midnight. Doug had been about as con-
trolling as a typewriter waiting for a typist. He was con-
siderate, affectionate, passionate...

What was that man saying to Josh to make him laugh
so, laugh the way he had with Doug?

And *why* did she feel so strange, so isolated and connected simultaneously, upon hearing the laughter?

She drew a deep breath of decision and shoved the
connecting door to the hallway open.

"And then, one time, Mom got so mad at Dad that she
stood in the kitchen, all in one spot, like she was hooked
to that part of the floor, you know, and then she jumped
up and down and called him a meanie. She really did.
'You're such a meanie, sometimes. Just a meanie.' That's
what she said. Honest."

"You're kidding," Steve said, chuckling.

"No, really. I mean, *yes,* she did. And Dad laughed so
hard he had to run to the bathroom so he wouldn't wet
his pants. *Seriously.*"

All Steve knew for certain was that Houston was some
seven hundred miles to the southeast. Everything beyond
that truth seemed in abeyance.

He'd interviewed the three Leary-Smithton children.
He'd *interrogated* them. And all he'd come up with thus
far was that their mother was beautiful, a good cook—
"she makes the best spaghetti this side of the Pecos."

She was fun, she was great, and sometimes she cried at night alone in her bedroom.

They'd thrown out tidbits about the afternoon nearly as an afterthought. The wounded man had worn fancy clothes and pointy-toed lizard shoes and groaned, "Cold dray horse," before gurgling horribly.

But inevitably, each of the boys had returned to praise of their mother. And, as if the memories were intertwined with their perceptions of their mother, the three boys had told him of their father. According to them, Doug Smithton had been perfect; the best dad, the best husband, the best cop, the quintessential father. He'd been the kind of man who worked all day and still wanted to play catch with his sons, the god who knew everything in each boy's mind, who knew by some psychic awareness how each of the triplets was different and how each was similar.

And knowing Doug as he had, Steve didn't have much trouble accepting this version of his old college chum. Doug was a big kid himself.

Despite the loss of their godlike father, according to the boys, their lives were joyful, easy and fun. Until that afternoon, when they'd seen a guy dying on the other side of Mr. Hampton's barn.

All three of the boys had described the "nearly dead guy" as wearing a "fancy" watch. Individually, all three had placed said watch on the guy's *right* wrist. Yet all three Smithton triplets were left-handed. Steve knew from long, hard experience that people tended to describe what they were most familiar with.

Individually and collectively, they had described the man as a dude. Steve wallowed through several possible meanings of the word before he finally realized the boys weren't using the current vernacular to mean any male figure they couldn't give a name to. They were using *dude* in the context of West Texas slang: the guy was dressed differently from anyone they'd seen before—outside of television—and looked "goofy" because he was so out of place.

After talking to each of the boys, hoping their stories jibed completely because they'd rehearsed their responses earlier, Steve felt conscious of that hunch feeling that prickled his spine. Their stories were similar but not quite the same. Each of them seemed to notice something slightly different about the wounded man. And very slight discrepancies in their collective recounting of events only lent weight to its veracity.

The same hunch that made him come to Almost rather than pitch the boys' letter in the trash can or call to see what their mom had to say played over his skin, making his brain feel slightly tight within his skull. It was also the same hunch that tickled his backbone when he'd rounded the corner of the barn, only to find an empty barnyard and a semilush sorghum field.

Cold...dray...horse.

No matter how many times he'd heard the words, Steve couldn't make sense of them. It didn't help that the boys were equally puzzled.

"Is there such a thing as a dray horse?" one of them had asked. Jason, he thought. The toughest one of the three.

Texas Ranger Steve Kessler didn't have the foggiest idea what a dray horse might be, though he had a dim notion that the word had something to do with labor. But, like the boys, he couldn't see what a dray horse might mean to a nearly dead guy.

The door to the kitchen opened and Taylor stood silhouetted in the light flooding in the kitchen windows.

Steve couldn't see her eyes and the shadows from the hall hid her expression. She held the door open with her arm outstretched, and her legs were slightly parted. Power seemed to exude from her entire body, an illusion augmented by the light creating an aura behind her.

"Are you all right?" she asked, and stepped forward into the light.

I'm toast, Steve thought, but aloud he croaked, "Fine. We're doing just fine."

The third triplet he was interviewing, not the brazen one, not the one with the labored breathing—Josh?—turned and beamed at his mother.

"He's gotta stay, Mom. To find the guy we saw dying. He practically believes us now—" Steve felt a stab of guilt in the boy's innocent acceptance of his own disbelief "—'cause he knows there could really be a bad guy out there. A killer dude. He can stay here, right?"

Steve had to catch his lower lip with his teeth to hide a grin at the look of sheer horror on Taylor's lovely face.

"Not here. I can stay in a motel," he said.

Josh piped up in triumph, "There aren't any motels in Almost. You'd have to go all the way back to Lubbock. Or Levelland."

Steve looked at Taylor. Taylor looked at a crocheted doily on a pillow.

"Of course, you're welcome to camp here," she said.

Southern hospitality was never more grudgingly offered, he thought. "Thanks. I accept."

As Josh whooped a hooray, Steve wondered what kind of fool he was to take her up on her less-than-alacritous offer. Kids, a marrying kind of woman, a nearly dead guy who disappeared and a whopping matchmaking effort...why was he staying?

Maybe because he'd never met a woman who talked to pillows before.

Or maybe it was because he wanted to stay with her.

Chapter 5

"He's staying with *you?*"

Taylor withheld a sigh as she wandered onto the front porch with the cordless phone. Would this afternoon never end? "It's either with me, or holing up in your garage, Aunt Sammie Jo," she said into the phone.

"No, no. I think it's wonderful, honey. The boys scarce talk about anything other than the famous, the wonderful Texas Ranger Steve Kessler. And now he's right here in Almost. Fancy that. And staying with y'all."

"The boys had a little scare this afternoon—"

"Oh, honey, I know all about that. Poor little old things. Charlie Hampton called in here come along five o'clock and told us the whole story. Seems there was some blood smeared on the tack-room door of that old barn a his and the ground appeared to be torn up from some kind of scuffle. He said he didn't know a thing about it till he saw the boys light outta there like they were fireworks on the Fourth of July, every jack one of them screaming bloody murder. And I mean that literally."

"There really wasn't any blood—the boys made that with their chemistry set."

Taylor's aunt chuckled. "Now if that doesn't sound just like that handful of yourn. Reminds me of when you, Craig and Allison were little. We never had a clue from one minute to the next what you three were going to come up with. One day it was space aliens landing in Homer Chalmers's backyard, another it was finding dinosaur bones out at your daddy's ranch, when you still lived out there.... Hang on a minute, honey. Well now, Mickey Sanders. How've you been, honey? Didn't you just love that picture? I swear I could watch Mel Gibson just read the phone book."

Taylor would never have dreamed of hanging up the phone while her aunt tended to a customer. If she had to wait thirty minutes, she would stay on the line with Aunt Sammie Jo.

The older woman was her father's only sister and the last of the former generation of Learys. She'd been surrogate mother to her nieces and nephews, filling in when they'd driven their own mom to utter distraction. Sammie Jo, an inveterate and unrepentant ranchwoman who now ran—with her husband, Cactus Jack—the Almost Minimart, Video Store and Gas Station, served as aunt to the entire community, probably the whole tricounty area.

And she was fighting breast cancer with every bit of gumption she possessed. She sported the most outrageous of wigs, a flamboyant, Dolly Parton look-alike, as garish on Aunt Sammie Jo as it was glamorous on the famous country-and-western singer. "It makes Cactus go plumb wild," she'd say, batting her eyes and assuming a Dolly pose. "And you know that old prickly pear still has quite a sting in him!"

Trying not to think about chemotherapy or the fact that one day Aunt Sammie Jo might not be there to pick up the phone and relate the latest in Almost gossip, Taylor patiently waited while Mickey Sanders and Sammie Jo discussed the merits of Mel Gibson's anatomy.

Several minutes later, Aunt Sammie Jo said, "I'm back, honey. That Mickey, she'll talk the tail off a jackrabbit." As far as Taylor had heard, Mickey had only primly said she hadn't noticed Mel Gibson's "cute buns" and asked how much she owed for the carton of milk and the Lubbock newspaper.

"Speaking of jackrabbits, you better have the boys come on by the store so I can stock 'em up with things you'll need for your fellow."

Taylor grinned, shaking her head. "I'm fine, Aunt Sammie Jo. I'm about as stocked as a person can get."

"As you say, honey, but it's been a goodly time since you cooked for a man," Aunt Sammie Jo remarked, blithely ignoring the dinner she and Cactus Jack had enjoyed just two nights before at Taylor's house.

"He can hardly eat more than three growing eleven-year-olds," Taylor said.

"But you can't feed him spaghetti every night he's there. Tell you what. I've got some purty chops Alva Lu's husband took off that yearling hog they put down. Makes my mouth water just thinking about 'em. That ought to be enough to feed your brood and a stray Texas Ranger or two."

Taylor knew from lifelong experience there wasn't a bit of use arguing with her aunt. And demurring was out of the question. "That'd be terrific, Aunt Sammie Jo. Thanks. I'll send the boys over in a few minutes."

"You do that. They can tell me all the news of the day, from the horse's mouth, so to speak. Why, Alva Lu! We were just talking about you.... You heard right. Blood and a scuffle out at Charlie Hampton's place. Yes, ma'am. And we've got a real Texas Ranger right here in Almost. Staying with Taylor.... No, I'm not pulling your leg one little bit. I'm talking to her right now.... Listen, *Taylor* honey, I gotta go. You send those boys, you hear?"

And with that, Sammie Jo hung up on her. Taylor tried to picture the pursy-faced Alva Lu Harrigan gathering the latest Almost news. For years, Taylor and her brother and sister had joked about tel-star, telephone, tell Alva Lu; she was a better gossip-spreader than Sammie Jo. And that was truly a feat. At the same time, Alva Lu made it a point of dropping around Sammie Jo's with a casserole at least once a week and always seemed to have an appointment of some kind in Lubbock when Sammie Jo needed to visit her oncologist.

Taylor knew that between Sammie Jo and Alva Lu Harrigan, whatever had—or hadn't—happened out behind Charlie Hampton's barn would be all over Almost within a matter of minutes. It was a sure bet that the rural telephone company would see nearly every one of the Almost circuits busy for the next half hour.

And by dinnertime, the story would have grown beyond all recognition.

"Boys!" she called, cradling the cordless phone and opening the kitchen door. Her gang pelted down the halls as if they'd been on alert for her summons.

"Yes, Mom?"

"What do you need, Mom?"

"We already cleaned our rooms and took out the trash."

And they'd washed their faces and hands.

They weren't just interviewing Steve Kessler for the position of dad, they were actively soliciting his acceptance. Even to the point of outright prevarication and the judicious use of soap and water.

"We're going to have a long talk about what you've done," she said sternly. Three cherubic faces fell. "But right now, Aunt Sammie Jo wants you to come to the store and pick up some things she's sending over for dinner."

Since going to Sammie Jo's invariably meant treats before dinner and sodas straight from the machine outside—those dispensers requiring quarters from Sammie Jo's cash register always producing far better tasting soda pops than any six-pack of the same brand in the refrigerator—the boys' faces brightened considerably.

"And come straight back home without dillydallying around," Taylor called to three retreating figures.

She shook her head and chuckled as she reentered the kitchen and nearly ran into six feet four inches of Texas Ranger.

"I'll bet it's been thirty years since I heard that word," Steve said, his brown eyes alight with humor.

"What word?" Taylor asked, feeling oddly breathless. The man seemed to take up every inch of space in what she'd always felt was a large kitchen.

"Dillydallying," he said, and grinned at her.

A bit of the child in him came out with that smile, as did the unvoiced admission that he was from the Southwest, probably West Texas. With the grin, his features didn't shift, making him tough cop one second and approachable man the next. But the smile lured her, made her want to lean closer to him, as if she could bask in its warmth.

"How about shilly-shallying?" she asked.

"Means the same thing but that your grandparents came from Ireland," he responded without a blink of an eye.

She chuckled. "And shimmy-shammying?"

He laughed outright. "Something circus performers can do?"

"Eleven-year-olds," she said firmly. "They can do all three without a pause. All at the same time."

"If today was any example, I'd say they would have had the toughest hombre shaking in his boots."

"Oh, you don't know the half of it," she said, managing to step around him without succumbing to the urge to touch him as she moved. If he'd been the boys, she would have rested a hand on a shoulder or towhead. If he'd been Doug, she would have trailed her hand across his flat stomach or maybe down the side of his muscled thigh.

But he wasn't the boys and he certainly wasn't Doug.

"Listen, if my staying here is a problem—"

"It isn't," she said curtly, her back to him. Of course it was a problem. Everything about him was trouble, the least of which was that her boys had singled him out as a replacement father and had brought him to this very house for that purpose.

"I'm going to head back to the Hampton place. I want to have a closer look."

"Without the boys' expert assistance?" she asked, turning back to face him, a smile on her lips.

He grinned and shrugged. "If I need any help, I'll holler," he said.

"If I'm any judge of the folks around here, you'll have enough help that you could have finished any investigation at least four weeks earlier."

A funny look crossed his face. Taylor didn't want to ask what caused the arrested expression.

"I gotta go," he said, and Taylor had the feeling he didn't mean out to the Hampton place.

The telephone rang, and as Taylor picked up the cordless phone, he left the kitchen mumbling a farewell.

"Oh, Carolyn... No, the boys are perfectly fine.... *Who* did you hear it from? How could Doc already have heard about it?"

Steve drove the short distance to the Hampton place, a grin still resting on his lips. And as he took the left fork of the drive, he wasn't terribly surprised to see two extra cars parked at Charlie Hampton's house and to catch a glimpse of two older men sitting in the shade of Mr. Hampton's front porch, watching him carefully.

Charlie Hampton raised his cane in a salute and Steve waved back after making a circling gesture with his finger. The old man nodded and pointed at his barn, granting Steve permission for another look around.

Steve wondered how many people had already been out behind the barn in the last hour while he'd been interviewing the boys. If the number of phone calls to Taylor was any indication, he'd be lucky to find much of the scene left intact.

To his relief, Mr. Hampton and whoever he'd brought out to show around had seemed to adhere to the principles of caution and had stopped well away from the scuffed area in the center of the empty barnyard during their inspection.

Steve held his broad-brimmed straw hat in his hands as he knelt cowboy-fashion at the edge of the empty, dusty stretch of ground between the barn and the sorghum field. He narrowed his eyes against the glare of the late afternoon sun. And instead of seeing the scuffed area, the pointy-toed footprints, he found the possible crime scene simply melting away and he was right back in Taylor Smithton's comfortable home, staring into her beautiful blue eyes.

He shook his head and replaced his hat low on his brow. The last thing he needed to think about was a woman like Taylor Smithton, the kind of woman that radiated an aura of commitment, promise. A wedding-bell kind of gal, his mother would have said.

And he just wasn't the wedding-bell kind of guy. Not anymore. He'd been down that particular bumpy road before and was lucky to have gotten back out with his skin intact. He'd said "I do" and meant it both times. His first wife, Jessica, had said "I will" and meant "Who's next?" Jessica wasn't a wedding-bell kind of gal, but she'd been carrying someone's baby and her mother had been pressuring her to find a daddy right quick. Steve, still wet behind the ears, and dazzled by Jessie's red fingernails and moist warm lips, had jumped to the front of her mama's long line of candidates.

Then, when Jessie lost the baby, Steve felt as though part of him were buried with that tiny casket. But Jessie didn't cry; if anything she seemed relieved. But she found plenty of shoulders to pretend to cry on, and other arms besides his to hold her close. And before too much time had passed, too much of their marriage lay in too many other bedrooms.

Tom Adams had nicknamed Steve's second wife the Barracuda, a title particularly suited to Charlena's ultra-slim form, her tiny, perfect teeth and her penchant for chewing men up and spitting them out in little pieces. Steve had swung her up on her pedestal just a few months after his marriage to Jessica had finally coughed its last dying breath. Three years later, he'd found himself apologizing for the brightness of the sky, clouds, if there were any, the heat in the summer, snow in the winter. There wasn't a single aspect of life that Charlena didn't find mildly or sometimes extremely irritating. And all of those irritations were somehow Steve's fault.

Steve knew it was a sad old story, and one not terribly unique. A thousand other guys went through divorces every day and went right back out there and found someone else. He couldn't. In the aftermath of two failed marriages, and sometime long after that tiny casket had entered the ground and he'd thrown his life's savings across two lawyers' tables, unable to so much as give one last look at Jessie's harder-than-hard face or at Charlena's sleek satisfaction, he'd found he'd sealed off the marrying side of his heart. He'd vowed then never to be vulnerable to that kind of pain again. Never to play the patsy in a strange con game. And if he'd wanted kids once, he didn't now. He couldn't bear the kind of torture that losing one would cause him. Far better to get clean out of the kitchen if he couldn't stand the heat.

Even if he found himself standing just inside the doorway, looking longingly toward disaster.

He stood up, dusting off his trousers, as if erasing the years. The sooner he figured out what the boys had or hadn't seen that afternoon, the better off he'd be.

Because Taylor Smithton seemed to have the knack of looking deep inside him. Right down to that sealed-off door.

Steve followed the pointy-toed footprints that seemed to lead from the barn to the scuffed area. Several other footprints—large and small—obscured any prints in front of the tack-room door. He shook his head, looking at the rust-colored stains on the doorjamb. Using a pen, he lifted the metal hasp and let the door swing wide.

Light leapt through the opened doorway and bounced across the plywood subflooring, revealing years of dust, a few boxes of what appeared to be tax returns that might date back thirty years or more, and a few perfectly clear pointy-toed footprints.

Stepping around the footprints carefully, Steve pried open a box the footprints apparently had stopped in front of. The box was empty, even of dust.

Steve tried working out a possible route for the footprints. The man had entered the tack room by the same door that stood open now, had walked across the room, apparently directly toward the empty box. Had he taken something out of the box? Was he going to put something in it? Had Taylor's sons made the prints themselves, and was their whole story simply elaborate window dressing for their matchmaking scheme?

And when had he started thinking of the boys as Taylor's, not Doug's?

Steve stepped out of the sunlight, half hoping the light would literally shed some glimmer of a clue that might help him understand what was going on in Almost. The man had walked to the box. Then what?

Still shifting far to the left to avoid blocking the sunlight, Steve knelt closer to the base of the box. There. At the corner. A swirled print fanned like a perfect bridge hand, as if the fancy dude had turned suddenly. Surprised? Interrupted?

His Texas Ranger curiosity running at full speed, Steve swiveled slowly, his eyes on the footprints just inside the opened door. He could see them clearly: the pointy toes, his own king-size boot prints and those of a third man, tennis shoes of some kind. Old Pointy Toes and Tennis

Shoes were roughly the same height, and to judge by the depth of the prints in the dust, probably fairly similar in weight. Steve's own prints were easily discernible by their sizable difference.

If he had to guess, he'd say Pointy Toes was interrupted by Tennis Shoes, though any fight didn't break out inside the tack room. No, they'd gone peacefully and slowly enough back through the barn door and outside. Had Tennis Shoes come back for Pointy Toes after the boys went screaming for Taylor?

Steve went back outside as if the empty sorghum field could supply the answer. A red-shouldered hawk silently circled low over the field, scaring up mice or insects. From a telephone wire high above, a meadowlark sang a melodious warning. The raspy drone of cicadas in Mr. Hampton's elm trees carried all the way from the house to the barn.

Maybe it was time to talk to Mr. Hampton.

Three older men were waiting for him as Steve drove up to Mr. Hampton's house and parked his car next to two others. Charlie Hampton lifted a hand in greeting. Steve tipped his hat and pushed it back on his brow a little. If there had been a woman present, he would have removed it altogether.

Steve introduced himself and offered his hand.

Charlie Hampton's grip was surprisingly strong and callused.

Steve then shook hands with the other two men Charlie named, Homer Chalmers and Sam Harrigan. Neither of them spoke, only nodded and tilted their hats back a notch. Harrigan spat a mouthful of chewing tobacco off the side of the porch without turning his head.

A man not raised in West Texas might have thought

the reception chilly at best. But Steve relaxed; these men were merely waiting for a report.

"Thanks for letting me have another look around," Steve said.

Charlie Hampton nodded but didn't waste any words on social amenities. "So what's been going on out back of my barn?"

"Frankly, I'm not sure," Steve said, and continued before the frown could fully settle on Charlie's already wrinkled brow. "But I think Taylor Smithton's boys may have seen the end result of a scuffle."

"A scuffle, eh?"

"They claim they saw a man who was shot in the chest."

"Dead?"

Steve shook his head. "Not when they left him. And since he wasn't there when we came back, they're either right about that or..."

"Or they're lying."

Steve didn't look away from Charlie Hampton's penetrating gaze. "I have to consider that possibility."

"Well, you can just unconsider it," Hampton said. "I've known those boys all their young lives. Oh, they're full of piss and vinegar, I won't kid you none about that. But they're Smithtons to the bone. Learys, too, for that matter. Hell, boy, their daddy was a cop hisself. Known him since he was a boy and came with his folks to settle here. And I knew Taylor's daddy and his daddy afore him. No, if they said they saw a bullet hole in some man's chest, then they saw it."

The other two men exchanged glances, then nodded at Steve solemnly.

Steve pushed his hat back another notch and leaned

against the railing of the porch. He smiled. "I roomed with Doug Smithton at Tech."

All three men nodded as if they'd known that bit of information.

"And I agree with you. If the boys are anything like Doug, I don't have any trouble with what you're telling me."

Charlie Hampton shifted his own hat to a more friendly position and mimicked Steve's easy lean against a post. "What do you suppose happened to the fellow with the bullet hole in him?"

"I was hoping you might know," Steve said. "Anyone besides us come or go this afternoon? In a car or van?"

Charlie shook his head. "Not that I saw. But I have to admit, I take a nap in the afternoons nowadays. The whole National Guard coulda come down the barn road and I wouldn't have heard a thing." He turned his head back and forth and pointed at his hearing aids. "Take 'em out when I sleep. Otherwise they whistle."

"The boys said they talked with you before they went out to the barn and found the man?" Steve said, making it a question.

"Well now, sure if they didn't." Again he waved at his ears. "I was watching my show. I'd just put my ears back in when they came around."

Steve didn't ask what show that might be; Charlie Hampton had a satellite dish on the side of his house. It could have been anything from "Montel Williams" to old reruns of "Perry Mason."

"Have the boys been coming out to your barn very often lately?"

Charlie frowned as he thought. "Now that you mention it, seems they have been coming round a bit more than usual. 'Course, the fact I planted something a little different this year makes for some interest. And the sorghum's not too high yet, making the going easier. And the careless weeds aren't grabbing at your socks like they do later. 'Sides, barns and kids just naturally seem to go together. Their mama used to come out here with her brother and sister. Same as *their* daddy did.''

"Seen anything else unusual? Strangers? The boys said the man was dressed fancy.''

"Aside from a salesman or two—and let me tell you, we still get 'em out here, even after these five years of drought—I can't recollect seeing any strangers.'' Charlie looked at his companions. Homer and Sam never looked away from Steve, merely shook their heads in unison.

"Does anyone else use your barn road besides yourself?'' Steve asked.

Charlie shook his head.

"Here's the deal, Charlie. I'd appreciate it if you'd let me block off that road so I can keep the scene clean. I'm with you in thinking the boys are telling the truth. And if this guy was as badly wounded as they say, then it's pretty good odds we'll need to have another look at your barn as a possible crime scene.''

"Gotcha,'' Charlie said. ''You go ahead and tape it off, or whatever you gotta do. There's no need for me to even go down to the barn this time of year. That field out there is doing just fine on its own. Nothing I can do about it now except pray for some more rain.''

The other two men nodded and looked up at the cloudless blue sky. Steve followed their gaze. ''Here's hoping,'' he said.

"Hear you'll be staying with Taylor,'' Charlie said.

Steve's heart seemed to hiccup. The matter had been decided less than an hour earlier and already the town knew. Steve felt rather than saw the speculative looks from the other two men. Charlie, on the other hand, simply waited for his reply.

"I have a flight booked for tomorrow. Unless we find something before then, I'll probably be taking it." He didn't want to consider why the realization made him feel flat.

"Unless we stumble across this guy running around with a bullet in his chest," Charlie said.

Steve nodded.

"Taylor's quite a lady."

The one-hundred-degree temperature didn't account for Steve's sudden discomfort. "Yes, she is."

"There's a saying about the Leary women—"

Homer spoke for the first time. "Two sayings."

"Two sayings," Charlie agreed. "The first is that there must be something in the water out at the Leary place. Every single one of the Leary women grows up to be a beauty with a heart to match."

Steve smiled crookedly. He'd just realized that both his wives faintly resembled Taylor. "And the other saying?"

"They say the Leary women are all unlucky in love."

Dinner was all but ready. The table was set, animals fed, boys bullied into clean T-shirts, and she herself had showered and changed into fresh jeans and a soft blue blouse.

Though it was already seven and the sun was far to the west, it still seemed midafternoon, thanks to daylight saving time and the summer season. Taylor lifted her shoulder-length hair and deftly caught it in a loose ponytail. A glance in the mirror to add a dab of lipstick told her she looked exactly what she was, a woman in her mid-thirties, mother of three boys who were about to receive the talking-to of their lives.

She corralled them in the living room, sitting them down on the sofa and taking the coffee table for herself. She waited until they'd quieted completely before leaning forward and resting her elbows on her knees.

"I want to talk about the letter you wrote to Steve Kessler," she said.

"We didn't know there was really something going on, Mom—"

"Yeah, like the nearly dead guy."

"We really saw him, Mom. You gotta—"

She held up her hand. "We'll talk about that later." She had to clamp her lips tight to keep from smiling. "Right now, I want to know what prompted you to write that letter to Steve Kessler."

All three of her sons hung their heads.

"I'm waiting," she said.

Finally, Josh spoke up, his guileless eyes meeting hers directly. Earnestly. "We saw him at school first, then on television, see? It was for some big fancy party in Houston. They were, like, raffling him off—"

"Auctioning him," Jason corrected.

"Same thing," Josh said.

"It isn't, either, huh, Mom?"

"Hush, Jason," Taylor said. "I've got the picture. Go on, Josh."

"Anyway, they called him Texas's most heroic bachelor. And some other junk, you know, like his arrest record and stuff, and they said he was just what any woman would want to find in her stocking at Christmas."

"It was a Christmas show."

Taylor blinked. "You've been thinking about this since Christmas?"

All three of her sons looked blank. Then light dawned.

Jonah half giggled. "Heck no, Mom! Just since what happened to Aunt Carolyn."

Taylor closed her eyes. Kessler had been involved in the raid on Carolyn's place last spring. He'd teamed up with the FBI to capture a local connection to drug runners using Carolyn's place as a drop-off and pick-up site for air transport of drugs.

She opened her eyes and focused her gaze on her three errant angels. "Talk to me," she said.

"And then, at school? We heard how Texas Ranger Steve Kessler was helping kids combat crime."

They'd talked of little else for at least a week, though she hadn't connected the name. Taylor hadn't thought anything of their obvious case of hero worship. She'd had a pretty good case of it herself for Wonder Woman back when. But she'd never written to Wonder Woman to try to fix her up with Taylor's daddy. Which was probably a good thing; her mother might have held one or two objections.

"And when did you come to the conclusion that you should write him lies?"

"About two weeks ago—" Jonah began, only to get an elbow dug into his side.

"This is what you've been up to practically since school let out?"

A mumbled assortment of affirmatives answered her.

"Do you three have any idea how wrong you were to have done such a thing?"

"But there really was a nearly dead guy, Mom!"

"Yeah! If we hadn't written the letter, Texas Ranger Steve Kessler wouldn't have been here—"

"And wouldn't be able to save the day now!"

"Nice try, guys. No cigar. If you hadn't written that

letter, you wouldn't have community service for the next three weeks.''

"Three weeks!"

"Aw, Mo-om!"

"I mean it, boys. Three weeks of doing all your chores first thing in the morning, then helping out around town, like at Mrs. Sanders's house, or Mrs. Harrigan's place, and then I want you out giving Mr. Hampton a hand with whatever he might need doing.'' Sending them to the site of the crime was her way of softening the blow, even if the boys hadn't noticed it yet. "Do I make myself clear?"

"But, Mom, all we did was write a letter. Where's the broken law about that?" Jason asked hotly.

She leveled a cool look at him. "Using the U.S. mail to perpetrate a fraud is a federal offense, punishable by imprisonment in a federal penitentiary.''

"But it wasn't fraud—''

"I suggest you look up the definition of *fraud,*'' Taylor said dryly.

"But we were trying to help you,'' Josh blurted out. "You've been real unhappy without Dad around. You still cry at night sometimes. We can hear you, even if you're trying to be real quiet.''

Taylor had to war with the urge to be sidetracked, the need to gather her sons to her chest and hug them and thank them for thinking of her. However misguidedly. Luckily, knowledge and reason won out.

"You're right. I still miss your Daddy. I always will, guys. But that doesn't mean I'll condone you telling lies to try to do something for me. How do you think that makes me feel?"

Three heads looked down. Jason's popped up first. "But don't you think it's a good thing he's here now?''

Taylor had to bite the inside of her lips to keep from

smiling. "What I think is that you boys owe Mr. Kessler a giant apology for writing him lies. And I think that I'd better hear you've been helping everyone in the community that you can possibly help. Every day for the next three weeks."

Her sons assented, and if the agreement was made with less than their usual enthusiasm, they knew they were lucky to get community service instead of incarceration, which was the family term for being grounded.

She and Doug had come up with the community service punishment when the boys were about four years of age. Neither of them liked the idea of spanking the boys as punishment for hitting one another. Somehow the concept of a hit for a hit seemed off balance. But helping others, becoming actively involved in someone else's troubles and needs, seemed less a punishment than a lesson in life.

And since the community service system was so well-known in Almost, the boys were treated to a host of unusual tasks and jobs and were rewarded for their efforts with hot lunches, cold drinks and freshly made fudge brownies. And since she had triplets, nearly every house in the small town of Almost sported freshly painted trim, weeded alleys and driveways and spotlessly clean attics.

"We're sorry, Mom," Jonah said. His brothers mumbled duplicate apologies.

She held out her arms then and gathered her boys against her chest. "Your apology is accepted," she said, hugging them. "I love you guys. Wild and crazy as you are."

Steve stood in the lengthening shadows on the front porch. He'd been stopped by the seriousness of their conversation, not wanting to interrupt, not wanting to intrude. And listening to every word.

He fought against feeling wholly excluded from such an intimate display of affection and family unity. Watching them, the four blond heads made golden in the light from a table lamp, the mother, her hair caught up in a ponytail, looking nearly as young as the boys sprawling across her lap, Steve felt a sense of isolation like none he'd ever encountered.

Far more than a screen door and a darkening porch separated him from this family. Past hurts, imagined and real, rooted him to the wooden slats outside. And while the temperature remained at something just below one hundred degrees, he felt chilled. And alone.

Lonely.

This is what a family is supposed to be, he thought, and immediately wished he hadn't. He still hadn't learned. No matter how many times he'd waltzed around the dance floor of bad choices, the gullible part of him still wanted to waltz again.

Damn.

"Now scoot and make sure the silverware's on the right sides," Taylor said, standing up and urging her brood to a room off the main living area.

As her sons disappeared through the opened doorway, Taylor turned around, shaking her head a little. She looked up at the ceiling and spoke. "And you said three would be easy. Fat lot you knew about it."

She let out her breath in a rush and grinned ruefully. Then she walked straight across the room and opened the screen door. And let out a little shriek when she ran right into him.

Steve would have given practically anything he had or had ever dreamed of not to have reached out and grasped her arms to steady her. She smelled too good, looked too beautiful, had somehow brought the warmth back to his limbs.

"It's only me," he said.

"It's...you."

He let her go, but the feel of her lingered on his hands.

Chapter 6

Steve wondered later if dinner was always the Mad Hatter affair it seemed to him. And always as enjoyable.

The food was terrific, a damn-all-consequences cholesterol-laden array of country-fried pork chops, mashed potatoes, gravy, broccoli with hollandaise sauce, thick French bread and an amazing array of assorted pickled condiments. Dessert, in the form of frozen yogurt, followed the meal as if in apology for the dinner's high-fat content. Steve couldn't remember the last time he'd eaten so well and with such satisfaction.

While the meal was superlative, the conversation was a hodgepodge of blood, gore, fantasy, speculation, non sequiturs and not-so-subtle matchmaking. Luckily for Steve's appetite, he didn't have a particularly weak stomach and told himself firmly that he was impervious to any lures a pack of hooligans might set out for him to join their chaotic family.

"That guy couldn't have gotten far."

"What I figure is…whoever shot the guy picked him up and carried him away."

Steve glanced up to see which of the three boys said this; it fit his surmise exactly.

"Yeah, well, how come we didn't see any tire tracks or nothing?"

"Anything," Taylor corrected, apparently selecting one grammatical error out of the hat and airing it. Steve wasn't surprised when she was ignored.

"There's millions of tire tracks out behind Mr. Hampton's barn. Shoot, we probably walked right over 'em and messed 'em up."

"Pass the salt. Please."

Steve handed one of them the salt and pepper.

"Ee-yuck, I hate pepper." At a look from his mother he smiled brightly at Steve. "But thanks for the salt. I *love* salt."

"Shoot, the killer coulda been right in the barn. We never even looked."

"That's too much, doofus. You're gonna turn into a pillar of salt, just like that Bible dude's wife."

"How come she didn't have a name, Mom? She's just Lot's wife. That doesn't seem fair."

"This is a really good dinner, Mom. You're the best cook in the whole world."

"Not just the world…the whole universe."

"Do you like your dinner, Ranger Steve?"

Steve swallowed hastily. "Excellent," he said in Taylor's general direction. "And you can just call me Steve," he added, despite rather liking the sobriquet.

"Cool."

"Way cool."

"Did you hear that, Mom? We can call him plain old Steve."

Taylor choked a little and met Steve's eyes and saw his appreciation of Jason's gaffe. He was anything but plain and far from old. And she liked the way his features softened when he smiled. For a few seconds she could actually forget plain old Steve was a Texas Ranger, a man with a badge and her sons' choice for a dad.

"So what happens next?" Josh asked Steve.

Steve looked momentarily blank as a slow flush stained his neck. Taylor wondered what he'd been thinking and then wished she hadn't, for her own cheeks grew overwarm as she saw he was having difficulty looking at her. If he had been an old family friend, a person she knew, perhaps they would have wandered outside after a while. Perhaps they would have reached for each other in the dark.

As her sons would say, where was she going with this thought? She didn't know this man, however well he'd known her husband. He was a Texas Ranger, lured to Almost by her sons' lies, and he was all but forced to stay the night—or nights?—in her house. No matter how much his smile might intrigue her, no matter how much his deep voice might play on her spine, she couldn't go *there.* Wherever *there* was.

She tried picturing him when he was younger, Doug's roommate, a tall, gawky kid who would have served as the perfect foil to Doug's antics. When had he developed the shadowed distrust in his eyes? Who had painted that coat of lacquer across his vulnerable soul?

And wasn't she being ever so clever in her probably misguided deductions?

"I guess we'll just have to wait and see if your nearly dead guy shows up somewhere. Doctors are required to report bullet wounds, so if a doctor, say in Lubbock or

Amarillo, calls in a report, we might have a lead. Beyond that...'' He shrugged.

"We'll help you investigate around here," Josh offered.

"Yeah, we know every hidey-hole round these parts."

"You'd be lost without us."

Again Steve raised his eyes to Taylor's and she felt a frisson of connection, of shared humor. She was grateful he didn't make light of her sons' statements. That afternoon they'd been truly frightened of the man they'd seen, and now, with the resilience of youth, they were masking any residual horror with boyish enthusiasm.

"Don't forget you have community service," she reminded them.

"Yeah, but see? We've been thinking."

"That's trouble," she murmured.

"Yeah, but see? We can investigate while we're working off the debt," Jonah offered.

"The debt?" Steve asked, though Taylor suspected that from his eavesdropping earlier, he'd figured out most of their punishment system.

"Yeah. Whenever we do something wrong—like writing you that letter was wrong...''

"'Cause we told you lies about us thinking murder was happening here in Almost—''

"Even though it turns out we were right—''

"But we didn't know it then, so technically we were lying then—''

"And we're sorry—''

"Except we were right—''

"So anyway, we have to pay for breaking the law, like owing a debt."

"Yeah, and we pay it back by doing stuff for people

in Almost. Like taking out their trash and painting their porches and junk like that."

Taylor felt Steve's gaze on her but didn't lift her eyes. Their community service system seemed somehow private, as if a bit of Doug still surrounded the plan. She'd often wondered if the plan might not have a backfiring effect, making helping others a personal albatross because it was linked with punishment. However, since her sons always embarked on whatever services the community required with enthusiasm and fervor, she had long ago accepted the belief that they would continue to help others in the far-flung future—without having to be punished to do so.

Feeling an unusual need to escape their chatter, she had the boys clear the table after reminding them to set the dishes in hot water to soak. She led Steve out to the back porch to escape the halfhearted arguments and clatter of plates against countertops, tables and other dishes.

Though Taylor's house sat in between two others on a road slicing through Almost, there were no homes behind hers. With the clear, clean air and the ultraflat ground at some three thousand feet above sea level, she could stand on her back porch and see nothing but open plains and uncultivated fields. From her back porch to the nearest neighbor behind her was some thirty miles to the west, and even the unpolluted high plains didn't allow her to see that far. The open land, stretching seemingly forever, made her feel at peace, at ease, as though endless possibilities lay before her.

One of her favorite luxuries—a puzzle to her energetic sons—was to slip outside after supper and simply sit in her rocker on the back porch and watch the last of the sunset.

And she'd taken Steve Kessler, a total stranger, a man

who'd already made her angry because he'd doubted her sons, out to one of her favorite spots on earth. She didn't want to question the reasons why.

She drew a deep breath, the rich summer air tasting far better than the "purty chops" Aunt Sammie Jo had sent over for their guest. And as she released her breath, she thought the day's sunset was as spectacular as she could have hoped for. The horizon itself was a rose color, and long, purple shadows streaked up from the ground in a splendorous fan, touching the few wispy clouds drifting by and, as if embarrassing them, turning them a bright, vibrant red.

"It's beautiful, isn't it?" she asked Steve, without turning around, forgetting for a moment that he was a stranger, forgetting everything but the need to share the sunset with someone. Anyone.

"Yes, it is," he said. Something in his voice made her think he was mildly surprised to find it so.

The boys' dogs, having heard their voices, raced across the broad expanse of back lawn and leapt around them as if the poor creatures hadn't seen humankind in ten years. Even the boys' cats—One, Two and Three—made an appearance, talking to one another and rubbing against Steve's legs as if discussing the merits of this stranger's presence on the porch.

"Goodbye," Taylor said firmly.

"What?" Steve asked.

Taylor waved her hand at the dogs and cats. "Goodbye," she said again, and grinned broadly as he watched, apparently amazed, when all three dogs reluctantly crept a safe ten yards away and the three cats leapt for the porch rails to groom themselves with utter disdain.

"The command to disappear," she said, settling down in a large pine rocker. Her rocker. The one she'd bought just for this porch, this place. She gestured at the other empty chair, though to do so made her feel slightly off-kilter.

"It's their one and only trick. Though, of course, the boys would tell you otherwise. According to them, each of those three mutts are Lassie, Rin Tin Tin and Scooby Doo all rolled into one. And all the cats must be Cat Woman in disguise."

She gestured again at the matching rocker and hid a smile as Steve sat down in it as if he were being sucked into a volcano. Reluctance didn't begin to convey his obvious discomfort. The man, by his accent and easy manner, was from the Southwest, probably right from the high plains of West Texas. Why would he feel so out of place on a back porch? Or was it something about *her* back porch?

A thought struck her. "Are you allergic to animals?" she asked.

He shot her a look of pure shock. "Allergic? No. Of course not."

She grinned.

"I mean it. I've never been allergic to anything."

She chuckled outright and held up a hand. "I'm sorry. I wasn't accusing you of a crime. You just don't look very comfortable out here."

He opened his mouth, as if about to tell her what was really bothering him, then closed it again. He shook his head, then asked, "Mind if I light a cigar?"

"Go ahead. I like the smell. My daddy smoked them all his life. I always keep an ashtray on the table behind you."

He gave her another of his unreadable looks, then reached for the ashtray. He made a slow game of lighting his cigar, and a few seconds later Taylor could smell the sweet, tangy odor of a good cigar.

Taylor inhaled the scent deeply, closing her eyes, indulging in a half-formed fantasy. She heard the rocker next to hers creak slightly as Steve shifted his weight in the chair, but with her eyes closed, it could be her father sitting there. Or Doug. Either of them. Alive again, sharing the shadows and the cooling of the evening with her.

She opened her eyes, not with reluctance, but with a slightly pathetic need to recognize reality. Doug was gone. Her father was gone. And the man leaning back in the still rocker was a stranger who had once known Doug but now lived in Houston and would be returning there in a day or so. Another peace officer. A walking target.

"I like that community service deal you have with your kids," he said after a few minutes.

Taylor smiled. "It seems to work."

He was silent for several moments, then he surprised her with his next question. "Were you stunned when the doctors told you triplets were on the way? I only heard from Doug after the fact."

Taylor wondered if she'd ever gotten to the place of "after the fact"? She smiled and answered honestly, "I was terrified."

He chuckled. "And now?"

She gave him a long, steady look, realizing that no one—not even Doug—had ever asked her how she felt about having *had* triplets. People might talk around it, they might look horrified at the prospect of baby-sitting them for more than fifteen minutes at a stretch—all except her sister-in-law, Carolyn, and her aunt Sammie Jo—but no one had ever wondered how *she* felt about raising triplets.

"After Doug was killed, I was scared to death. I was

afraid I'd screw up and ruin them somehow." When he didn't comment, she continued, "But then I rallied. Kids are just grown-ups with growing bodies."

"Do they ever play tricks on you? Pretending to be a different one?"

"Not if they don't want to clean out Mr. Harrigan's pigsties."

Steve chuckled. "What law would that be breaking?" he asked.

"Impersonating a son. Impersonation comes under the penal code governing fraud."

He laughed outright. "I have to admit, to me they're as alike as—"

"Don't say peas in a pod...I know. But they really aren't. For quick reference, Jason is about half an inch taller than both his brothers. Jonah has asthma—which is why the animals stay outside most of the time—and Josh is the 'like, way cool' one of the bunch, the echo."

The back door banged open and her sons shattered the peace of the back porch. "Dishes are done."

"Like, really done."

"Yeah, we even dried 'em and everything."

"You guys looking at stars or what?"

"What's that smell?"

"A cigar, doofus. Don't you know anything?"

Taylor smiled. "And Jason says doofus a lot, even though he knows it's wrong. And no, boys, we're just talking."

"Oh. *Oh*," Josh said, and roughly nudged his slower brothers. "We gotta, uh—"

"Do homework?"

"School's out, doofus!"

"Go to bed now?" Jonah supplied.

"Yeah," Jason agreed, then yawned elaborately,

blowing his ruse by adding, "That's good, Jonah. Maybe you're not such a doofus, after all."

"You're the doofus." But Jonah imitated Jason's huge yawn. "I don't know about you guys, but I'm dead tired."

"Yeah, like, we're all dead tired. It's okay, Mom. You don't have to tuck us in or anything. You guys just stay out here."

"Yeah. Talking."

All three boys giggled delightedly.

She suffered three crushing hugs and kisses, then, before they could close the back door, she—and undoubtedly Steve—heard one of them say, "Now all he's gotta do is kiss her and they'll fall in love."

The door slammed shut, leaving the two adults outside with the dogs, cats, night insects and a solid wall of embarrassment between them.

Darkness had stolen in completely in the short time since they'd come to the porch, and now the only light came from the millions of stars overhead and the window from the kitchen.

But the night was anything but peaceful. Crickets hummed, a dog in a neighbor's yard desultorily barked, and tension crackled between Steve and her like downed electric wires.

The strange thing was that, while she didn't want to consider the rest of her sons' intended package, now that the boys had put it in her mind, she found she did want Steve Kessler to kiss her. A very real part of her wanted to feel his lips pressing against hers, warm, perhaps slightly curved in a smile. But nothing this side of a level four tornado would propel her to cross the few feet separating them.

Steve cleared his throat. "They miss their dad. Doug."

She knew their father's name. She smiled crookedly, trying to defuse the tension. "Yes."

"It's not really me," he said.

Taylor tried reading his expression, but shadows hid his face. She saw the glowing ember on the tip of his cigar. "I don't know," she said finally. Honestly. "It might be."

"No," he said. Too firmly?

She sighed, at a loss to explain the pang she felt at his denial.

"Tell me about him."

"Doug?"

"Yes." And when she didn't say anything, he added a soft, "I mean, we didn't really keep in touch as much as we could have after graduation. Tell me about your life together."

Was he asking her this as a balm to her sons' embarrassing remark or as a possible deflection of the lonely widow concept.

"Please?" he asked.

From the safety of the darkness, she found she could talk about Doug to this man whom she'd wished would kiss her only seconds before. "He was a good man. Kind, resilient. Flexible."

Her sons would take Steve's asking her about Doug as a sign of his wanting to know about the competition. She told herself to take it as a bridge over awkward waters. "And, of course, he liked to play practical jokes." She remembered the afternoon the state troopers had come to her door and she'd believed it to be one of Doug's pranks. A sick prank, but a joke nonetheless.

Steve said, "He always had a picture of you in the dorm room. Tom—Tom Adams, I'm sure you know him, he's with the FBI now—he and I were jealous, I think."

Taylor didn't know what to respond to that remark. She said something about the years flying by.

"How long were you two together, anyway? What... fifteen years?"

Taylor suddenly felt old and tired. "Twenty, counting our courting days in high school." Her twenty years with Doug somehow seemed to say it all and yet still managed to leave everything out.

"I went to his funeral," he said.

She nodded, though she doubted he could see her. She'd felt so unsynchronized that day. She'd risen from her too empty bed, somehow gathered her sons and attended Doug's funeral. It hadn't seemed a farewell so much as a ritual to be survived.

"You look different in black," he said.

She thought about that for a moment, not certain if he was complimenting her or merely making an observation. "It seemed like half the country was there in uniform. When they did the twenty-one gun salute, every armed officer drew for his gun."

Steve made a sound between a grunt and a chuckle. "I know I did. Someday the brass is going to figure out that those farewell salutes send more guys to the shrink than..." He trailed off.

"Than attending a funeral does," she finished for him. "The boys were impressed, though. It was the only thing that seemed to take their minds off the fact that Doug wasn't going to come waltzing in the front door later that night and ask them what they'd been up to all day. Jason even asked me that night when Daddy was coming home, that he had a lot to tell him."

Somehow she'd known he wouldn't say that two years was plenty of time to get over the loss of a husband and for the boys to get over the loss of a father.

"Must get lonely sometimes," he said.

"Lonely?" she asked, not admitting, even to herself, that his statement left her feeling that way for the first time in a very long time. So she lied to him. "Not with triplets and enough family scattered here and about to trip over every time I walk out the front door."

"You lived here with…Doug…before…?"

"In this very house. We pretty well had our pick of any empty house in town. That was after the oil crunch and Almost practically folded up and blew away. This house seemed big enough to accommodate the boys. When they came."

Steve felt the weight of her life with Doug settle on his shoulders. He tried telling himself that he felt sorry for her; she had several challenges to overcome if she was to try a second chance at marriage. She had three exceedingly precocious preteen sons. She lived in a dinky town in the middle of nowhere, dwelling in the same house she and her husband had chosen and fixed up for a life together. Nearly every man he knew would feel daunted by such a prospect.

His estimation of her soared upward a couple of notches. And on the danger scale, she was already in the red.

Then she chuckled. "Watch Elephant—" she instructed, pointing a slender finger at the smallest of their three dogs, who was belly-crawling toward Steve's crossed feet. "He thinks we can't see him."

At her mention of the dog's name, the small mutt whined a little and started backpedaling until he reached his pals.

"They're well trained," Steve said, wondering how she'd managed to command order from both children and animals, especially when everything seemed to come in sets of three.

"They're terrible," she said, and he could hear the smile in her voice. "But they're loving. And that's all that's important, isn't it?"

He couldn't answer her; he was suddenly, inexplicably afraid she might be right.

She stood and walked to the edge of the porch to lean against the rail. The rocking chair she'd abandoned continued to rock gently, as if some part of her had stayed behind, would stay there forever.

Steve realized that if he pictured her in the future, he would see her in that chair, face serene, a small smile playing on her lips, her eyes closed as if dreaming.

His list of her obstacles to a second marriage was pure hooey, he realized. Maybe he'd come up with that list just to scare himself off. Lord knew, around her, he needed scaring. Something about her made him want to forget consequences, made him want to just pull her against his chest and kiss her senseless.

He set his cigar in the ashtray and stilled his chair as he stood up. He wasn't sure why he'd stopped the rocking, though he suspected it had something to do with leaving part of himself behind to rock beside her.

He straightened to find her steady gaze on him. Now that she was standing, the golden light from the kitchen illuminated her features. A light breeze tugged at a stray strand of her blond hair and lifted it. Her eyes darted from his to his lips and back again. Her tongue darted out and wetted them.

Unconscious as it may have been, no invitation had ever been clearer. He took a step toward her.

"Thanks for dinner," he said.

"You're welcome." Her cheeks seemed to pale a little. Her lips parted.

He was close enough to smell her perfume, a scent that strangely reminded him of autumn mornings. A scent that lured him yet another step closer. What in the hell was he doing? This woman was as off-limits as a woman got in his book. She was his college roommate's widow, she was vulnerable...and he was an idiot. A gullible, pedestal-raising, country-boy fool.

"I'd better turn in now," he said, yet didn't make a move toward the door. One touch, he told himself.

"Yes." She sighed, as if answering his inner thoughts, not responding to his statement of fact. Of safety.

Her rapid and shallow breathing caused her blouse to rise and fall. And for the life of him he couldn't help glancing down. Call him a politically incorrect son of a sea cook.

Damn, he thought. "Good night," he said aloud.

If he'd been out drinking all night, he might have been able to explain the compulsion to keep moving forward, to ignore every rational thought in his brain. And, if he'd had anything to drink but iced tea that evening, maybe he'd have been able to rationalize why his hands were reaching for her.

Taylor found she could scarcely breathe. She was vaguely aware of the old saying warning dreamers of wishes coming true.

As if their bodies were in perfect harmony, she leaned forward at the precise moment his hand slid into the curve of her waist. While everything in her rational mind told her she was making a mistake, everything in the shadowed night told her she could lean still farther, arch into his arms, close her eyes, feel his warm breath playing on her skin.

He slowly, carefully pulled her closer, cupping one large hand over her cheek, fingers slipping beneath her hair, drawing her upward. And then his lips brushed hers. Slowly. Gently. A question, perhaps a quest.

For a shocking, startled second, she wondered what she was supposed to do with her hands. Then, as if they had a will of their own, they found his muscled forearms and rested there, lightly at first, then with gathering strength, pulling him, drawing him to her as he was enticing her to him.

He groaned a little, as if in pain, then deepened his kiss, his hold on her, enfolding her in his arms, tasting her, drawing a passion from her she'd thought long buried.

She literally felt dizzied by his touch, by the contact with him. Whatever electricity had flared between them earlier crackled anew, setting her body aflame.

She was suddenly, sadly conscious of how long it had been since she'd been kissed, the kind of man-woman, deep, strong-attraction *kissed*. The awareness of the kiss, the man behind it made her knees weaken, made her cling to him even more. She felt she was drowning and part of her never wanted to come back up for air.

She didn't know when her hands left his forearms and linked around his neck, her fingers burying themselves in the soft hair she'd wanted to touch since her first glimpse of him. And she didn't know when she drew him down still more firmly, fully acknowledging the passion he inspired in her. All she was aware of was the feel of his lips against hers, his hot tongue warring with hers, his hands roaming her back, her waist, steadily stroking her, inciting the fires in her.

And when his hand slid upward to cup her breast, molding her to his palm, she moaned a sigh of pleasure into his waiting mouth and pressed against him. The flames rippling over her were liquid now, molten in intensity, and the very blood in her veins seemed to run hot and fiery.

He lowered his lips to a wildly throbbing pulse at the apex of her collarbone. Her fingers dug into his shoulders as he blew hot, shallow breaths into the vee created by her blouse. He raised his head again, looking at her through half-closed eyes, eyes as glazed with desire as her own must have been.

"You are so incredibly beautiful," he whispered. "I've wanted to do this from the minute I first...since you opened the..." The rest of his sentence was lost in his kiss.

"Maybe the boys weren't so far wrong, after all," she murmured in response, capturing his lower lip gently between her teeth.

He didn't suddenly still. Taylor thought he seemed to stiffen slowly, pulling away from her as cautiously as he'd approached her originally.

"What?" she asked, scarcely able to see him through vision clouded with desire. But she knew he was frowning. Still holding her, but frowning.

"The boys *are* wrong," he said.

Confused, she could only let her hands trail down his muscled chest.

"People don't fall in love after just one kiss, Taylor."

That hadn't been what she meant when she'd said the words, but it didn't matter. What mattered was his distance now. Though still touching her, he might as well have been on the other side of a great chasm, the far rim of the Grand Canyon.

And it seemed somehow sadder that he'd used her name for the first time as he ran from her.

She smiled crookedly. Sadly. Because he didn't know

what he was talking about. "What are you trying to tell me?" she asked. But she knew. She *knew.*

"People *don't* really fall in love at first sight," he said, almost angrily. "They can't."

"Who are you trying to convince? Me or yourself?" she asked softly. She dropped her arms to her sides, pinning his hands against her for a moment. It surprised her how much it hurt when he drew his hands away.

"I just don't believe in the kind of things you do," he said.

"You don't know what I believe in," she replied. She nearly smiled. While she knew from personal experience that it was entirely possible to fall in love after one single, blissful kiss, he seemed to feel a great need to deny the possibility.

"Sure I do," he said, stepping back from her and running a hand through the hair she'd so thoroughly disarranged for him. "You'll tell me you believe in those old classic values. Raising kids in a small town. Having sitdown dinners. You'll tell me you believe in families, community service, doing things for people. That you believed—still believe—in marriage."

"I do," she said.

"It's ludicrous to think that sort of thing is possible."

"So call me ludicrous," she said, and smiled to take the sting away. She didn't understand what he was trying to tell her, but she knew it came from some part of his bruised heart.

"God, you're more gullible than I am," he said.

She resisted the urge to stroke his cheek. "What a crime," she said softly.

"It's not a crime, Taylor. It's just not for me. I've been around that block twice."

She was certain he had no idea how wistful he sounded.

Tough guy Texas Ranger Steve Kessler reminded her of a little boy locked outside on a cold night, staring in at a warm family scene.

"And you don't believe people can know love the moment they see it, the second they feel it?"

He closed his eyes, and when he opened them, he didn't look at her. He said raggedly, "No, Taylor, I don't."

"I see," she said.

"I'm just not into the whole marriage package. I'm just trying to be up-front here."

She raised a hand to cup his face. "Who hurt you so badly, Steve?"

Chapter 7

Steve lay on his back on the folded-out sofa bed, his head resting on his hands. He stared at the ceiling as if expecting it to answer the myriad questions roiling in his mind.

He still ached with want of Taylor and was still reeling from her question about who had hurt him so badly. He'd only been trying to warn her that she shouldn't read anything into their kiss. He'd only wanted to let her know straight-out that he wasn't the marrying kind of man.

He might have been once. But he'd tried it too many times. Twice too many times. Once, shame on you. Twice, shame on me. Third time...

He should never have given in to the impulse to kiss her. And once there, he should have pulled back immediately. But he'd been stunned at the depth of her passion, at the intensity of his own. He'd been lost in her sweet taste, the heady scent of her perfume, the feel of her soft skin. And he'd felt like he'd come home, finally arrived at a destination he'd desired for years.

The house seemed to sigh around him, a soft soughing. He glanced at the window and saw, through a crack in the curtains, that a tree gently bent at the caress of a stray night breeze. A breeze. He'd heard a light breeze. How many years had it been since he'd heard anything less than a full-force hurricane?

But in Almost, with no one traveling down the well-maintained county road—that could more accurately be termed a farm-to-market road—and all houses in the village dark, dogs asleep and even the insects silent, he found he couldn't hear anything but the breeze. If he listened closely, he could probably hear Taylor breathing from her room down the hall.

He tossed and turned restlessly.

Less than twenty yards away, Taylor also lay awake, staring at the stars through her opened curtains.

She had the disconcerting feeling that, like Sleeping Beauty, Steve had wakened her with his kiss. She wasn't a young girl, as she'd been once, flushed from the throes of unfamiliar feelings and desires; she was a woman now, all too aware of her body, alive to the possibilities inherent in the passion that seemed to flare so effortlessly between them.

It saddened her to think that Steve claimed not to want the same things she did. And it saddened her more to realize that until he'd voiced them, she hadn't known she'd wanted them herself. If he'd never cataloged the fundamental desires in her life, would those wants never have surfaced?

If he didn't find a nearly dead guy with a bullet wound in his chest, Steve would be returning to Houston. He would go back to his life, his condo probably, and, un-doubtedly, his bevy of pretty women. Men who con-demned marriage seemed to revel in that rigidly imper-manent life-style. Even men who had tried marriage twice. Maybe especially those men.

And, aside from three boys who would talk about him for days afterward, her life would go back to the exact same routine it had carried for the past couple of years. Wake, cook, visit, cook some more, clean some more and go to bed, sometimes to fall asleep, sometimes to cry her-self there.

Except her life wouldn't be quite the same now.

By kissing her, he'd infected her with a restlessness, a longing she'd managed to sublimate for so long, so well and so perfectly that she'd nearly forgotten it existed.

She pounded the pillow, ostensibly to make it more comfortable, but more likely in lieu of hitting one prob-ably soundly sleeping Texas Ranger. The sooner he left Almost, the better it would be for her. And for her sons. Better for them to learn that many men would rather live alone all their lives than to commit to a family.

"That's just fine with me," she muttered. She might not have realized, until he'd told her, just how deeply she did want a new life, a second chapter, but she understood how firmly ingrained was her reluctance to hook up with another peace officer. One life blown to bits had been enough.

Oh, but how she'd liked having a man sitting at the dinner table again. And rocking on the back porch with her. And having him holding her in his arms, his lips pressed to her collarbone.

Taylor groaned aloud and sat up. If Steve wasn't in the living room, she'd simply get up and go to the kitchen for a glass of lemonade. And maybe sit outside on the back porch for a while.

A scream pierced the stillness.

Taylor was out of bed and across the room before she fully recognized the sound as coming from one of her sons. She flew out her bedroom door and down the hall, flicking on the light as she went, and before the second scream rent the night she threw open the door to her sons' room.

She hesitated on the threshold of the boys' large bedroom. Because the three boys had never wanted separate rooms, she and Doug had simply knocked out the walls dividing three bedrooms and turned the space into one very large room. Each boy had a wall for dressers and bookcases, but the three of them had long ago pushed their twin beds to the center of the room to span out like spokes of a wheel with a nightstand and three lamps as a hub.

The second scream still echoed in the air as she paused, wondering which of her sons was being murdered.

"Jeezly crow—what's going on?" Jonah asked.

"It's Jason," Josh answered.

Taylor rounded Jason's bed and swiftly sat down on the edge of it. He was tossing his head back and forth as if trying to escape a monster, and his mouth was wide open, ready to loose another terrible scream.

"Jason...sweetie...Mom's here," she said. She repeated her words a second time, stroking his forehead and rubbing his exposed shoulder. She didn't want to wake him abruptly.

"What's wrong with him, Mom?"

"A nightmare," Taylor said.

Jason stopped thrashing but began mumbling loudly,

"Don't come any closer, mister. I mean it. Oh, God, he's gonna touch me!"

"No one's going to touch you, Jason," Taylor said firmly as she lightly shook his shoulder. "I'm right here, honey. Nothing can hurt you now."

His eyes popped open and he stared at her through the shadowy light from the hallway. He gasped at seeing someone so close to him, then realized who it was. "Mom," he croaked gratefully.

"Yes, honey. I'm right here."

"That dude was chasing me. His face was all covered with flies and he had dirt under his fingernails like he'd crawled out of a grave or something."

Taylor's other sons exchanged murmurs of appreciation for the fright.

"I was afraid he was going to touch me."

"It was a dream, Jason," Taylor said. "Just a nightmare."

"He was all covered with blood. From his bullet wound. I kept thinking that's how Dad must have looked. All covered with blood."

"Oh, honey."

Jason pushed himself to a sitting position and threw his arms around her, squeezing her painfully. "He didn't look like that, did he, Mom? Dad, I mean. He didn't, did he?"

Taylor hugged him tightly, trying to subdue his trembling, trying to convey with her body what words could never do. "No, honey. No, of course he didn't. It's okay now. I'm here," she said.

"It really creeped me out."

"It would have creeped me out, too."

"Where is he, Mom?"

"Yeah, Mom, he can't come in here, can he?"

"No. We're safe here," she said.

"How can we be sure? What if he breaks in the window?"

"What if he kills our dogs and sneaks in the back door?"

"What if the real killer saw us out there and thinks we know who he is? Like in that movie...?"

"What if he does something to you, Mom?"

"Nothing's going to happen to you or your mother," said a deep voice from the hallway.

All four of them jumped and whirled to face the door.

Steve Kessler stepped into the doorway, silhouetted by the light from the hall. He literally filled the space inside the door, his hair brushing the lintel, his bare feet on the threshold.

"Jason had a scary dream," Josh explained.

"It was a *nightmare*," Jason said hotly, as if the distinction conferred adult status.

"The nearly dead guy was coming after him," Jonah said.

"What if he does come after us?" Josh asked.

Taylor held her breath as Steve stepped into the room, approaching the spokelike beds. His chest was bare, revealing a broad expanse of male musculature. She closed her eyes briefly. He seemed determined to drive her insane.

"And what if the real killer is on, like, a spree?"

"Number one, I can't think of a single reason why the nearly dead guy would want to come here. All you boys did was try to help him," Steve told them.

"But what if—"

"Number two, if you'd seen who shot the guy, than he would have seen you. Since you boys weren't witnesses to the actual crime, you don't have to worry about him, either."

"Yeah, but—"

"Number three, if the shooter saw you, he's sure not going to want to come around here and bother you. Especially with me in town."

"Yeah, but—"

"And number four, if you three are going to help me with my investigation tomorrow, you'll need to get some sleep."

"Help you?"

"No fooling?"

"Way, *way* cool!"

All three boys hurled themselves back under the covers and closed their eyes tightly. The sight reminded Taylor of the way the boys used to act when she told them Santa wouldn't come until after they went to sleep.

She patted Jason's shoulder. "You okay now?" she asked softly.

Jason shrugged nonchalantly. "'Course, Mom. It was only a dream. That guy wouldn't really come after us."

"I love you," Taylor said.

"I love you, too, Mom."

Watching them, Steve felt his heart constrict. Taylor said the words of love with such ease and with such obvious feeling. What would it be like to have a woman like Taylor saying such words to...say...a man like him?

Had she said the words to Doug after all their years together? Somehow, he thought perhaps she had. The thought troubled him on many levels he didn't care to explore.

"Good night, boys," she said, rising to her feet. She stepped around the edge of the bed, moving toward him.

Steve's heart gave a jolt and started beating too rapidly.

"G'night, Mom. Love you."

"Love you, too, guys. Sweet dreams. Really sweet ones this time."

Steve found himself smiling crookedly as her sons laughed. He backed out of the room to allow Taylor to draw the door partway closed.

One of the boys called out in a falsetto Freddy Krueger imitation, "I'm coming to get you, Jason. And I've got dirty fingernails!"

Steve had to bite off a laugh as Taylor choked, then said, "Cut it out, Josh." He knew she couldn't have been heard over the swearing and giggling in the darkened bedroom.

He waited as she pulled the door closed with a soft snap and raised her eyes, not to his, but to his chest. Her gaze landed there and skittered off. She studied the wall just beyond his shoulder.

"Thanks."

"For nothing," he said.

Her eyes flicked to his, then away again. "You don't still have any doubts that they saw somebody wounded, do you?"

He smiled. "About that, no."

He thought her smile was wistful. "Sorry we woke you," she said.

"You didn't. I was awake."

She darted a glance at him, then looked away. "So was I. It was too hot to sleep."

Since Steve reckoned her central air-conditioning was probably set on something just above freezing, he couldn't help but grin a little. Luckily, she wasn't looking at him.

"I'm going to get some lemonade," she said. "Want some?"

He knew he should just decline and climb back in that lumpy sofa bed and toss and turn some more, but ever since he'd walked through Taylor Smithton's front door, his rational mind seemed to have taken a vacation. "Sounds good."

On the way through the living room, he grabbed his shirt and shrugged into it. It seemed the lady couldn't look at him when he wasn't fully dressed.

But it seemed he was wrong about that. When he pushed through the doorway into the kitchen, she shot him a quick glance, then looked back down to find herself carefully pouring lemonade all over her countertop.

She righted the pitcher with an oath he'd have sworn couldn't escape her lips, then set it on the counter with a sharp thud. "Try to hit the glasses next time," she muttered, reaching for a drawer. Inside it, he saw some thirty or forty neatly folded tea towels.

She blotted the lemonade from the counter, rinsed the cloth and vigorously scrubbed the Formica. "Ants," she said.

Even from where he stood he could see that her eyes were bright with unshed tears. "I beg your pardon?" he asked.

"If I don't get it up right away, the ants will find it. Summer, fall, dead of winter. They're always waiting for a speck of sugar. I've heard horror stories of people having to move just to get away from them."

Steve blinked. This didn't quite seem like her. Her house was tidy enough, but not meticulous. It was impossible to be meticulous in dusty West Texas. The person who tried would go crazy.

She rinsed the tea towel again and wrung it dry before draping it over the bar in the center of the sink. She leaned against the counter, her back to him. She seemed completely unaware that her silk nightgown was not only clinging to her skin, revealing every rich curve and sleek line, but affecting him like a shot of stiff whiskey, leaving him strangely breathless and burning all over.

"That was a terrible nightmare," she said.

"Yes," he said slowly, trying not to undress her the rest of the way with his eyes, telling himself not to be a fool, not to fall into the gullibility zone.

"The boys never saw Doug…after. I made sure they kept the casket closed."

He remembered Jason's question about how his father had looked.… *He didn't, did he?* Steve didn't know what to say, so said nothing at all.

"I lied to him. All of them." She waved her hand. "It's not like I haven't lied to them before. Everyone lies. 'Oh, that's a cute horny toad, Josh. I don't really hate that cartoon, Jonah.' Stuff like that. Little lies. But you see, I never told them what Doug looked like. I didn't want them to know. So I lied to them. I lied to Jason tonight. All I told them at the time was that he was killed instantly, that there was no blood because of that."

Steve closed his eyes. He realized a part of him had always wondered, too. She should never have had to see such a thing. No one should. "You did the right thing, Taylor."

A shudder worked down her spine. It took every inch of resolve in him not to cross the room and take her into his arms. And then some.

"Was it right? I always thought so. Then tonight, because of that stranger they found—oh, how I wish he'd just show up and tell us it was all a nasty joke, the kind Doug thought was funny sometimes—but because of him, the nearly dead guy, I mean, Jason's having nightmares and wondering if his father looked like that after he was…was k-killed."

All Steve's resolve evaporated when her voice broke.

He crossed the room and drew her back against his chest, wrapping his arms around her, cradling her shoulders, rocking slightly. And, unconsciously, he used the very same words she'd said to her son earlier. "It's okay, honey. Sh. It's okay."

But it wasn't, he thought. He pressed a kiss to her temple and kept his lips against her velvet skin. He closed his eyes. "It'll be all right," he murmured. As she'd asked earlier, just who was he trying to convince…her or himself?

When Taylor felt his warm arms enfold her, drawing her against his broad chest, she'd felt vaguely humiliated at breaking down in front of him. Especially because of his denial of emotional involvement. His calling her "honey," his rocking motion, a slow, gentle swaying left and right, his warm lips murmuring soothing nothings against her temple, smoothed over her embarrassment.

It felt so *right*. So permanent, somehow.

Steve Kessler might profess not to be the marrying kind of man, but he was the very kind of man a woman wanted to marry. She smiled slightly and raised a hand to wipe away the tears that had broken free.

"I'm okay now," she said. "It just threw me."

He didn't let go of her. If anything, he held her tighter. "It'd throw anybody."

"Thank you," she said, referring also to his calm support in the bedroom, and signaling him that he could take those arms away from her now.

He stopped the rocking motion but didn't turn her loose. The cessation of the slow undulation thrust their contact onto a different plane. Between one heartbeat and the next, it transformed from neutral nurturing to a sexual attraction.

She realized suddenly, and with a catch in her breath, that she could feel his shirt buttons through her thin nightgown. She could feel his heart thudding against her back. She could feel the long line of his legs. And could feel his awareness that things had just changed.

And still he didn't move.

Her breathing came a little faster, and every nerve ending on her body called out a need for immediate contact.

He kissed her temple, a far different sensation from the comforting, gentling pressure she'd felt earlier. No less gentle, but infused with a deliberate, tantalizing intention now, he trailed feather-soft lips down her cheek, her jawline, her bared throat.

She felt simultaneously enervated and energized. Her entire body trembled in reaction, her legs threatening to buckle, her head dropping back to rest on his shoulder, granting him even greater access.

He ran his hands along her arms, warming her, heating her, turning her into clay for his careful sculpting. He slowly massaged her fingers, her palms, her numb arms, all the while nuzzling the soft hollow beneath her ear, the sharp curve of her collarbone.

If he hadn't been standing behind her now, she would have collapsed to the ground, such was her intense languor.

Slowly, steadily, he massaged her arms, her shoulders, her hands, raising his head only to kiss her temple again, to rub his cheeks against her hair, to brush a kiss near her lips, to lightly flick his tongue at the nape of her neck.

Feeling weightless and yet strangely heavy, Taylor tried telling herself to stop him, to run and hide in her safe, lonely bedroom. She knew she was too vulnerable, too unprepared for a physical relationship with any man, let alone one who wore a badge and who had already made it clear he didn't want any involvement. Most of all, she knew she should cry a halt because this man, this one man, made her feel alive again, and to feel alive was to risk everything.

But she didn't run. She couldn't.

His strong hands slipped from her arms to her waist, and his massaging, caressing, stroking continued. Her stomach, her breasts, her trembling thighs...his hands roamed over her, exploring her, finding rills and valleys, lingering at her breasts then molding her to him, letting her know he was as aroused as she.

And yet, she had the strangest feeling that mere arousal was the very least part of what he was doing to her...and what she was doing to him. She wanted to close her eyes forever and savor every nuance of emotion that flowed between them.

This, she thought, *this* was what it was supposed to be like. Love, life, *feeling.*

With a groan that seemed to come from deep inside him, he abruptly whirled her around to face him, pulling her sharply against his full length, plundering her mouth with a kiss that seemed born of desperation.

Hungered beyond thought, she returned his kiss with the clear impression that only this moment existed in all of reality. His touch, his taste, the rich scent of this one man filled her senses and left them reeling.

"Oh, man!" a voice muttered.

"Sh, can't you see they're *kissing?*" another whispered.

"Wa-ay cool!"

She felt dropped from a cliff's edge as Steve released her and pivoted, automatically blocking her from the boys' sight. "What are you doing up?" he growled.

"Nothing," said one.

"Getting a drink," lied another.

"We're outta here!" said the third, and a wild elephant stampede couldn't have more loudly announced their departure. Their bedroom door slammed shut, though whoops of triumph could still be heard.

Taylor leaned against the counter, her legs trembling too badly to support her. She watched through heavy-lidded eyes as Steve raised a hand and smoothed back his hair. He let out a large whoosh of air.

"I didn't mean to yell at them," he said. He shot her a sideways glance, then looked at the still-swinging kitchen door.

Taylor half smiled at his back. "They didn't sound as if they minded."

He turned then, a rueful grin on his face. "No, I think they believe we're halfway down the aisle already."

His words shot a pang of regret through her; she wasn't sure why. Perhaps because they carried too much reality in them, and for those beautiful few minutes, she'd been transported beyond the mundane world. But it could have been because he looked as stricken as she felt.

"I'd better turn in myself," he said. His eyes dropped to her nightgown and back up again.

"Yeah," she said, wishing she didn't want to argue with him, wishing she could simply step back into his arms and forget the universe.

"Yeah," he echoed, and left the kitchen without looking at her again.

She stayed where she was for a moment, then pushed herself away from the counter and walked, somewhat unsteadily, to where she'd left the lemonade pitcher. She put it away, doused the lights, drew a deep breath and bravely walked into the darkened living room.

"Good night, Steve," she said, hesitating at the entrance to the hall. She couldn't see more of him than a largish shadow in the center of the sofa bed.

She clicked off the hall light, plunging them into total darkness.

"Taylor...?"

"Yes?"

"Have you dated much since...?"

Her heart rate accelerated anew. "No. Not at all."

"The men around here must be blind."

She smiled, and it felt awkward on her lips. "There aren't any single men around here except Doc Jamison, and he seems more like a brother than a..." She trailed off, unable to complete her comparison.

"I agree with the boys about one thing."

"What's that?" she asked, her heart thundering now.

"They have the most beautiful mother."

Taylor closed her eyes, savoring his words. "You're not so bad yourself."

"Cool," he said, and she could hear his grin.

"Yeah. Way cool," she said. But even to herself, the words sounded bittersweet.

Chapter 8

After a confusing, restless night's sleep, Steve woke with the firm conviction that the sooner he got out of Almost, the better. What happened in the kitchen couldn't happen again. Taylor was too vulnerable, still too fragile following the loss of her husband. Just as she was the kind of woman to marry and raise a family, she was also the kind that could devote her whole life to one man. And that man had been Doug Smithton.

Steve knew, if he was completely honest, that she shook him up, made him want things he knew better than to wish for. Again. She didn't have sparkling, witty conversation that made him uncomfortable, searching for some new quip or retort, yet she was light-years from unintelligent. She had a gift for making a stranger feel right at home. Too right.

She didn't go along with everything he said, just to strengthen his male ego, yet one kiss, one touch, and she made him feel more male than he'd ever felt before. She didn't seem combative—except when he'd barked at her kids the afternoon before—and yet he felt oddly challenged.

She wasn't like anyone he knew, in fact, and yet she made every woman he'd been with seem a little shallow by comparison. Look-alikes or not.

He shook his head and slid the sofa bed back into place with a little more force than necessary. Hell, he didn't know why he was analyzing this woman to death; he would be back in Houston that evening and would, in all likelihood, never see her again.

Except in his dreams.

He squared his shoulders and headed for the kitchen, the scent of coffee and the sound of three eleven-year-olds plotting some new scheme. He pushed open the door.

The three boys were slouched against counters and the table, semicircling their lovely parent. The picture they presented, one of relaxed harmony, a togetherness that somehow seemed to come straight out of a Currier & Ives painting, didn't seem to isolate Steve as it had the night before. A person could adjust to anything, he thought, and then wondered why the impression troubled him.

He looked at Taylor, who hadn't noticed him yet. Dressed like a thousand other women in West Texas, in jeans, tennis shoes and a cotton blouse tucked in at the waist, her hair caught up in a ponytail, she looked fresh and inviting. And too alluring.

"Maybe Mr. Hampton's barn loft needs cleaning," Jason suggested hopefully.

"Hey, yeah. Mom, did you know Mr. Hampton's barn has a loft?"

Her face softened, causing Steve to suffer a long-unfamiliar pang in his midsection. "Yes. We used to play there when we were kids."

"You, Uncle Craig and Aunt Allison?"

"When we were little. As I recall, we weren't allowed to play in there. Too dangerous."

"That's kinda what Mr. Hampton said yesterday."

"That's when we found out he had a loft. We didn't know about it before."

"Is it cool, Mom? Like way cool?"

Steve remembered her parting words from the night before, and how that undefinable something in her voice had wiped the grin from his face. Famous last words, he'd thought then, and felt slapped by them now.

"I suppose so," she said. "He used to store cottonseed in the barn proper. We'd climb up in the loft and jump down into that mountain of seed. It was like jumping into a huge, scratchy pillow."

"Wow."

Taylor's faraway gaze refocused on her avid listeners. "But don't you boys go jumping out of there, you hear me? Allison broke her arm one time. In two places. She had to wear a cast all that summer and couldn't run through the sprinkler or go swimming over at the Harrigans' or anything. It still bothers her sometimes...at least, I suppose it does."

Steve watched as the three boys exchanged glances. Another mystery? Why did Taylor look so sad?

"You promise me," Taylor said, frowning now. Steve had the oddest desire to smooth the frown from her brow with a gentle kiss. He would press his lips just between her mobile eyebrows, right on that—

"We won't," three voices chorused.

"I mean it."

"We promise," Jonah—at least Steve thought it was Jonah—said, and received two sideways glares from his brothers, who apparently *didn't* promise any such thing.

Steve let the door fall behind him and found he'd been waiting for the exact moment Taylor would look up at him and smile.

Just like that.

His heart seemed to skip a beat and he swore inwardly. If he was anticipating the way her smile would make him feel, his afternoon flight couldn't come soon enough. He'd be asking her to marry him in less than five minutes, he thought sourly.

"Steve!"

"Hey, Steve, we've got a great plan."

"Yeah, we're going to do community service with Doc Jamison first. He goes everywhere."

"See? And we'll spread the word that we're missing that nearly dead guy."

"Yeah, like, people will start talking and looking for him and stuff—"

"And we'll probably find him in time for dinner."

"Doofus, we're not going to eat him."

"Ee-yuck, who said we wanted to do that?"

He felt his grin spreading. "A little ketchup might make him taste better," he said.

"Good morning, Steve," Taylor managed to interject over her sons' lack of appreciation of a bloody, nearly dead guy for dinner. "Boys, let the man have some coffee before you talk him to death."

"Yeah, but—"

"Scoot on outside. Run off some of that energy with the dogs."

Human tornadoes couldn't have contained more energy than the three bounding out the back door, calling for their faithful companions.

Taylor calmly closed the back door. "Coffee?"

"You bet," he said, leaning against the refrigerator, careful not to displace various notes, drawings and photos.

"How do you take it?"

Funny, he thought, the night before they'd kissed like there was no tomorrow. He was lighting out of town because he was scared to death she'd somehow ensnare him in her warm, too comfortable world, and she didn't even know how he took his coffee.

"Black," he said. To match his ever shifting mood.

She handed him a large, steaming mug.

He sipped at it and signaled his appreciation.

"I feel like we're doing a coffee commercial," Taylor said, joining him at the table. "We can talk about Paris now, or something romantically nostalgic."

He wanted to ask her if the boys had said anything about the impassioned kiss they'd witnessed the night before, but didn't have the slightest clue how to bring it up, or what to say if she did. He settled for a grin.

Her answering smile seemed to exacerbate rather than ease the tension between them, though he couldn't have begun to guess why. He was actually grateful when the telephone rang and she rose to answer it.

After a few perfunctory questions and answers, she laughed and said, "You're sure you don't mind having the pack riding with you this afternoon, Doc? I can always rope somebody else into coming up with chores for them. I suppose I could spring for another can of paint for the school playground. It can always use one."

Watching her ease with this unknown veterinarian, Steve was conscious of a stab of what could only be jealousy. Sure, she'd told him the night before that she thought of Doc Jamison like a brother, but with the man on the other end of the phone she didn't exhibit any of the uneasiness she did with him.

"Well, just don't let them drive you too crazy," she said, then, in response to something he said, she laughed again, a delicious, throaty chuckle that severely undermined Steve's determination to run as far away from her as his two legs and an airplane would take him.

"Well, that's one problem solved," she said, rejoining him at the table. "Doc's going to run straw boss for the community service stint today."

Steve grinned uncertainly, again conscious of a stab of jealousy. The boys were a handful, sure, but somehow in his short stay in Almost, he'd already found he rather liked the heavy dose of hero worship they had for him. While he was in town, they were supposed to be *his* handful.

The telephone rang. This time it was for Steve from Doris Ledbetter at the Houston office. "So, how many more Almost dead bodies have you found?" she asked.

"Only the one," he said. "And he's still missing."

Taylor rose and busied herself at the kitchen sink, creating a false impression that she couldn't overhear his conversation. Steve briefly wondered if she was reacting to his laughing conversation with Doris as he had to Taylor's camaraderie with the veterinarian.

"Almost triplets," Doris said, chuckling. "Sounds like you have your hands full. Should I call Lubbock and rally the troops? You'll be running for the nearest exit in minutes. I can already hear your feet in motion."

Steve frowned slightly, wondering why the quip pricked him. Because he *did* always run? Because it was far too close to the truth?

"No, it's not like that," he said a bit too firmly. "If the guy doesn't turn up before my flight, it's pretty good odds he's not in the area anymore. Somebody'll patch him up somewhere and we'll get a lead then. The boys are spreading the word that, as they put it, we're missing a nearly dead guy."

Doris chuckled. "Admit it, Steve, you're having fun."

"In a one-horse town in the middle of the high plains? You've gotta be kidding." He wished he could take back the words when Taylor's spine stiffened and she tossed her ponytail as if annoyed.

Doris said, "City life's not all it's cracked up to be. And you know you hate it."

"Neither is living in the country," he shot back, ignoring the truth of her second statement.

"Already running. Like I said, I can hear your big old feet. Okay, boss, but here's hoping you trip. A pretty widow with three rambunctious kids could be exactly what the doctor ordered. I have to admit, I'd love to see the day when you fall. It would save me holding another dinner party with some dreary, anorexic excuse for a woman."

Steve didn't comment for the simple reason that he couldn't formulate a retort. Anything he said in denial of her words would, at that moment, be a lie. And Doris had just admitted she'd never liked the women she was trying to fix him up with.

"So, see you in the morning?"

Steve's frown deepened and a depression seemed to grab hold of him. Leaving Almost was exactly what he wanted to do, so why should Doris's reminder that tomorrow he would be hundreds of miles away bother him so?

He hung up the phone and turned to find Taylor studying him. "What?" he asked.

"You're leaving today," she said. She voiced the words without a nuance of inflection.

He wanted to apologize for the sky being a bright, undying blue. But he wouldn't. "If nothing turns up by mid-afternoon."

"I see."

Steve felt a familiar pang of guilt, for the kisses the night before, for his desire to leave, for leaving before everything was resolved. And the pang was followed by a stab of irritation. He'd told her he wasn't the marrying kind. Why should he feel guilty about warning her ahead of time? Why should he feel guilty about not wanting the things she did?

Taylor felt slapped by him, by his rejection of her home, her town, but mostly by his blatant disregard of the kisses they'd shared the night before.

She told herself not to question it. She wasn't the first woman to be kissed, then ignored, and she wouldn't be the last. She told herself to be wise and let it go. Let *him* go without letting him know that the kiss had meant something to her, had left her soul-searching and hungry.

Doug had often told her that her greatest fault was not knowing when to let well enough alone. "What are you doing?" she asked.

He stiffened, as if anticipating a blow. But he was the one dealing the blows.

She felt glued to her side of the floor. She wanted to walk over to him, touch him, if nothing more than to convince herself he was real. Or maybe to convince herself that the night before had really happened.

He turned away from her and stared out the kitchen window, watching her sons romping with their dogs. He sighed heavily. Then, without looking at her, he said, "I've been married twice, Taylor."

She frowned, not at the news, but at his delivery of it. He jerked away from the window as the back door banged open and her troupe of wild elephants thundered into the kitchen.

"Did you call Doc?"

"Are we going with him?"

"Did you find anything new, Steve?"

"How are we gonna find out who killed that dude?"

The boys seemed to sense the tension between the two adults, for they faltered to a silence unusual to them.

"Everything okay?" Jason asked.

"Uh, maybe we better feed the dogs or something."

"Yeah, like they're probably hungry."

"Outside."

"Yeah, outside."

The three scuttled for the back door and went out, worried frowns volleying back and forth at Steve and her.

"What are you trying to tell me?" she asked when he didn't say anything more.

The back door popped open. "Forgot something," Jonah said, dashing inside and grabbing the huge sack of dog food. He wrestled it outside and slammed the door behind him.

"Steve?"

The telephone rang. Taylor swore aloud and yanked it from its cradle, barking a hello into the receiver, never taking her eyes from Steve's back. "Oh, Aunt Sammie Jo. I'm sorry. No, everything's fine. I just...what? When?"

Steve turned slightly, almost looking at her.

She listened awhile longer then covered the mouthpiece with her hand. "Kurt, Martha Thompson's boy, found a gun in Charlie Hampton's sorghum field."

"Did he leave it there, I hope?" Steve asked, turning to look at her finally. But this was a different Steve, all business and hard Texas Ranger.

Taylor asked, and paled a little at Sammie Jo's answer. She again covered the receiver. "No. Martha Thompson told Sammie Jo—she didn't call here because her cell phone batteries are down and she lives close to Sammie Jo. Anyway, she said Kurt carried it all the way home by holding a number two pencil through the trigger."

Steve closed his eyes for a second, but when he opened them he looked much more like the Steve she thought she'd come to know. A slight, nearly imperceptible smile tugged at the corners of his mouth. "Tell her I'll be right there. And tell her *not* to touch the gun."

Taylor did as instructed and hung up the phone.

"How do I get to her place?" Steve asked, reaching for the swinging door.

"By way of explaining what being married twice has anything to do with the price of eggs in Almost," Taylor said.

He smiled crookedly. Sadly, she thought. "When you fail at something twice, you learn to leave it alone," he said slowly, meeting her eyes directly now.

"I'm not a something," she said.

"Oh, you are, Taylor. You're very much something." His smile was still sad.

The back door burst open. "You guys done talking yet?"

"You going somewhere, Steve?"

"Kurt found a gun," Taylor said.

"Kurt *Thompson?*"

"Oh, man, he has all the luck."

"We found the nearly dead guy."

"Yeah, but he disappeared."

"But we saw him first."

"Yeah, that's cool. But a gun..."

"You know this Kurt?" Steve asked.

"Yeah, he's in our grade at the Almost School."

"A friend of yours?"

The boys looked blank, then two of them shrugged. If Steve didn't know what the blank looks sprang from, Taylor did. Almost was too small a town to designate people as friends or otherwise. To the boys, Kurt was simply a kid, like themselves, a part of the town, a piece of the whole.

"Hey, are you going over to Kurt's house?"

"Can we come?"

"Yeah, we can translate for you."

"Translate?" Steve asked. "Doesn't he speak English?"

"Yeah, but not as good as us."

Steve actually chuckled. Taylor felt the boulder resting on her heart shift slightly.

"So we can go with you?"

"Please, Steve?"

"Way, way please?"

Steve's eyes softened and his grin seemed to relax. He lifted his eyes and met hers. In the split second before he apparently remembered what they *hadn't* been discussing, he seemed to be sharing his enjoyment of her sons with her. Then his smile faded slightly, not an abrupt cessation, just a withdrawal. From her.

"Sure," he said. "Why not?"

Sure, she thought, why not make them fall for you, too? Make it a clean sweep.

But then, they already had him pegged for their new father.

And he was already out the door with them.

Steve herded the Smithton triplets into his rental car with a strange reluctance to end what had probably been the most bizarre evidence-gathering mission he'd ever been on.

Doug would have loved it, he thought. Hell, he'd loved it. It was a scene right out of Monty Python. Four boys, three identical blondes, one dark and overexcited, all talking seventy-five miles to the second and killing off half the town with blithe insouciance, underscored the innocence of this town, the total naiveté of the inhabitants.

The gun Kurt found lay in a freezer-safe Ziploc plastic bag with a picture of Rudolph the Red-Nosed Reindeer on the front. The festive plastic, out of season and out of Steve's context, only served to underscore his sense of unreality. What other case in the universe would have him placing recovered weapons in such an evidence bag?

But the gun *was* evidence. He had no doubt it had belonged to the boys' fancily clothed nearly dead guy. A nickel-plated, pearl-handled .45, the weapon was an expensive dilettante's toy, designed for more noise than damage, and looks rather than intent. A pretty thing, but largely ineffective if someone really needed to be stopped. It hadn't been fired. Steve wondered if it ever had been. But it was a sure bet fingerprints could be lifted from the fancy handle.

"Are we going home—"

"Or gonna check out the crime scene—"

"Where, like, Kurt found the gun?"

The last place Steve wanted to be at that moment was inside Taylor's too comfortable home. "The crime scene," he said.

"Kurt said he found the gun in as far as his dad is tall."

Steve blinked, trying to first unravel the sentence, then work out the mathematics.

"His dad is real short."

"Yeah, like we're gaining on him—"

"So, the gun had to be pretty close to where we saw the nearly dead guy."

Steve grinned a little. Doug's kids were pretty sharp. They had a clean, fresh way of analyzing situations that plenty a team of Rangers could have used. Good witnesses, good eyes and good regrouping skills.

Once out at Charlie Hampton's place, the boys were suitably impressed with the crime tape blocking the road, extending from two fence posts. And they were nearly struck dumb by the footprints Steve had discovered inside the barn and exceedingly careful not to touch any of them.

And it was the boys who discovered a set of tire tracks on the front side of the barn, tracks that revealed no particular speed coming to the barn but considerable departing.

Damn, Steve thought, Doug would have been proud of these kids. *He* was proud of them and had only known them twenty-four hours. And just as their father had years before and their mother now, they had a way of getting right under his skin.

Taylor's hints on how to tell them apart helped enormously, and by the time they left the barn to head back to the house, then on to Levelland to have the gun fingerprinted, Steve prided himself on the notion that he could actually discern physical differences as well as those of personality.

And by the time they were driving back from Levelland, two hours later, Steve found he wasn't seeing his old college roommate in the boys, he was seeing Taylor's mobile eyebrows, her generous mouth and a myriad of small traits that she seemed to have passed directly to her sons.

Shortly after making the right-angled turn at Anton, the

boys began yawning. The two in the back seat seemed to fold into each other, a loose tangle of arms, legs, tennis shoes and freckled faces. Jonah, holding out longer than his brothers, yawned hugely and slumped across the front seat. Hitching himself into a more comfortable position, he rested his head on Steve's leg, sighed heavily, tucked a fist under his chin and fell deeply asleep.

Steve held his arm up awkwardly, not knowing where to rest his hand, not wanting to wake the boy, uncomfortable holding the wheel the remaining thirty miles. Finally, he gently placed his hand on Jonah's shoulder. While his hand was nearly the same size as the boy's entire upper arm, it seemed to fit there naturally.

He looked up at the road and corrected his erratic driving, even if he couldn't do a thing about the hiccup in his heart.

Chapter 9

From the second Steve returned to her home with her three sleepy sons, the phone had rung incessantly, the doorbell had dingdonged repeatedly, the dogs had barked, the cats had yowled and her boys had been thoroughly rejuvenated by their run to town with their hero.

"Is it always this chaotic around here?" Steve demanded of her as the phone rang for the fifth time.

Taylor tried assessing his mood, the reason for his irritation. He'd returned in a quiet, pensive state. She didn't know him well enough to know if this was common for him or if the boys' enthusiasm had worn him to a frazzle. But he hadn't looked harassed, simply contemplative.

And he looked as if he wanted to say something to her. Something that might explain his curious admission earlier that morning?

"Thanks for the warning," she told her aunt, and hung up the phone in time to answer the door. It was Doc Jamison, there to collect the boys for their community service.

He shook hands with Steve and the two men exchanged quick background information before Doc herded her crew to his mobile clinic.

The instant they drove away, the house seemed to fall into a tense, watchful silence. Taylor suddenly felt more than alone with Steve Kessler, she felt nakedly alone.

He cleared his throat.

She smoothed her jeans.

He ran his hand through his hair.

She chewed on her lower lip.

"I like your kids," he said.

She didn't know quite what she'd expected him to say, but it wasn't this. Not in the wake of last night's kiss and this morning's statement of hard fact.

"Their eyebrows move—just like yours are doing."

It wasn't a compliment exactly, just another of his rhetorical comments. "I know," she said anyway.

The doorbell rang.

"Damn," he said, as if they'd been interrupted from a serious discussion.

Taylor couldn't help smiling as she headed for the door. Why was *he* so upset? He'd made it perfectly clear he didn't want any part of what they had to offer in this "one-horse town in the middle of the high plains." What difference could it possibly make to him if it was chaotic or peaceful?

Though she'd smiled sweetly enough before she moved to the front door, Steve had caught enough of her raised-eyebrow censure to be reduced to about the same age as Taylor's sons. As she greeted the people standing outside the dusty screen door, he found himself smiling. Taylor Leary-Smithton wasn't quite as vulnerable as he'd thought; she could pack a heck of a wallop with a single look.

So as not to eavesdrop, he went into the kitchen, ostensibly searching for a cup of coffee. He settled for what was left of the lemonade Taylor had poured all over the counter the night before. Before he'd kissed her a second time.

Before he'd drowned in that kiss.

He gulped at the cold liquid and stared at her infinite view out the back window, hoping one of the neighbors in this one-horse town in the middle of nowhere would find something. Something to keep him around just a little longer.

Taylor's unexpected company was her sister-in-law, Carolyn, her new husband, Pete Jackson, and Taylor's nieces, Shawna and Jenny.

"We thought we'd come to see how the crime squad is doing," Carolyn said as she brushed Taylor's cheek with a kiss and moved into the living room.

"Anything new?" Pete asked after a brief hug.

Taylor murmured a negative as she pulled the two girls, roughly the same age as her sons, in close for a quick snuggle.

"Did the boys really find a dead guy?" Shawna wanted to know.

"Nearly dead," Taylor said. "But he wasn't there when we went back to check it out."

The girls exchanged knowing glances. "Told you," Jenny said.

"Oh, no," Taylor quickly corrected. "We're fairly certain there was a scuffle of some kind. Whatever else the boys concocted—" she thought about their admission of planting sandwich bags of baking soda behind the school work shed "—they really did see a man wounded out behind Mr. Hampton's barn."

"What about the Texas Ranger...Steve Kessler, was it?" Carolyn asked. "We met him last spring, didn't we? Tall man? Is he already gone?"

"No," Taylor said, remembering his derisive words about Almost on the phone that morning. Why couldn't she just be angry at him for his snobbery and hustle him out of town with a firm wish that some vaguely humorous evil would befall him? Why should an even smile and a pair of warm brown eyes make her anger melt as quickly as it rose to the surface?

Carolyn was looking at her strangely. Taylor tried a smile. The two women hadn't known each other all that long, despite being sisters-in-law. Carolyn had married Taylor's brother, Craig, and except for the rare holiday, they'd stayed in Dallas. Until Craig was killed in a car accident and Carolyn packed her daughters up and moved into the old ranch house where Taylor had been raised.

Taylor still didn't know all the details surrounding Carolyn's obvious poverty after Craig's death, but she suspected her brother had lived his married life much as he'd done during his growing years, as recklessly and as thoughtlessly as possible. Luckily, shortly after moving to Almost, Carolyn had found Pete Jackson, a former FBI agent, and he'd brought the bloom back to her cheeks and, after saving Carolyn's life, he'd saved her heart, too.

The two women were close friends now, closer even than Taylor was to her own sister, Allison, she thought wistfully. But even that closeness wouldn't allow her to reveal how thoroughly shaken she was by Steve Kessler's presence in her home. Especially not in front of Pete and the girls.

"Sammie Jo did call to warn you about this, didn't she?" Carolyn asked, then turned suddenly. "Oh, girls, I forgot the deviled eggs. They're out in the truck."

The girls pelted out the door, looking so much like she and Allison must have as children that Taylor found herself holding her breath.

"We'll stay young forever, won't we, Taylor?"

"As long as we can, Allie."

But Allison hadn't been home in twelve years. She'd never met her nieces and nephews. She'd never met Carolyn or Pete. She hadn't even come home for Daddy's funeral. Or Doug's.

"Where are the boys?"

Taylor grimaced, but was glad to be brought back to the present. "They're out with Doc. They're doing community service again."

Pete chuckled. "The guy at the paint store in Levelland can send his kids to college on what those three cost in paint."

Carolyn smiled. "Almost has the best-dressed porches in West Texas, thanks to their service."

Taylor shook her head. "They, of course, are vastly proud of themselves for having the foresight to have considered murder and mayhem in Almost before it even happened."

Pete frowned. "Does Kessler think it's related to what happened last spring?"

"I'm not sure—oh, here he is," Taylor said.

Steve had come into the living room from the kitchen and was soon standing too close to her for any degree of comfort. She glanced up at him and thought she could read a measure of apology in his gaze. A slow flush stained her cheeks as she recalled her telling glance, her embarrassment at hearing what he thought of her beloved little town. And a deeper blush flared across her face as she realized just how thoroughly she'd revealed that she'd been eavesdropping, and how deeply his constraint around her troubled her. It should have made things easier, she thought, but it didn't. Not at all.

To cover her discomfort, she introduced everyone, despite the fact they'd already met before.

The men shook hands and Pete repeated his question.

Steve shrugged. "It's hard not to make a connection. We certainly didn't collar everybody in that little roundup we had. But without a body, without anything really, all I'm doing is playing guessing games."

"If I know the boys, they're driving Doc crazy, searching for the body in every nook and cranny in the county," Carolyn said.

"They've got the right idea," Steve said, smiling, "Spread the word we're missing our nearly dead guy and maybe someone will find him."

Carolyn gave him a speculative look. "You don't seem terribly daunted by the boys." And she laughed aloud at the mock look of horror he gave her. "Oh, you're hooked already."

Taylor didn't know which of them she wanted to hit first, her sister-in-law or the Texas Ranger, who seemed to be able to manage her sons with a single raised eyebrow yet pretended he couldn't tell them apart.

The girls returned with Carolyn's famous deviled eggs, accompanied by their Aunt Sammie Jo and her husband, Cactus Jack, who was carrying a huge Dutch oven filled with barbecued brisket.

"Everybody in town will likely be dropping by this afternoon to hear what's going on around here," Aunt Sammie Jo said, kissing Taylor and sizing up Steve with an appreciative stare. "So we brought a little something to fill their stomachs. Cactus, did you remember the paper plates?"

Cactus hadn't. The girls were dispatched to run to the car and collect them.

Sammie Jo was right. Ten minutes later, Mickey Sanders dropped by with a Crock-Pot filled with beans. "It's so hot outside I considered bringing a salad, but the way I figure it, beans go with anything. Now, Taylor, shall I just take them in the dining room? I know a few other people will probably be dropping by and I might as well get dibs on the plug-in."

Mickey Sanders and Sammie Jo were both right. Less than five minutes after Mickey got the Crock-Pot situated where she wanted it, Alva Lu Harrigan made her careful way up Taylor's steps with a sheet cake covered with aluminum foil. "It's a 7 Up cake," she said, holding the pan over the girls' heads, apparently not trusting them with it, and handing it to Taylor directly. "Don't set it on the table without a hot plate, it's still warm."

Taylor hid her amusement as she accepted the offerings and directed the girls to dig in her buffet cabinet for hot pads and warming plates. If they had this much food already, by five the table would be covered.

The girls were in fine fettle, enjoying the responsibility of hostessing. Darting in and out of the dining room, greeting neighbors and family, they happily arranged the table, peeked beneath Tupperware lids and peeled back aluminum foil wrappers with all the glee of children at a holiday party.

As people continued dropping around, Taylor's house did take on the atmosphere of a fully planned party. The last time she'd had so many people in the house was a reception she'd thrown for Carolyn and Pete's wedding. And the time before that had been minutes after Doug's funeral.

On the first occasion, conversation had centered around

congratulations to Carolyn and Pete, and on the second, commiseration on the loss of her husband. The group now gathering in her living room, talking with the ease of old friendships and enmities, and swelling with each passing moment, was there for one purpose only: gossip.

Homer Chalmers leaned his cane behind the front door and handed Taylor a bag of shelled pecans. "From my trees," he said as he walked past her to shake hands with Steve. "Met yesterday out at Charlie Hampton's. Found that fellow yet?"

Sam Harrigan brought a case of soda and took some time on the front porch moving the cans into a large cooler filled with ice. He handed Steve a chilled can and said, as if their conversation the day before had never ended, "Could be that fella the boys saw downed was that fancy-dressing salesman that comes round selling fertilizer. Comes by about once a month. Fancier duds, I never did see."

Cactus Jack sent the girls running to the Almost Mini-mart for a box of cigars he'd been keeping in the cooler for a special occasion. "Somebody showing up nearly dead then going missing warrants a cigar all around, don't you think? And don't go getting in the cash register, hear?"

Taylor felt a rush of gratitude for her family and friends. These were real people, men and women of heart. They would gather this way if someone's house had burned, if someone died, someone married, someone had a problem that needed solving, or if the sky turned cloudy and promised rain. Food, one of the basic human needs, would be mounded on empty tables, and conversation would smooth away all woes.

Sure, they were curious, but mostly they wanted to support her, make her feel nurtured by her fellow humankind.

Every laugh, every bit of food consumed, every touch on her arm conveyed their love for her, their concern that she and the boys would be safe and happy.

Aunt Sammie Jo asked Carolyn, "Doc has the boys with him?"

"Community service," Carolyn answered with a grin.

Sammie Jo rolled her expressive eyes. "My porch has been five different colors in as many years."

Charlie Hampton picked up Sam Harrigan's speculation about the fancy-dressing salesman. "That salesman fella sells fertilizer for an outfit by the name of ChemCon. Probably got his card somewheres. What's that you say?"

Homer nearly shouted, "Foreign-sounding name."

Charlie nodded and glanced up at Taylor with a wink.

Sam Harrigan asked if anybody had "seen that fella that runs the antique store? Martha Thompson was telling Alva Lu yesterday that she dropped by with something to sell and said nobody answered the door."

Alva Lu nodded. "Maybe that was him the boys saw—what's his name, Sam?"

"Jose. And it couldn't of been him. The boys said the man had fancy clothes on. Jose Caldrerros don't have enough money for basics, let alone frills. Never seen him outta coveralls and that yellow shirt in the three years he's been here."

"Think we're gonna get some rain?" Dallan Sanders asked Pete, pointing out the front door.

"God knows we need it," Pete said, giving the one and only proper response.

Cactus Jack asked the farmer he was talking to, "What's the world coming to when a quiet little old place like Almost has drug dealers and killings?"

Sammie Jo turned around from her position behind an easy chair, where she'd been telling Mickey Sanders about the latest Brad Pitt release. "Now, Cactus, we don't know for sure anybody's been killed."

Sam Harrigan said, frowning, "You know, now I come to think of it, Jose goes out of town a lot, buying stuff for his store. That's probably where he is."

"Seems strange he goes and buys stuff when he don't sell a blessed thing."

"Martha Thompson bought a doodad for her sister's birthday at that store just last month."

Homer said, "I did see a stranger in town the other day. Yesterday, maybe the day before. Don't remember. Saw him buying gas at Sammie Jo's."

"That wasn't a stranger, that was my nephew up from Midland to pay his respects," Alva Lu said, and sniffed. "He's in the oil business, you know."

"Not Jimmy. I know Jimmy. Known him since he was knee-high to a fence post. No. Somebody else. In a white four-door Chevy. Think it was a ninety or ninety-one model. Hard to tell nowadays. So many danged makes and models."

"Must've been some teacher going out to talk at the Pep Alternative School."

"When are you going to put another bathroom in this place, Taylor? You know how I hate to stand in line. Never mind, I'll just go home and use the facilities there."

"Well, I should think so," Alva Lu said. "You live next door."

Steve felt as if he'd strayed into some bizarre universe. Possible murder, missing wounded, and the entire town of Almost had turned up at Taylor's house to discuss the matter. And the weather. And anything else that crossed their minds.

He watched with a renewed sense of having fallen

through the looking glass as elderly women with carefully
arranged hair and flower-print dresses over support hose
and stocky shoes set out steaming casseroles in the dining
room, instructing Taylor to fetch a pie server or a slotted
spoon or a knife. Younger women, wearing jeans or
shorts, followed the directions of their seniors and stacked
paper plates and napkins on the table and went searching
for plastic flatware and paper cups. One of the older
women directed a young girl of about twenty to dust off
a lovely cut-crystal punch bowl.

"I remember Taylor's mama using that bowl at Extension Club meetings. That was...oh, a thousand years ago.
Taylor! Do you have any orange sherbet? Wasn't that
what your mama used in her punch? That and ginger ale.
And something else..."

"Pineapple juice," Taylor called out from across the
room.

"Now, Trixie, set that bowl at the far end of the table.
Careful. Good. Now, why don't you run down to Sammie
Jo's and get the things we need. Just leave this five-dollar
bill on the counter. That should more than cover it."

The men, both young and old, gathered in the living
room until the Leary-Jackson girls returned with Cactus
Jack's box of cigars, then moved as one to the front porch.

By the time Taylor's living room clock chimed the fifth
hour of this strange afternoon, some fifty or sixty people
were crammed into every available space both inside and
outside the house. And Steve had met each and every one,
shaken every hand, had tried answering every question,
no matter how rhetorical.

Charlie Hampton walked past him, heading out to the
shade of a broad elm for a chew of tobacco, and as he
passed, he gave Steve a slap on the back. "Good to have
you here, boy."

The words and the gesture were executed in exactly the same way his grandfather had slapped him on the back when he was a kid. The same way he might slap a fellow Ranger on the back after a particularly hard case...a bit of sympathy, a bit of bracing up and a lot of fraternity.

Gullible Steve stared after him, feeling adrift, his furious adherence to caution and self-pity evaporating a bit more. He liked it here. He really liked being around these people, their warmth, their friendliness. Yes, he liked these hardworking, caring folk.

Cynical Steve shook his head. He had the sinking feeling he'd made the biggest mistake of his entire career by coming to Almost to follow up on a poorly written letter hinting at trouble in the small town. The place and all the people in it were a vortex of some kind, sucking him in.

A trill of laughter attracted his attention and he swiveled to see Taylor across the crowded front porch, laughing at something her sister-in-law was saying. She was the strongest magnet of them all, he thought. Not just for him, but somehow for everyone in Almost. She seemed to embody the warmth of the town, the heat of the summer day.

All eyes seemed to linger on her and, regardless of West Texas geniality, no one seemed to miss an opportunity to touch her, to stroke her arm or lean against her shoulder for a moment. Women reached sun-scarred hands to adjust her hair or pet her cheeks. Men drew themselves up a little straighter, sucking in their bellies when she walked by or looked their way. She couldn't turn to walk anywhere without an elbow being held out for escort.

It was as if Taylor, with her honesty, her warmth, her serenity, was the very heart of their little town, the best of all of them.

And because he was a stranger, summoned by her children and wearing no wedding ring, speculative eyes followed his every gesture and watched his every move around "our girl."

As if aware of his regard, Taylor looked up suddenly and met his eyes in a nearly electric connection. The high color seemed to fade from her face for a moment. Her lips curved in an uncertain smile and she raised her hand to her chest in what Steve knew as an unconscious gesture of protection.

Steve became conscious of several heads turning in his direction. Eyes ping-ponged from Taylor to him and back again. An equal number of smiles and frowns appeared on faces. And still he couldn't take his gaze from hers.

They might as well have kissed.

Steve heard a screech of tires and dragged his gaze to a battered pickup sending up a cloud of dust to obscure the road. A tall, exceedingly thin man slipped through a cracked-open door and hitched his way to Taylor's house, bending forward slightly, as if afraid the light breeze might blow him from the ground. He stopped at the front gate as if confused by the mechanism.

The impromptu party grew silent in waves of awareness as people became alert to something unusual going on.

"That's Delbert Franklin."

"He never comes to town."

"With Delbert, it's all work, no play."

"Sh. He's looking all business now."

Unerringly, the skinny man's gaze zeroed in on Steve. He pushed the gate open, using it as a prop for a moment, then moved on toward Steve.

"You the Texas Ranger Doc and the boys were telling me about?"

Steve nodded and held out his hand.

The man looked at it for a moment as if he'd never seen a hand before. He rubbed his own work-stained palm on his trousers, then took Steve's hand in a bony, single-pump grip.

"After Doc left this morning, I got to thinking about a car I saw yesterday afternoon. White Chevy. Swerved right into the highway side of my maize field. Don't have a fence up in that stretch of the field. Never needed one before. I thought the guy was drunk or something. Never saw the car before." He paused for a deep breath and glanced at the silent, listening crowd on the porch. He nodded at a few of them, murmured a few of their names. They nodded back, mouthing his name in return.

"Anyhow, after Doc came by this morning, I got to thinking about the way that car swerved into the field, and decided to go have me a look." He paused again, this time to shake hands with Charlie Hampton, who had apparently finished his chew and had come up behind Steve to join the two men.

"Delbert," Charlie said, nodding and pushing his hat back a notch.

"Charlie." Delbert's eyes flicked toward Charlie and back to Steve. "Anyways, so I went out there and poked around. At first I didn't find nothing, just a couple of deep tire treads. Some white paint on a fence post—he's gonna have one heck of a scrape on his front left fender. Didn't see the tracks right off, 'cause it's so dry, you know. Anyways, I was steaming mad 'cause the blamed fool had broken a good dozen or more plants."

"But you found something?" Steve interrupted finally.

"Well, yes, sir. I hope to tell you I did."

Steve resisted the urge to shake the information out of the scrawny farmer.

"I think I found that fella you're looking for," he said in a wheezy, gravelly voice. "And there ain't no doubt...he's deader than a doornail this time around."

Chapter 10

Steve half expected the entire party to rush for their cars and follow Delbert Franklin and him out to where the farmer found the body. Instead, they drew together in small clusters, talking softly, speculating, nodding sagely and lifting hands in unison as he drove off behind Franklin's dirt-encrusted pickup.

Some ten miles south of Almost, the whipcord-thin farmer pulled his pickup off the road, perching it at a precarious angle on the side of a weed-filled ditch. If Steve had been late arriving on the scene, he would have been able to spot the location by the huge cloud of red dust obscuring Franklin's vehicle and field.

"Come on," Franklin said, not looking at Steve as he stomped into the field, "He's right back in here."

Steve was struck by Franklin's thoughtfulness in avoiding the tire treads that had damaged the man's maize crop. Unlikely as it might seem, Steve had secured plaster of paris imprints of tire tracks before and had locked in a case or two because of them. He was doubly glad the boys had spotted those tire marks in front of Charlie Hampton's barn. He was no expert, but these looked like a perfect match.

"Thanks for avoiding the treads," Steve called out, having to walk quickly to catch up with the man.

"I watch TV," Franklin said, stopping abruptly beside a semierect plant. Steve thought the man could have hidden behind the shoot and been overlooked. Franklin pointed downward. "There's your man."

Steve stepped forward and caught his first sight of the "too fancily dressed nearly dead guy."

It didn't take a quantum leap of intelligence to see that the man hadn't come to this location on his own. Aside from the tire tracks, nobody could have thrown himself into such an awkward position.

"Want me to call the coroner on my cell phone?" Franklin asked.

Steve dragged his gaze from the sprawled, spent body and looked at the thin farmer. He, better than most, should have known that farmers, ranchers, housewives—people with Southern drawls and laconic speech patterns—were as intelligent and as up-to-date as any city dweller, but somehow he'd forgotten this truism. And yet who more likely to possess a cell phone than a farmer, sitting alone all day in his combine, needing to call home, call the shop or perhaps phone his multimillion-dollar partner to remind him of the state dinner later that night?

"Please," Steve said, remembering his words to Doris about a one-horse town, words he hadn't meant, words that Taylor had shown the decency not to call him on.

Even as he inspected the site, careful not to mar any possible footprints—though he didn't see any—he thought of how he'd treated Taylor's sons the day before.

He'd disbelieved them, he'd sworn at them—according to Taylor—and he'd only half accepted the scuffle concept as true.

But here, crushing five or six stalks of maize, lay a man dressed in Armani casual wear, and who was, as Delbert Franklin had phrased it, deader than a doornail.

Sure, out behind the Hampton barn, Steve had seen the footprints, the darkened patch of ground that could have been—or not been—bloodstains. And he'd heard Jason's nightmare and seen and felt Taylor's heartfelt response to it. And he'd driven all the way to Levelland with three precocious preteens with a nickel-plated .45 in a plastic bag. And still, despite everything, the cynical side of him had refused to completely accept the truth of the evidence. He'd accepted that something had happened, but not really the full weight that the boys had witnessed the death throes of a man wounded by a bullet.

He tried not to think of what the boys might have felt upon seeing this man sprawled out on the dust behind Charlie Hampton's barn. No wonder Jason had had a nightmare. The boys would be lucky not to be having nightmares for the rest of their lives.

And no wonder they'd barreled into the house screaming for their mother. No kid should ever have to see such a sight. And following this thought came another: especially not those kids. They'd been through enough with the loss of their father. They'd already paid whatever dues kids had to pay to grow up too early. They hadn't needed the vision of this man dying before their eyes.

He had to wrestle with a surge of anger at the unknown assailant, the person who had shot this man and allowed three young boys to stumble across his remains.

Steve wrapped his handkerchief around his fingers before sliding his hand into the dead man's dusty and bloodstained Armani sport jacket to feel for a wallet, something to reveal the man's identity. And as he did so, he tried picturing what kind of apology he would offer the boys.

He withdrew a slender, leather folder and wondered if he could just play the coward and not say a word about his disbelief to the boys. Aside from one comment among themselves—and calling him mister yesterday, in a subtle and momentary revocation of his hero status—they hadn't seemed to take offense at his words, actions or patent distrust.

He flipped the folder open. Ordinarily, he would have left this evidentiary gathering to the homicide detectives that would be on the scene within the hour, but he was positive this was no ordinary case; this wasn't the original crime scene. The dead man had obviously been tossed here.

Steve's eyes didn't see the cards inside the folder he was holding. Instead, he pictured three mischievous boys whooping and hollering, waving bamboo poles at imaginary snakes and rounding the back side of the Hampton barn.

He could too easily see the wounded man lying in the dusty barnyard, holding his manicured hand toward them for help, saying "Cold dray horse" and expelling blood from his mouth.

And as he felt the blood in his own veins seem to freeze, he could all too easily picture the killer hiding nearby, in the field perhaps, or maybe back in the barn, listening, watching the boys as they tried making sense of a man dying before their young eyes.

And he could picture the man wondering if the boys had known he was hiding inside that barn, right behind the tack-room door, hoping they hadn't seen him shoot his victim and wondering what he should do about them.

If those kids had rounded the backside of the barn five minutes earlier...would they have witnessed the actual shooting? Would they have been the next victims?

Steve's hand tightened around the folder, bending it like a cheap deck of cards, picturing Taylor's grief-stricken face as she learned her sons had met their fate at the hands of an unknown murderer.

Steve's gaze crystallized on the folder. If he had anything to say about it, the boys would never know how close they'd come to life-threatening danger. And their mother, try to pry it from him as she might, would never hear such a thing from *his* lips.

The folder was filled with various business cards, different names, different towns, even different states and countries. The only one that caught Steve's eye was one with the name Richard DuFraunt, designating him as a salesman for a company out of Canada...ChemCon.

Sam and Charlie's fancy-clothed fertilizer salesman made the rounds for ChemCon. The same guy? It seemed likely.

Unfortunately, when Steve patted down the man's bloodstained jacket, he found another hidden pocket containing something, and when he tore the lining, he discovered four different passports. All four pictured the man lying in the dirt. All four bore different names. Two last names were Richards, the other two were DuFraunts. All were from Canada.

Steve didn't know of too many fertilizer salesmen who needed even one passport, let alone three more with identical pictures and subtly altered aliases. Everything about the man, from the bullet hole in his chest to his taste in clothes and jewelry, screamed a connection to money. And because of what had happened in Almost last Spring, money screamed a connection to drugs.

"Mr. Franklin?" Steve asked, swiveling a little on his boot heels.

"Delbert," the farmer suggested.

Steve nodded, accepting the friendly gesture. "Delbert, would you do me a favor and use your cell phone to call Tom Adams. He's with the FBI in Lubbock. I think he should be here."

"Done it already," Franklin said.

Steve turned to squint up at the beanpole faintly resembling a man. "You what?"

Delbert Franklin shrugged. "Told you. I watch TV. Figured this here fancy pants must've had something to do with what went on at the Leary place a piece back. So I called the FBI while I was coming to get you. He's on his way already."

Steve looked back down at the dead man and smiled. If he could have witnesses and bystanders like Delbert—and Taylor's rambunctious triplets—he'd never have to worry about making a case again. They would all be made for him.

Taylor watched as shadows stretched across her front yard, underscoring the length of time that Steve had been gone. Still, while she could see the tips of several cigarettes and cigars glowing in the darker regions of the porch, the day was far from over. In high summer, with a goodly portion of the country adhering to daylight saving time, nightfall wouldn't come for another couple of hours.

Yet it seemed Steve had been gone for days.

"When will·Steve be coming home?" Jonah asked. Doc had dropped the boys off at least an hour earlier and would be returning to join the party as soon as he fed the animals recuperating at his clinic.

Jonah lifted his arm and wrapped it around her waist. Like her, he'd come to the front lawn to stare hopefully at the empty road leading south of Almost.

His question struck Taylor on at least three different levels. On the most basic level, she was wondering the same thing herself. Delbert must have really found the dead man out in his maize field.

They'd all seen at least four state trooper units pass by in the course of the afternoon. And the entire impromptu party had offered directions to the Lubbock coroner after he'd driven past the house going both north and south at least three times.

And Taylor had seen Tom Adams, the FBI agent in Lubbock, the man who'd helped Steve and Pete with the trouble at Carolyn's last spring, drive by. He'd been either talking animatedly to himself or singing along with the radio.

But it wasn't the troopers, the coroner or even the arrival of the FBI that made Taylor ponder Jonah's question on a second level. It was Jonah's frown of worry. She knew he was sincerely concerned that something terrible had happened to Steve. Her son had good reason to worry; he'd been down that sad road before.

Since Taylor didn't believe Delbert Franklin to be the kind of closet psychopath who might do away with a Texas Ranger, especially in front of a host of state troopers and an FBI agent, she wasn't concerned that Steve had come to harm. And Delbert had made it perfectly clear to one and all that the man was truly dead this finding.

No, she thought, Steve wasn't hurt, but she was more than half-convinced that he might seize this opportunity to turn his full attention to duty and use duty as an excuse to escape this one-horse town in the middle of the high plains.

But the level most disturbing to Taylor, the third level, was the subtle nuance in Jonah's innocent question, "When will Steve be coming home?" *Home.* As if Steve lived with them. As if he were already the father the boys wished him to be. As if he belonged with them. The notion made her shiver despite the still-boiling hundred-degree temperature. Was that because it too neatly fit her own feelings about Steve?

"I don't know, honey," she said. "Soon."

"I hope so. I'm *dying* of curiosity."

"We all are," she said truthfully. But her curiosity extended a good deal beyond the discovery of a dead man in a maize field. Would Steve be staying now? Would he bolt? And which did she want him to do?

"Think it's the same guy?" Jonah asked.

"I don't know," she said again. He and his two brothers and half the population of Almost spending the day at her home had asked the same question at least thirty different times in the past few hours.

She made up an errand for Jonah and his brothers and watched them coerce their cousins into assistance before they all headed to Sammie Jo's store to fetch more unneeded paper plates.

Carolyn waved her over and patted an empty chair someone had carried out to the shade beneath the large elm. When Taylor joined her, Carolyn was smiling fondly at the backs of their disappearing children. "I wish they could stay this age forever."

Taylor smiled, though she didn't agree. Each year seemed to reveal some delightful new trait in her sons. She'd loved every minute and looked forward to the next phase with quiet anticipation mixed liberally with trepidation.

"You like him, don't you?" Carolyn asked softly.

"Yes," Taylor said simply. She knew who Carolyn referred to and didn't bother trying to play guessing games.

"I thought you'd sworn to never so much as look at another law enforcement type."

"I did." Her use of the past tense seemed to say it all.

"Ah. The boys like him, too."

"Yes."

"I wonder how long he'll be staying, now that they've found the man."

"I don't know," Taylor said for what must have been the thousandth time.

"I wish..." Carolyn fell silent, but the space between the two women seemed filled with unspoken wishes.

Taylor turned to look at her sister-in-law, and was sorry she had when she met Carolyn's sympathetic gaze. Then she admitted, "He's made it very clear he doesn't want anything to do with families and commitments. And he's not crazy about one-horse towns in the middle of nowhere."

Carolyn smiled, her eyes crinkling a little at the corners. "He's lying."

"I don't think so," Taylor said slowly, remembering. Remembering too much...the feel of his strong arms around her, the warmth of his lips, the passion imperfectly checked.

"Deep down, there isn't a man alive—or a woman, for that matter—who doesn't want the whole enchilada."

"Steve Kessler may be the exception to that rule," Taylor said.

Carolyn shook her head. "It would be nice to think so. Saves everyone trouble."

Taylor didn't ask what her sister-in-law meant, because she knew, and she had the feeling Carolyn was right. If she believed Steve's rejection of all the homier sides of life and he went back to Houston without a backward glance, his going wouldn't be *her* fault. The rolling stone simply would have rolled on.

"He says he's been married twice."

"That's a good sign. Shows he wants commitment, even if it hasn't worked out for him."

"I think he might have decided not to travel that road again."

"Well, you said you'd never deal with another cop. People change their minds."

Thankfully for her peace of changed mind, their aunt Sammie Jo strolled over to their shady nook at that moment. "There you are," she said. In unison, Carolyn and Taylor started to rise to offer their chairs to Sammie Jo. She waved them back down.

"Sit. Sit. My fanny's sore from having to sit listening to Mickey going on and on. Lordy, that woman can chatter."

Carolyn grinned at Taylor, who shifted her gaze to smile up at her aunt. "I'll bet she never got a word in edgewise. Mel Gibson or Brad Pitt?"

Sammie Jo chuckled in appreciation of the direct hit. "Oh, Brad Pitt today. He's got the cutest behind. Darn near as cute as that Texas Ranger you've got holed up here."

Taylor laughed outright. "He'd be flattered to know you think so."

"Not that one. He knows," Sammie Jo said. "And that's good. A man who doesn't know his own worth ain't much of a man. Remember that."

Taylor nodded.

"And a woman who would let such a man get away from her isn't using the gifts God gave a monkey."

Taylor shook her head. "That cart's *way* before the

horse, Aunt Sammie Jo. Steve's only been here overnight and he'll be leaving as soon as he can. Today, possibly.''

"Don't let him go," her aunt said with devastating simplicity and total disregard for anything remotely resembling reality.

But for just a moment, having listened to the comments of her sister-in-law and aunt, the two women closest to her in life, she wished what they believed was possible.

"Are the boys spending the night out at your place tonight, Carolyn?" Aunt Sammie Jo asked pointedly.

Taylor couldn't help her exclamation of protest, but her sister-in-law serenely nodded. "Yes, it's my turn tonight. You took the girls last week," she added, turning a too innocent face in Taylor's direction. "Remember?"

"They're fine here," Taylor said, wondering if she was protesting because she didn't want to be left alone with Steve Kessler or because she did.

"Nonsense," Sammie Jo said. "Give the man a break. I love those boys to death, but they'd wear out a dead man."

"Speaking of dead men," Carolyn said, lifting her chin in the direction of the highway, her eyes on an ambulance coming from the south. Its lights were flashing, but the driver wasn't using the siren. Which told all of them all they needed to know: no amount of speed would revive the passenger in the back of that van.

The party at Taylor's house once again fell silent as the ambulance headed north, returning to Lubbock or Levelland. All eyes shifted back to the south and followed the progress of the black-and-white state trooper unit that came next. And the one after that.

"That leaves two of them still out there, plus your Ranger and that Adams fella from the FBI," Sammie Jo said, taking inventory. "Wonder who that man was. And how he came to be killed right here in Almost."

Pete joined them, dropping his hands on Carolyn's shoulders. Despite the heat of the summer day, he wore a long-sleeved shirt. Taylor knew he did so to hide the death's-head tattoo on his forearm, the tattoo proclaiming he'd been in prison and had killed there. She smiled as her sister-in-law reached up to lace her fingers through his. Taylor wondered if her leaning her head against the painted forearm was an unconscious gesture or if Carolyn was remembering the days when she hadn't understood the reason for her husband's tattoo or his stay in prison, the time she hadn't known he had been with the FBI.

"Kessler just called," he said. "He wanted to know if you'd mind if he stayed a couple more days."

Taylor opened her mouth and closed it again. She thought of Carolyn's offer to take the boys for the night.

"I told him it would be all right," Pete said. "If there's a problem, he can always stay out at our place."

Carolyn kissed his hand. "The boys are staying out there tonight."

To Taylor's relief, Pete didn't so much as blink an eye at his wife's obvious matchmaking efforts.

"Well, at least you won't have to worry what to feed him," Aunt Sammie Jo said. "There's still enough food in there to feed an army."

Taylor felt as if an army had just taken over her life. An army of well-intentioned, utterly misguided loved ones.

"Mom! He's coming!"

"Steve's back!"

The boys and Carolyn's daughters raced down the strip of grass outside Taylor's fence and slid to a halt at the gate as Steve pulled his rental car to a stop in front of Taylor's house.

"Steve!"

"Did you find him, Steve?"

"Was it the same guy?"

"Was he still wearing that watch?"

"Was he really dead this time?"

"What's his name?"

"Who shot him?"

A strange expression crossed Steve's face as he looked down at the boys and their cousins. To Taylor, he appeared to relax slightly, as if in relief, and a smile tugged at his lips as he raised his hand to subdue the clamor, only to lightly rest that giant hand on Jason's head, then Josh's.

"We found him. Yes, he's really dead. He's already on the way to Levelland to the county hospital. Yes, he was still wearing his watch. And he has at least four different names. And it was thanks to you boys that Delbert Franklin found the man."

"Yeah?"

"Way cool. Hear that, Jenny? We're famous."

"He didn't say you were famous, he said—"

"Was he all gross?"

Steve shook his head and pushed through the five kids and the gate. He looked around, not as if for help, but the way a drifting boat might seek an anchor. His eyes linked with Taylor's and she saw him relax yet another notch.

He looked back down at her sons. "I owe you boys a big apology," he said. "I'm afraid I didn't believe you right away yesterday."

"Oh, that's okay," Jason said magnanimously. He waved his hand and released an admission of his own. "Mom warned us a long time ago about the boy who yelled wolf. I guess that's kinda what we did, huh?"

"Did he have, like, lots of false IDs?"

"Yeah, like, he did," Steve said, smiling down at Josh.

"Cool. Way cool."

Steve's grin broadened. He looked up and met Pete's gaze. "And to answer your earlier question...I'd say our boy was very likely involved in the shenanigans that went on here last spring. Think you could remember the guy who ran with the Wannamacher brothers? The Canadian?"

Pete nodded solemnly.

Steve dug a large plastic bag containing the four passports from his jacket pocket. Using the plastic to open one of them, he held out the photograph for Pete's inspection. "This the guy?"

"That's him," Pete said. He lifted his hand to rub his jaw. "I remember him rather well. He had a punishing left hook."

To the entire party's disappointment, Steve slipped the plastic bag back into his pocket. He looked over at Taylor then and smiled crookedly. "Any objection to my hanging around here for a few days?"

She had a thousand of them, she thought, her heart beating too rapidly. "Of course not," she said aloud.

The boys dashed to the front porch to spread the news to the assembly gathered there. Over the exclamations of surprise and wonder, and the loud recapitulations of her sons' activities both the day before and that morning, the entire crowd distinctly heard Jason's smug pronouncement. "And he kissed her last night. You know what *that* means. Now he has to marry her."

Chapter 11

Taylor's chair creaked as she rocked slowly back and forth. Darkness had finally come to Almost, masking the town, cooling down speculation and curiosity. Now that everyone was gone, the townspeople to their own homes and beds, the boys to Carolyn's and Steve into the bathroom for a shower, Taylor should have been able to relax.

Instead, with every motion of the rocking chair, the tension within her seemed to spiral another turn tighter.

In the heat of the afternoon, with Steve out in Delbert Franklin's field monitoring the discovery of the dead man, she had more than half believed Carolyn and Sammie Jo's faith that Steve would somehow transform into the kind of man who would want to spend his life in the middle of nowhere with a widow and three identical boys.

And somehow, sitting in the shade of the elm tree, listening to neighbors chatting, laughing and arguing good-naturedly, she'd thought it was possible to simply relax and believe that wishing for something could make it so.

But with everyone gone and Steve alone in the house with her, at this very moment naked in her shower, she was all too keenly aware that wishes were a far cry from the real McCoy.

The very last thing she'd wanted in the world was to fall in love with another law enforcement official. The boys might idealize the profession, as she perhaps had encouraged them to do. But she knew the pitfalls on a far too intimate level.

And yet, she had the sneaking suspicion that his very profession was one of the attractions for her. He laid his very life on the line every time he walked out the door.

The boys had said all it would take was one kiss. Just one.

They hadn't come up with the notion from television or videos. They'd heard the story of their father kissing her one night after a school dance. And they'd heard the story of how she'd fallen in love with their dad during that kiss. How he'd fallen in love with her.

That was how she had known Steve was wrong the night before, when he'd kissed her and then said that a person couldn't fall in love after a single kiss. She'd done it herself. And had spent some fifteen years in a wonderful marriage to a lovely man and had three great kids to show for it.

Now, she was more than half-certain she'd gone and done it again.

She'd never felt as lonely as she did right then. Not even the day Doug was killed had she suffered such a feeling of utter isolation. She didn't believe a chasm of different needs and wants separated her and Steve; she suddenly felt an entire universe yawned between them.

And she'd never missed Doug as much as at that moment. Strangely, she wanted to hear his opinion of Steve, what he thought about his old college roommate—and what he thought about *her* feelings for the Ranger. She wanted to hear her husband's advice. Most of all, she ached to hear him utter a benediction, an acceptance, as if he would stretch out to her after all this time and give her the go-ahead to live life again.

The screen door creaked behind her and Taylor closed her eyes in sudden fear. Her heart jolted then beat threadily. She gripped the arms of the rocking chair with a painful grasp. What was she so scared of?

"Taylor...?"

That's who she was afraid of, she thought wildly. Herself, Taylor Leary-Smithton. She was afraid that the lonely woman inside would demand freedom that night...solace and companionship. Maybe even love. And she was afraid she wouldn't have the strength to deny those wants.

He let the door softly close behind him. She could smell the scent of his soap, his shampoo. It was a clean, sharp odor, and it made her inhale deeply and frown at the hunger that leapt up in her. She knew that if she touched him, his skin would still be warm from the hot water, his face would be smooth after a shave, and his hair would be damp against her fingers.

A ray of light from the kitchen fell on her profile. Steve held his breath as he took in her closed eyes, the long lashes fanning across her rounded cheeks, the slightly parted lips, the frown on her forehead.

Something twisted inside him, a painful wrenching sensation that propelled him forward and forced him to bend over her rocking chair. For a last sane moment, he hesitated, remembering Houston, remembering his long-ago vows to avoid the dangers of another involvement, remembering his failures, telling himself that he didn't dare take the leap again because this time, all safety nets would be gone.

Women like Taylor Smithton were one in a million, and if she took the same route as his previous wives, he would be left in ashes, no longer a phoenix, this time never to rise again. Then his final vestige of reason fled as he lowered his lips to her furrowed brow, slowly, deliberately trying to kiss away the frown.

She sighed and stiffened slightly. Then, as if suffering something similar to his internal struggle, she suddenly lost whatever inner war she'd waged. She raised her face and opened her eyes. Her gaze was steady and her eyes a silvery blue in the shadow cast by his body. She seemed to appraise him for a moment, then a soft, almost sad smile curved her lips. "Do you want to hear the reasons why you shouldn't kiss me? Why I shouldn't kiss you again?"

"No," he said honestly. He knew all the reasons. Every one of the thousand and two reasons he should stand up straight and go back inside her house, pack his things and head for a sterile motel room in Lubbock, or even relinquish the investigation, as the FBI wanted him to do, and fly all the way home to Houston. "No," he repeated.

"Then, please…would you kiss me again?"

Her simple question inflamed him as easily as a match set to kerosene-soaked paper. He knew he should discover what she believed were the reasons not to go ahead, because they had to be vastly different from his own, but he told himself he could taste her now and still draw back, still walk away intact. He lied to himself, convincing himself that he still had the strength to call a halt before he plummeted headlong over the cliff she represented.

She moaned a little as his lips brushed hers, and he

heard an answering groan coming from deep within his own throat. His kiss deepened even as she pressed upward. For all the sorrow in her voice, for all the doubt etched on her face only moments before, her lips let him know that she'd crossed some Rubicon of hesitation.

This kiss tonight was no shy, I've-been-alone-a-longtime meeting of lips. This was a kiss to drown in, a kiss to bring a man to his knees. And Steve felt his weaken.

Instead of sinking to the wooden floor, he cupped her face in his hands and buried himself in her flowered scent, in the heady taste of her mouth, flicking her tongue with his, then warring with it in a driving, demanding rage of hunger. He could feel her trembling beneath his touch and knew he was shaking, too. With want, with need. With fear.

And he realized he'd wanted her, had dreamed of this exact, precise moment since the first time he'd glimpsed her shining face in the frame on Doug's nightstand all those years ago. And he realized why he'd been struck the previous afternoon by his ex-wives' resemblance to Taylor; he'd been drawn to them because they'd vaguely looked like the glowing girl in his fantasies.

He felt a tear escape from her eye and withdrew to look at her. He didn't know why she cried, but ached for her because of the hot tear snaking down the side of his hand. It seemed to scald his skin.

"What...?" he asked softly, pressing his lips to the tear, tasting the salt, trying to absorb whatever pained her. And yet a part of him—perhaps the part that tried to understand the tears, that long-restrained part of him that understood that wanting a shared life meant sharing vulnerabilities, frailties—knew why she cried, knew why something inside him felt flicked raw.

She shook her head, her damp cheeks touching first one of his palms, then the other.

"Please?" he murmured, lightly brushing her lips with his own. "Taylor...I really want to know what you're thinking. What you're feeling."

Instead of answering, she returned his kiss with fervor, capturing his mouth this time, thrusting her tongue against his, arching upward as she raised her hands to his chest.

He growled softly as she ran her palms across his fresh shirt, and groaned when she thrust her fingers through a gap between buttons, long, tapered tips brushing against his bare chest. He raised his head to pull at the night air, half-certain he was dying in his thirst for her.

She looked up at him with glazed, half-closed eyes. Her tears, and perhaps whatever had caused them, were absent now, though her gaze was liquid and trapped somewhere between confused and shockingly determined.

"Will you tell me why you cried?" he forced himself to ask.

She sighed and deftly unfastened a button on his shirt. Then another. Her eyes lowered to her task.

"Taylor...?"

"Because I want you so very badly," she said simply. "And I'm scared."

She freed a third button before sliding her trembling hands across his upper chest. "Oh... I knew you'd be this warm."

Even if he had wanted to stop now, her hands touching him, her candid words and the tears that had preceded them would have made it impossible. He all but dragged her from the chair, leaving it rocking madly behind her as fast as his heart was racing in his chest.

He pulled her into his arms, aching for the feel of her against his chest, needing to draw her against his full length, to press into her, to arch her body to his. And to press his lips to the throbbing pulse at the base of her throat.

Gripping his shoulders, she arched back, allowing him access to her collarbone, to her velvet skin, to her full, firm breasts. He fumbled with the buttons of her blouse, forcing himself not to rip the material apart in his need to touch her, to see her.

Finally he had the blouse opened, and he closed his eyes as he pressed his hands over her sharply defined nipples, feeling them jutting against his palms through the lace of her bra. Bracing her, keeping her pressed to him with one hand, he slid the other beneath the wisps of lace at her shoulders, pushing the straps from her shoulders.

Her head lolled back making her defenseless, guileless. Wholly woman and, because of that, wholly vulnerable. Reverently, he pressed a kiss to the bare column of her slender neck.

A childish part of him wanted to beg her not to hurt him, even as the protective side of him ached to assure her he would do everything in his power to shield her from any more pain in her life. "I'm here," he said, and thought the words illogical, no matter how important.

Her eyes closed and her lips parted as she sighed. She released a whispered plea as he stroked his hands across her shoulders, lowered them to smooth her chest, grazing the rounded tops of her breasts with his knuckles. He slid his fingers between her breasts and into the thin hollow between her bra and her satin skin.

Impatient suddenly, resentful of this barrier separating her from his gaze and touch, he jerked the restraint downward, causing her to gasp and her breasts to spill free. Holding her all but draped across his arm, he gazed down at her bared torso, so hungry, so wanting her that he shook with the need.

She moaned a little, inflaming him anew, and as if the sound released him from a spell, he swiftly cupped one breast, massaging it deeply while lowering his mouth to the other and capturing her turgid nipple between his already suckling lips.

Close to fainting, Taylor felt inchoate phrases slipping from her lips, begging him to continue, perhaps just begging him, arching still further back as he laved her sensitive skin with his wickedly knowledgeable tongue. At her plea, he recaptured her lips, and she tasted a hint of her own perfume before she felt the heat of his mouth searing away all tastes but their own commingled desire.

Steve's skilled hands roamed the curves and valleys of her body, releasing a raging torrent of want and need. If she had any doubts about the rightness of what they were doing, about tomorrow and next year, this would be her last moment to voice them. Questions flitted across her dazzled mind and were driven away unanswered by his sure touch.

Her every nerve ending quivered for him, her body singing as pulse after throbbing pulse of pure adrenaline coursed through her veins.

Years before, after a school dance, she'd fallen in love with a headstrong, impulsive boy with laughing eyes and a good heart. But she wasn't a girl anymore, and this was no boy kissing her now. Nor did she want him to be.

He swore suddenly and propelled her across the porch until her back met the smooth, recently painted clapboards. And he growled a low imprecation as she buried her hands in his silky hair, gripping it as surely as his hands molded her form to his.

His hands strafed her body, brushing her blouse from

her arms, abandoning it to the porch floor, letting her bra fall to her waist, ignored by both of them. He lowered his head to the chasm between her breasts, cupping her fullness to his cheeks, then pressing her breasts together to kiss their hardened tips, suckling her, nipping at her, nuzzling until her knees buckled and he ground his body to hers, catching her, pinning her to the wall.

He swore again and dragged the screen door open, half carrying her, half falling over her as he push-pulled her inside. She knew she'd never felt quite as dazed before, drugged with his scent, with want of him. This wasn't a product of her loneliness, this was a tornadolike, violent storm raging through her body and mind. She yanked his shirt from his waistband and swiftly unfastened the last of his buttons, moaning at the feel of his broad, muscled chest beneath her fingers, his flesh as hot as flames. She both heard and felt his swift intake of air as her arms encircled his waist and she drew herself sharply against him, straining to meet him, arching back to allow him full access to her naked upper body.

"Taylor..." he murmured, sweeping one hand over her breasts, dipping lower and gripping the button securing her jeans. "I want..."

"Yes," she whispered, raising a leg to hook him still more tightly against her.

"Oh, God," he muttered, seemingly abandoning whatever restraint he had left to begin pulling at her jeans, unzipping them and plunging his hand behind her, into her waistband and lower, beneath her panties to grab her bottom in a swift, almost angry need. He arched his own back, his hips thrusting against her, letting her know the full extent of his desire for her. "You're driving me insane, Taylor."

"Yes," she whispered again, agreeing with him as she

would have agreed to anything on earth at that moment. He lifted her leg higher, hitching her up, running his hands down the back of her thighs, then back to her waistband to tug at her jeans.

She slid from him and he swiftly stripped her remaining clothing from her, shoving it to the floor in a ruthless, utterly determined sweep of his hands and feet. Instead of grabbing her to him, as she'd expected, he ceased all motion and simply stared at her.

Totally nude now, bathed in the light of the overhead lamp, she was suddenly shocked into awareness of how far they'd traveled in such a very short time.

"You're so beautiful," he said, making her somehow more naked beneath his raw gaze. Hunger, want, even supplication were evident in his eyes. And a huge question.

And the question freed her from her momentary panic, her brief return to a glimmer of sanity. She stepped forward and pushed his shirt from his shoulders, letting it fall to join her own clothes on her kitchen floor. Somehow it seemed fitting that their clothes tangled together before their bodies met.

She suspected he had no idea how terribly vulnerable he was, how precarious his hold on his self-enforced solitude. But his doubts, his fears and his desire for her were etched clearly on his face.

"Steve..." she murmured, giving him the gift of his name. "Oh, Steve."

He did sweep her to him then, kissing her hungrily, with a passion that verged on desperation. And when her knees buckled this time, he lifted her from the ground completely, wrapping her legs around his waist, kneading her bare bottom, drawing every nuance of desire from her lips.

Never breaking his kiss, he strode from the kitchen, pushing her against the swinging door and through to the other side, down the brightly lit hallway to her opened bedroom door.

"Taylor?" he rasped, pausing for a second at the threshold.

She didn't know what he was asking her exactly but dimly understood that some further acceptance or affirmation was needed before he would carry her into her cool, dark bedroom.

She was half-aware that he might be thinking of Doug, perhaps of the nights she'd cried alone in this room. And maybe he was remembering his divorces, *his* losses. She pressed a kiss to his lips, breathing heavily against him, straining to meet him, aching to feel his naked flesh against hers.

It seemed all the answer he needed, for he swept through the doorway and into her bedroom. He lowered them both to the bed, leading her, following her, dancing with her in the most ancient of dances, crushing her against the cold quilt covering her sheets.

Her turn now, she grappled with the button at *his* waistband, released it finally, then slowly eased the zipper open. He muttered something between a plea and a curse when she slipped her hands beneath his shorts and slid both shorts and pants down his long, muscular legs.

Before she could kick the pants free from the bed, he snatched them up and plunged his hand into a pocket, withdrawing his wallet. He flipped it open. His Texas Ranger star gleamed briefly in the dim light from the hallway, freezing her, reminding her. He reached in a flap behind it and withdrew a plastic packet and tossed the wallet aside.

She felt a rush of embarrassment sweep across her

cheeks, inflaming them. She had never thought of protection. Not once. And here she was with a man whose entire profession spelled protection...who was protecting her.

She followed his hand as he slid the thin sheath over his length, and he groaned as she enfolded him completely, murmuring his name against his ear, whispering his name, pleading for him to come to her.

Steve could no more have resisted that plea than to jump into an icy lake at that moment. Some dim thought of prolonging things crossed his mind, of needing to imprint himself on her or perhaps the reverse, so that in the future, they would each have this one perfect memory. But when she fell back upon the bed, all rational thought fled.

In the dim light from the hallway he could see her body dewy with a sheen of desire, her eyes lidded with languor.

"Please, Steve..." she murmured, restlessly moving her head, stretching a hand up to him.

He'd never wanted any woman as much as Taylor. Never had, never would.

Her hands found him and guided him to her, and he lost hold of thought totally and plunged into her, burying himself in her hot core, rasping her name as her molten body encased him.

Theirs was no easy, gentle meeting of bodies and souls. It was like a fiery conflagration, consuming the both of them. She matched him thrust for parry, lunge for withdrawal. He could feel her hands digging into his back, his buttocks, and felt her satiny long legs wrap around his, fiercely holding him deep inside her.

The passion that flared between them burst into full flame, searing his mind, his soul, burning its way through his body and into hers. This was where he'd wanted to be since that first time he'd seen her, where he'd wanted to be two years ago when he saw her standing alone and in black, and where he'd dreamed of being the night before. And where he'd wanted to be all that time ago back in college. He could now admit he'd spent his entire adult life wanting her.

God only knew what would happen on the morrow, when sanity returned and bridges were thoroughly burned. But now, right now, he was in the one place on earth he wanted to be. The only place. And she was with him. Totally, completely with him. He covered her mouth with his, catching her ragged breathing with his own, his tongue thrusting against hers in exactly the same rhythm as his body met hers.

Faster and faster they rocked together. Swiftly and surely they locked into a rhythm as endless as the sands that blanketed the West Texas plains. And when her breathing deepened and hitched and she arched back, he held her tightly as she cried out, clinging to him in utter abandon.

He savored the expressions flying across her face, the joy, the pain, the ecstasy, the fierce exultation, and then he couldn't think at all as her body claimed his. He couldn't do anything but give in to the need she'd roused in him, the throbbing, desperate release that shook him to his very soul and seemed to shatter the universe with the intensity of its explosion.

Gasping, then stilling abruptly, shuddering as spasm after spasm drew him ever deeper into Taylor, he cried her name aloud as she had called his. He was dimly aware that she held him, drawing every last bit of strength from him, then gently restored it to him with long, stroking fingers and soothing kisses.

Shuddering, he slumped against her, trying not to crush her, chuckling as she shoved at his elbows so that his full weight pressed her against her bed. And still she held him tight. So tight and warm. And so lovingly.

Her body still quivered with the force of her release and his shook in response to her diminishing spasms. She chuckled and he smiled and pressed a kiss to her temple, only to feel tears.

"Are you crying?" he asked, freezing.

"Mmm. Because it—you—were so wonderful."

He kissed away the remnants of her tears, not entirely sure he understood them, only half believing her words. Afraid of believing them. Afraid because he could too easily buy them, too readily accept a fantasy in lieu of reality.

Her hands on his back tightened then dropped to her sides as if she had no strength left. She sighed heavily and he felt her breasts press against his chest. He started to withdraw from her, but she swiftly raised her hands again to stop him.

"Don't leave," she said.

"I'm not leaving," he answered, and his words seemed to echo in her cold bedroom, in the warm bed, like a vow. Like a promise.

She sighed and he felt her smile. "I'm glad," she said.

He felt like every kind of proverbial fool when he smiled in response.

Drowsily she kissed him.

Dazedly, he kissed her back.

Nearly asleep, she murmured, "I think I love you."

Shocked awake, he held her without speaking while she slipped into sleep.

Chapter 12

Taylor tried not to stare at Steve as he listened to someone on the telephone. Though he'd risen early and showered and dressed before she ever came into the kitchen, he looked more haggard than he should have. Dark circles rimmed his lower lids and his mouth was tight and hard.

Not at all the way it had felt the night before. Then, his lips had been warm, as soft as heated velvet, and they'd pressed tenderly against her throat, her mouth, her breasts.

She'd expected not to sleep, to wake at his every movement, but she hadn't; she'd slept deeper and more soundly than she could remember having done in months and months. Maybe years.

When she'd glanced in the mirror to brush her teeth and hair, she couldn't help but see the change in her. Everything about her seemed different. Her eyes glowed a brighter blue, her cheeks appeared rosier. She somehow felt a whole woman again. Together inside and out. Steve had wrought this change; he had done this for her.

And Steve hadn't once looked at her since she'd walked into the kitchen.

He muttered a quick thanks and hung up the phone. And still he didn't turn in her direction.

"The police in Lubbock found a car fitting the description I called in yesterday," he said, gazing at her open-faced cabinets, his eyes resting on a collection of the boys' action figures.

"What car was that?"

"One of the men at the party here yesterday said he'd seen a strange car in town the other day. He was vague about when, but specific on what…a white four-door Chevrolet, a ninety or ninety-one. And then, Delbert Franklin described having seen what sounded like the same car. Not much to go on, but the Lubbock force found one at the airport this morning. Red dust on the tires…blood on the left side of the back seat."

Taylor wanted to ask him to look at her, to just turn and meet her eyes, affirm what had passed so beautifully between them the night before. She started forward, her hand outstretched, but as if he had radar where she was concerned, he shifted slightly to the left, checking her touch.

"They're going to check with the morgue in Levelland, see if an autopsy's already been done. If it has, they might be able to work up a match on the blood work."

She shoved her hand into a pocket and curled her fingers into a fist.

He shrugged as if he could feel the tension in her and was shaking it off his broad back. "The front fender has several scratches on it, scratches that could have been made running through a barrow ditch, into a fence post and on through a maize field. But the real kicker is that it was rented by one of the names we found on the guy yesterday. Richard DuFraunt. The police have already run a fingerprint check. The car was wiped clean. Except for the blood.''

''Steve…?''

He stiffened, as if anticipating a blow. Or hoping she wouldn't talk? He spoke quickly, ducking emotion. ''Which leads us back to exactly where we were…one dead guy in Armani, the same man who helped work Pete Jackson over last spring, apparently heavily connected with the drug cartel working through Almost, and not a single clue as to who shot him and threw him in Delbert's field.''

Taylor felt as if she were standing in quicksand. One wrong word, one wrong gesture and she would slip deeper into a quagmire of uncertainty. Watching him, silently begging him to just look her way, she felt afraid that everything magical that had blossomed between them might evaporate into the bright morning light.

Surely that couldn't happen. Steve wouldn't do that to her. Couldn't.

She hadn't been alone in that darkened bedroom. He'd been right there with her, in every way, physically, emotionally. Lovingly.

''Steve, I—''

The front door banged open and her troupe of wild elephants thundered down the hallway and burst into the kitchen.

''We already ate breakfast at Aunt Carolyn's. We had pancakes!''

''What did you guys have? Is there any left?''

''You should see everybody in town, Steve. I swear

every field around Almost has somebody out in it looking for dead guys. Honest.''

''We looked all in Jenny and Shawna's barn, but we didn't find nothing.''

''Anything,'' Taylor corrected automatically, wishing her boys anywhere on earth but in her kitchen at that moment.

''Mom, a guy can't think about grammar when there's dead guys around!''

''A guy had better,'' she suggested with a look.

The boys, as they had the day before, seemed to sense the tension between the two adults. Taylor would have granted them full reprieve from community service if they had followed their instincts of the day before and disappeared. But this time, they apparently psychically and collectively decided that direct action was needed.

''What's going on?''

''Something wrong?''

''Nothing's wrong,'' Taylor lied, finally looking away from Steve's brick wall of a back to move to the sink. ''Nothing at all.''

She tried not to turn around, tried not to look. But she couldn't help herself. She felt as if a part of her died a little when she found he hadn't moved.

''Are we going to go out for more investigating today?''

''You know what I think, Steve? We should check out Mr. Hampton's loft. I'll bet the killer hid the murder weapon up there.''

''Hey, yeah, that's a good idea!''

''Or we could see what we find in Delbert Franklin's field. You know, past where he found the dead guy and all. Like Kurt Thompson found that fancy gun in Charlie Hampton's sorghum.''

"What do you think, Steve?"

He turned then, not looking at her but at her sons' bright, eager faces. His own was somber, shadowed by far more than mere sleeplessness. A humorless smile quirked his lips into a grimace. "I'm afraid the FBI is taking over this case," he said.

If he'd dropped a strange bomb that robbed preteen triplets of speech, Taylor thought he couldn't have hoped for greater silence than his words produced.

It was Jonah who finally broke the spell. "You're leaving," he said, his rigid stance an accusation.

Steve flicked a glance in Taylor's general direction, though it fell far short of meeting her eyes. As he looked back down at her sons, she had to close her own eyes. To hide the pain his words caused. He was *leaving*.

"That's right, Jonah. I've already done all that I can here. The case is linked to an FBI case that went down last spring. The one at your aunt Carolyn's. If I stick around, I'll be horning in."

Taylor opened her eyes to look at him then, wondering if he was lying to spare her children or simply to hide from the truth their union had created.

As if he heard her mental question, he said, "Really. Tom Adams asked me yesterday to step out of the picture. This is an ongoing FBI investigation."

"Yeah, but—"

"We asked you here—"

"So, like, it's *our* case, right?"

Steve shook his head and raised his hands…hands that had brought life to her the night before, hands that now seemed to be taking that life away. "I wish it was, Josh, but it doesn't work that way."

"What way does it work?" Taylor asked hoarsely, then as he looked across at her, his eyes devoid of emotion, his mouth tightened into a rigid line, she wished she hadn't asked.

He straightened, his hands falling away from the boys' shoulders, a giant among three blond, adoring pygmies. "It's an FBI case. The FBI should handle it from here on out. And besides, when I phoned my office this morning, Doris told me they want me back in Houston. A case I was working on needs my immediate attention."

He looked half apologetic, half defiant. "Really," he said again.

Taylor thought if she heard that word another time she would scream. Nothing was *really* like anything remotely real at this moment.

But she refused to look away, refused to let him off the hook. This was the man who had taken her to places she'd never dreamed of going, made her feel like a woman again, and who had promised, however drowsily, not to leave. All too aware that her sons were listening to every word they might exchange, she drew a shallow breath, managing to squeeze a bit of air into the space crushed by her heart. "I've always wondered about something," she said.

He didn't say anything, merely waited, tension radiating from him like excess electricity from an overcharged power transformer.

She fought tears of abandonment, tears of anger. And conquered the urge to fall to her knees and beg him to explain what was happening, why he was acting this way. "I've always wondered how some people can start something and go away without finishing it?"

Steve's head reared back as if her words had been rapiers marking his cheeks. But the boys misunderstood her.

"Yeah...how can you stand not to be here when we find the killer?"

"That would be, like, *boring*."

"You're really going to go away? Back to Houston?"

Steve felt a shudder work through him. This was pure, unmitigated torture, he thought. He hadn't lied about the FBI wanting the case. Hell, it was theirs to begin with. It was only the boys' letter that had propelled him into it in the first place.

And he hadn't lied about his Houston case demanding his swift return to the home office. He'd been working on cracking that pornography ring for a good three months now. Who would have guessed the thing would break now?

But neither of those considerations was the reason for his leaving. The simple truth was that if he didn't leave right then, he knew he never would. And no matter how he might feel, a person didn't—couldn't—fall in love in two days. It was impossible. A pipe dream. An illusion. And he'd bought two tarnished illusions twice before.

All they have to do is kiss, and they'll fall in love. Isn't that what the boys had said, or something very like it? He'd told Taylor they were wrong. They had to be. It didn't matter that he felt they were right...he'd been proven wrong twice before.

"But you don't have to leave right away, right?"

"Come on, Steve...say you'll stay awhile."

"Yeah, like you could just live here and commute or something?"

Steve felt impaled by their pleas, tortured by their faith that all could work out just the way they'd planned, the way they wished it could be.

The look of hurt in Taylor's eyes and the triplicate looks of incomprehension on the boys' faces flayed him like a whip on an already wounded and raw back.

"You don't *really* have to go away, do you, Steve?"

Did he? The job said yes. And every safety factor in him screamed for him to go *now*.

"I'm afraid so," he said. "Today, anyway."

"But you'll come back."

"How come you have to go today?"

"Yeah, Uncle Pete said yesterday that you wanted to stay a couple of extra days. Aunt Carolyn told us."

Something dawned on Jonah and he turned an accusatory look at his mother. "Did he do something wrong and you don't want him around anymore?"

The tension in the room encompassed her children. Jason shoved Jonah in a rough push. "Doofus, we saw them kissing. He didn't do anything all *that* wrong."

Steve's heart seemed to break as Taylor raised a hand in question, in denial…or was it in a wavering plea?

"No, he didn't do anything wrong," she said. And her voice caught on the final word.

What did she want of him? He'd told her he couldn't go through another failed attempt at commitment. Maybe he hadn't said the exact words, but the meaning had been perfectly clear. As perfectly clear as her words of love had been the night before. Words that meant absolute perfection…ultimate doom. She'd never know how deeply everything in him had craved the sound of those words on her lips. *Her* lips only. And she would never know how agonizing it was to leave her with those words unanswered, unacknowledged.

For a split second he considered canceling his departure, ignoring the summons back to Houston, letting other Rangers handle the pornographers. The thought flashed through his head that he could simply stay. Just stay. With Taylor, with the boys, with a town full of half-crazy, half-wonderful people. He could make a life there, live it fully and enjoy it. And the gullible side of him begged him to do just that. *Just stay.*

But the cynical side of him, the failed side, the part of him that could never reveal how much it hurt to see his wife leaving on a supposed vacation and knowing she was going less than two miles down the road to a local motel, demanded he leave now, his heart only partially bruised, not irrevocably destroyed. Leave now, that side of him urged, while any vestige of pride remained.

"I gotta go," he said desperately, and pushed his way out of the kitchen before he gathered this precious family into his arms and begged Taylor and her sons to keep him with them forever.

Taylor felt as if her heart had acquired a terrible weight. That organ beat in her chest, still pumping life-giving blood through her veins, but every part of her felt so heavy, so tired, living, but only numbly. What had transpired between the loving, poignantly sweet good-nights and the hard-featured reality of the morning?

Unable to force herself away from the countertop in the kitchen, relying on it to hold her erect, she listened as Steve packed his gear and deflected a host of questions from her worried sons.

"When you finish your case, you're gonna come back, aren't you?"

"Your other case can't be nearly as interesting as dead guys in maize fields."

"You are coming back, aren't you?"

"Doofus, he doesn't know how long it will take."

"Yeah, but, like, when he's done…you will come back, won't you?"

Steve mumbled something.

"Yeah, all right, but *when?*"

He mumbled something else.

"What if we're not here? What if we're out at Aunt Carolyn's or over at Aunt Sammie Jo's? How'll we know if you came back?"

"Doofus, we never lock the door. We don't even have a key."

"Oh, yeah. Right. Well, then cool. You can just come in, and when we get here, you'll be here already."

"Home."

"Yeah, like right at home."

A betraying tear trailed down Taylor's face. She rubbed it away with the back of her hand, staring hard at the action figures that had commanded Steve's attention earlier. Angry at herself, angry at Steve, she felt humiliated and far more. A country cousin, she thought. That's what she'd been. A princess who'd fallen in love with the dashing prince only to watch him ride off into the sunset—alone. In a rental car.

Oh, this prince had tried to warn her. *I've been married twice. I've failed twice.* And she'd been too naive, too caught up in a simplistic belief system to understand that the warning had been part of the game, that his words were merely part of the illusion he created before slinking away, getting what he wanted without having to stick around for the pain that came later, aftermaths like heartbreak and crushing hurt.

And yet, she couldn't believe this. Not of Steve. Not of the man who had held her so fiercely in his arms the night before, held her as if his very life had depended upon it.

No, Steve was no love-'em-and-leave-'em sort of man. One look at his averted face and pain-filled eyes told her he was in as much agony as she. She just didn't understand his. If only he would talk to her. Just talk. And if only she had the courage to voice her fears, her questions. Her overwhelming doubts.

"Can I carry your bag?"

"I'm gonna carry it, Jonah. You got to sit in the front seat with Steve on the way back from Levelland."

"Yeah? Well, you sat in the front seat on the way there."

"That means it's *my* turn," Josh said.

Taylor heard a scuffle and closed her eyes. Steve brought this squabbling on with his leaving. Upset, not knowing how to contain their uncertainty, unable to analyze their confusion, perhaps even their anger at him, they were releasing those emotions on one another.

Steve would be leaving Almost as swiftly and unremarkably as he'd arrived there. But all of their lives had been touched by him in some indefinable way. The boys, because their fantasy had been transformed into reality. Her neighbors and family, because they all had felt more comfortable with the notion that she wouldn't be alone. And Taylor herself, because she had still believed in love.

"Dang it, Josh! *I'm* carrying it!"

Her spine stiffened as she decided to let Steve diffuse the tension among the triplets. If he could. As if it were possible to diffuse separation anxiety and the loss of a dream.

Taylor watched as Steve slipped behind the steering wheel, tossed his cowboy hat into the back seat, adjusted his visor, cinched his seat belt and checked the rearview mirror before pulling out onto the deserted road. His every gesture displayed a methodical caring. He'd displayed that same consideration with her friends and family, the same concern with her children. And the same thoroughness with her.

He raised a hand in farewell, but didn't look back as he settled into the right lane and accelerated. As if he couldn't get away soon enough.

"He'll be back," Jason said.

"Yeah. He's gotta," Jonah murmured, his eyes still on Steve's diminishing car.

Steve's final words to her had been a mumbled, "I'll call you."

"He's gonna come back, isn't he, Mom?"

"I hope so, Jason," Taylor responded automatically. "I...hope so."

"He will. It's, like, duty and stuff."

"Yeah, like that."

But the boys' lack of conviction matched her own.

As if Steve's departure sapped the boys' energy—and she suspected that it truly had, for she felt lethargic and ready to crawl beneath the covers herself—they listlessly performed a scissors-rock-paper routine to decide what kind of soda they wanted from Aunt Sammie Jo's machine.

"Can we go, Mom?" Jason asked, his voice lower than usual, his young face drawn in a way she hadn't seen for almost a year.

"Sure," she said, trying to force some measure of enthusiasm in her voice. She failed miserably. "You guys are off community service today."

They all looked at her in dulled surprise and with an element of suspicion. "How come?"

"Because, thanks to you, they found the dead guy."

They smiled, pleased, but it seemed to Taylor the smiles didn't hold their usual boyish credulity. These smiles seemed adultlike in their knowledge that she was throwing them a bone to distract them from missing Steve.

As she watched them plod down the hot, dusty lane, she wished someone would throw her one.

Chapter 13

Every day that long week, the weatherman on television pointed to a large capital *H*, signifying a high system parked over the dot representing Almost on the weather map. Temperatures soared above the hundred mark by nine in the morning and reached one hundred and ten at the apex of the day.

The mercury continued to rise slowly and painfully until, by midafternoon, plants watered just that morning wilted and drooped to porches and sidewalks. Mothers wouldn't allow their children outdoors between noon and four, and Sammie Jo's Minimart did a land-office business in long-lasting PABA-free sunscreen.

The heat pressed down on the Smithton family as harshly as it did on the maize and sorghum fields, the cotton, the corn and the miserable cattle, lowing in their hot, dry corrals or out on the parched ranch land. Not allowed to go outdoors during the "funnest" part of the day, with nothing they liked on the only television channel Almost could receive, the three boys listlessly played board games in their air-conditioned bedroom, only occasionally coming out for something cold to drink or something cool to snack on.

For Taylor, the oppressive heat outside seemed an extension of her inner turmoil. She'd felt cold the morning Steve had left. Cold and cast adrift. But now, four days after his departure, the well of pain deep within her seemed to boil with conjecture, second-guessing and a too spicy dose of wishful thinking.

She'd even found herself wishing that something terrible would happen in Almost, another stranger's body discovered, the killer revealing himself, anything that might draw him back into their circle. But day after day passed without a discovery.

The phone had rung as many as fifteen or twenty times a day. Carolyn, Sammie Jo, Tom Adams with the FBI, even an old friend from high school who had heard about the Almost happenings from her mother-in-law...but never Steve. And sometime in the past twenty-four hours, she'd quit jumping every time the infernal machine sounded the alarm that someone was calling her.

And the nights, without the phone ringing at all in the thick silence of an overwarm darkness, seemed even worse. Because then she couldn't even pretend that he would call. As he'd promised.

Now, as she hung up the phone from a check-in call on one of Almost's oldest citizens, Dorothy Bean, Taylor was suddenly acutely aware of the silence in the house. Even as depressed as they were, her three sons were seldom *quiet*. She rapped on their door, hesitated, then pushed the door open.

All three boys looked up from where they sat on their individual beds, notebooks in their laps, pens or pencils in their hands. Determination set each of their jawlines, and their blue eyes seemed steely with resolution. Strangely, they didn't look so much like her or Doug; they resembled Steve on the morning he'd left their home. They all wore his "nothing you can say or do will make me change my mind" expression.

What an odd legacy to leave her children.

"What's going on, boys?" Taylor asked, aware that the last time she'd caught them writing something, that something had brought Steve Kessler hotfooting it to Almost.

"We're writing Steve some letters," Jonah said, breathing heavily.

Even as her heart gave a slight leap of mingled hope and sorrow, Taylor realized that Jonah hadn't suffered an asthma attack since the day he and his brothers had discovered the nearly dead guy. Or was it more closely connected than that? He hadn't experienced the loss of breath since Steve Kessler's arrival. And now that he'd departed...?

She shook her head. That thought was ridiculous. Jonah's asthma was a *physical* condition. The doctor in Lubbock had stressed this to her and Doug when Jonah was first diagnosed with the troublesome ailment. No, his improvement had been a matter of less dust in the air, more moisture...not anything to do with Steve Kessler, Texas Ranger.

"Can we take 'em over to Aunt Sammie Jo's to mail when we're done with them?"

Taylor frowned, wondering what they were writing Steve, somewhat envious of their courage in doing so and wishing she could steal a measure of it. "It's too hot to go out," she said.

"Yeah, but if we wait, these won't get out of Almost until tomorrow."

"And besides, we've got community service at Almost Antiques this afternoon. We *promised* Jose."

"You'll be working indoors?"

The boys brightened. Taylor thought it was a pretty sad state of affairs when performing community service was preferable to sitting around contemplating the failure of their grand scheme.

Jason wheedled, "And Jose's got air-conditioning. Kinda. He's got an old swamp cooler anyway."

"As long as you promise you'll go straight there after dropping off your letters at Aunt Sammie Jo's."

"We promise!"

Those promises again, Taylor thought. She wished she could ask what the boys had written in the letters.

"Can we have three envelopes, Mom?"

"Yeah, and some stamps?"

"Aunt Sammie Jo has stamps," Taylor said, "And why don't you just put all three letters in one envelope."

The boys looked at her aghast. Josh said, "Well, like, it wouldn't be the same. You know, like we each wanted to send him a letter but were too cheap or something to send them out all by themselves."

The logic escaped Taylor, but she fetched them the necessary three envelopes.

As her sons took off for Sammie Jo's and then to Jose Caldrerros's Almost Antiques, she found herself grateful for their absence. Their enforced tenure indoors combined with their depression over the loss of Steve Kessler only served to underscore her own restlessness and despondency.

For the first time in her adult life, Taylor found Almost too small, too restrictive. Maybe a little too cloying. The caring, the nurturing, the day-to-day details of a daily life suddenly felt pointless and shockingly meaningless. Taylor told herself she had no reason for thinking this way. Then, because of that no reason at all, she began to cry.

Steve had thrown himself into the pornography investigation with a desperation only matched by his loneliness once he had to leave his high-rise office and go home to his sterile, empty condominium.

During the day, hard at work, pressing everyone on his team to resolve this case as soon as humanly possible and probably sooner than that, Steve could tell himself that he hadn't run from Almost, from Taylor, that he'd only done his duty and gotten out of that single-gas-pump town in the middle of nowhere.

But at night, alone in his bed, he couldn't hide from his longings, couldn't duck any truths. He'd been scared. Pure and simple. Taylor Smithton had touched him in ways he'd given up believing possible years before, back in the days when he'd been content to dream of a woman in a photograph, sorry he couldn't have her, but glad, if anyone did, it had been Doug, his friend.

And when he'd married her look-alikes, however unknowingly, he'd attributed the failures to something lacking in him, rather than seeing that he'd married women who were the exact opposite of Taylor's warmth and sincerity. And yet he'd been hurt when they hadn't been like the way Doug had described Taylor. He'd been hurt when they hadn't conformed to his image of Taylor.

Then, once in Almost and inundated with the force of her personality, he hadn't been able to hack the raw, unvarnished honesty ever present in her clear eyes. In her kisses, in her touch, in the love for her children...and him?

And he hadn't been able to hack the idea that someone...Taylor...could see the soft side of him. He'd been terrified that vision would come back later and lay him flat out.

He told himself that if he was stupid enough to resort to his youthful fantasies and fall for a girl-next-door type in a pissant town politicians didn't even bother to visit, then at least he'd been smart enough to get out before his ultimate destruction had come to pass.

The trouble was, he thought, he didn't believe this garbage. For it was garbage. Taylor might be the girl-next-door type and the town might be so small as to warrant only an unnamed dot on a road map, but she wasn't the kind of woman a man should run from. She was the kind of woman a man, a whole, honest man, would grab hold of and never, never let go.

He'd been worried about revealing his inner feelings and having them used against him, so he'd run as far and as fast as he could. And *that* had proved to be the most torturous route to have taken.

During the past five days, he would occasionally hear a throaty glissade of laughter and turn his head, searching for Taylor, his heart beating faster, his fingertips tingling with the need to touch her, to draw her into his arms and promise her the sun, moon and stars forever, if she would only agree to love him. Her laughter lingered in his mind. Her honest tears lingered in his heart.

He'd used the excuse of his hotter-than-hot investigation to cancel all his Kids versus Crime speeches the past week. But the true reason he'd ducked them was he'd been aware of a burning need to see the boys again, to hear *their* laughter, to listen to their sometimes absurd, sometimes wise observations. To feel a sleepy head lolling on his shoulder, to shake hands with a grubby, dirt-encrusted boy who grinned through lips stained with milk and the remnants of a chocolate bar. He missed watching them romping with their bizarre assortment of pets. He missed his own game of trying to tell them apart.

He missed *them*. It was that simple. And because of them, he didn't want to be around other kids right now, any kids, because short, freckle-faced, shining faces would now, and probably forever, remind him of Jonah, Joshua and Jason.

Doris came into his office then, signaling him that his current case had just escalated up a full flight of stairs.

He grabbed his files and stormed out of the office, ready for battle.

Sure, he thought, he could fight the bad guys; he just couldn't confront one wonderful woman and three enterprising boys and beg their forgiveness for walking out on them.

Chapter 14

Two more days passed, making Steve's time away from Almost exactly one week, and the pornography case had worn to a sordid, anticlimactic finish at roughly midnight the night before. Anyone remotely suspected of involvement in the pornographic ring had been arrested, Miranda rights had been read and repeated, and the smut dealers were hauled off to spend the remainder of the night in jail. Their attorneys would have them back on the streets by the time the day really warmed up. But the evidence secured the night before would eventually lock them away for a healthy portion of their lives.

The case in Almost wasn't going along quite as neatly, Steve discovered, after placing a quick phone call to Tom Adams. *That* phone call hadn't been difficult, utterly unlike trying to contact Taylor. According to Tom, Richard DuFraunt—and assorted aliases—*was* aligned with a Canadian chemical company, ChemCon. ''Get this, Steve, ChemCon is the primary focus of a widespread investigation of drug smuggling. Different division, of course, which is why we didn't snap right away."

Also, Tom said, the Almost citizens' search of their town had yielded one or two more interesting items. Sam Harrigan had discovered a satchel in his barn, a backpack containing bundles of cash, another couple of false passports, some film containers filled with heroin, and to no one's great surprise, a change of Armani casual wear.

"Thanks to Pete Jackson's memory, we're pretty sure this DuFraunt was the Canadian connection to the case last spring. And we're fairly certain, given the discovery of the backpack and his murder, that he was caught skimming some of the proceeds from a haul," Tom said. "Our boy liked the good life. His tastes in clothes, hardware, even manicures, were expensive. Taking some of the product and creaming off some of the cash in the process must have been too great a temptation for him."

"Why Almost? You'd think the heat after the incident in the spring would have kept him a million miles from there."

"The case was essentially folded up. We got the local connection, stopped the drops, basically pulling the plug on the whole shebang. This guy already had an established route, probably ranged as far north as Canada and then on down to Mexico. Almost has a dozen or so barns where he could easily stash his skim-offs. Then all he had to do was dance in later and pick them up with nary a suspicious glance in his direction."

"So you're thinking his death was a hit?"

"Could be. Or it could be we missed the real local connection back then."

Steve had frowned at that notion. He pictured the group of people at Taylor's house, the food providers, the caring neighbors, the concerned citizens of Almost. It was impossible to see any one of them, for any reason, condoning dealing in white death.

"Listen, Tom," he said, "do me a favor, will you?"

"Just name it, Ace."

"Keep an eye on Taylor Smithton and her boys for me, okay?"

Without hesitation, Tom agreed, then added, "Taking the plunge again, Steve?"

"Just watch out for them."

"Actually, I have a guy watching their place already. We were afraid the killer might think the boys may have witnessed a little too much for comfort."

Steve felt his heart constrict at Tom's words. He should be there, he thought. If there was the slimmest chance their lives were in danger, he had no business being six hundred miles away, no matter how pressing his current case had been.

He sat up straight. Hell, he should be there anyway. Danger or no. What was he doing in a high-rise building a day's full drive away from Almost? The only real happiness he'd encountered in his adult life he'd encountered in that little one-horse town in the arms of a beautiful homemaker named Taylor.

He lifted the telephone receiver and punched in Taylor's number before he allowed himself to consider the consequences. And he could picture the exact location of the phone in her kitchen. And her slender hand reaching for the receiver.

He saw Taylor as she'd been on her front porch, a smiling, radiant woman. He saw her rocking on her back porch, her face golden in the light from the sunset, her features serene and smooth with inner peace. And he saw her stricken eyes when he'd announced he was leaving, her lip caught between her teeth when he'd said he would call and then just drove away. *Without a single word about the night before.* Without a word about how she'd turned him inside out, made him wholly defenseless in her honesty, her beauty, her passion.

And he pictured the triplets, saw them playing with their unlikely pets, heard them giggling in their darkened bedroom. *He's coming for you, Jason...and he's got dirty fingernails.* He thought of their determined matchmaking efforts, remembered how easily he'd succumbed to them. How readily he'd gone along with their plans and how swiftly he'd fallen for them.

Hell, he'd fallen for the whole town. That silly little one-horse town in the middle of the high plains, a speck on the face of the Texas-New Mexico map, and he'd give anything to be back there again, walk right out of this bust and be there, sipping iced tea or drinking a cup of steaming hot coffee, surrounded by chaos and clamor, encircled, as Taylor and her sons were, by love and concern and human warmth.

But the phone had gone unanswered, ringing into a silent house. And echoing in his heart.

Doris stuck her head through his opened door. She held out three envelopes to him. "These are from Almost. From your Almost triplets, I'd guess, being the eagle-eyed assistant that I am."

Steve practically hurdled the desk to get hold of them. He was surprised at the depth of disappointment he felt to realize there were only three envelopes. Closing the door against Doris's blatant curiosity, Steve opened the letters as he went back to his desk. He was touched by the fact the boys had sent their letters in separate envelopes. It was as if each of them was extending him an individual and separate friendship.

He pulled out the first crumpled and imperfectly folded

sheet of notebook paper and flipped it over to read the signature, wanting to be able to conjure up an image of the right boy with the right letter.

Jonah. Steve smiled, though the smile would have been there had it been either of the other boys' names, as well. An image of Jonah burst readily into his mind. Jonah the conscience, Jonah the mediator. Jonah the cautious and methodical. Jonah the trusting.

> Dear Steve, How are you? I am fine. We're still sad because you had to go back to Huestin.

Steve grimaced at the message but grinned at the spelling.

> But we've been working real hard on comunity service. Jose—

The poor man's name had been written and marked out at least five times, with Jonah finally settling on "Colthroses."

From his years in the Southwest and from memory of people talking at the nearly-dead-guy party, Steve automatically supplied the correct Spanish pronunciation of Caldrerros and continued reading.

> He runs the antique store. Jose called Mom and said we could work off some of our community servis.

Steve grinned again.

> He has a gun just like the one Kurt Thompson found in Mr. Hampton's field. We all hope you can

come back to Almost soon. Mom's real sad, I think, but won't talk about what's wrong. I think she misses you a lot. Love, Jonah.

Frowning now, Steve ripped open the second envelope, this one from Josh. Steve could more readily hear Josh than picture him. *Way cool. Like, just way, way cool. Yeah.*

Dear Steve, Like, gosh, you shoulda been hear. Jose Cauldrenhose has us like working in his junk shop. Rember, he was like out of town when we found the nearly dead guy, but he like came home yesterday. He asked us all about it and stuff. Jason said the killer could still be after us 'cause we mighta seen something, like him killing the guy. I hope you can come back to Almost like soon. We need to solve this case. Your fan, Joshua Smithton.

Steve smiled at the full moniker. Only Josh. "Now Jason's," he said, opening the final envelope and smoothing out the letter, picturing the bravest but most sensitive of the three. Jason so readily took on the older-brother role that he often forgot they were only minutes apart and he was just as much a kid as the other two.

Dear Steve. How's it going, man? We're in the middle of a heat wave around here and it's BORING BORING BORING cuz we can't go outside or anything.
Doc gave us up to Jose Cuhdrayros—

Steve stood up without being aware of doing so.

And blood was coming out of his mouth...and he held out a hand toward us and said, "Cold dray horse."

"Oh, dear God," Steve muttered, gathering the letters together in a tight fist. He was out of his office and racing down the hall in less than three seconds flat.

"Where're you going?" Doris called after him.

"Book me a flight to Lubbock," he called, jabbing his finger at the elevator button. "Those kids are working community service with the man who murdered Du-Fraunt! And call Tom Adams—have him meet me in Almost. And call Taylor and tell her to get her kids out of that antique store!"

The elevator door finally opened and he all but flew inside, stabbing the button leading him to the parking lot. By the time the door opened in the basement garage, he'd already checked his weapon, made sure his cell phone battery was charged and was fully prepared for action.

And as he screeched his car out of the garage, he began to smile. As excuses went for showing up where his reception might be understandably chilly, this one was a doozy.

Chapter 15

Taylor was leaning against the broad counter at her aunt Sammie Jo's minimart, listlessly absorbing another lecture on the benefits of picking up the telephone and simply calling Texas Ranger Steve Kessler, when he walked into the store.

When Aunt Sammie Jo broke off speaking at the tinkling of her miniature cowbells hanging on the door, Taylor didn't bother to turn to see Alva Lu, Mickey or Martha. But when Aunt Sammie Jo's hand automatically lifted to adjust her wig, Taylor felt the transfer of tension and somehow just *knew* Steve was there.

She couldn't move, couldn't turn around.

"Sammie Jo..." he said, his voice low and gravelly and fitting too perfectly in the grooves etched in Taylor's heart.

She closed her eyes, picturing him removing his hat, dusting it gently against his muscled thigh as softly as a caress. *Why had he come back?* He'd made it clear in his absence and his sustained silence that the happenings in one tiny town in the Panhandle didn't concern him.

"Well, Taylor honey, lookit who's here." When Taylor didn't look, her aunt shot her an inscrutable glance, then shifted her gaze back to Steve. She continued tartly, "Forget something, Mr. Kessler?"

For the past week, Taylor had heard every possible discourse about her own cowardice, her lack of gumption, her own ineptitude at "catching the only good thing that's likely to come down this road in a century or two" and her apparent stubborn need to cling to the past. But the moment the man returned, all Sammie Jo's ire was reserved for him.

"Like a bad penny," Steve said, "I just keep showing up."

"You've got that right," Aunt Sammie Jo snapped, but she smiled nonetheless and fished a couple of quarters from her cash register. "My, it's a real scorcher today. Think I'll go get me a soda." Without another word, she left the counter and went out of the store via the back door.

"Taylor…?"

Half hoping that when she turned around she'd find she'd been mistaken about his looks, mistaken in her feelings for him, mistaken about everything, Taylor finally pivoted to face him.

As she'd pictured, he filled the space in the doorway, six feet four inches of solid muscle and broad shoulders. His hair shifted in the draft from the ceiling fan a scarce five inches above his head. His lips were parted slightly, as if he were somewhat out of breath. And his jaw was set in that harshly determined line she'd caught glimpses of on her children's faces only a few days before.

She schooled her own features to what she hoped would

be read as polite impassivity. "Hello," she said, and was vaguely pleased to find her voice sounded neutral, collected. If he'd been able to hear her heartbeat, he'd know exactly how shattered she was just to be seeing him again.

"I tried to call," he said.

Liar, she thought.

"There was no answer."

She wasn't about to tell him how many excuses she'd dreamed up so that she could spend the day indoors, sitting and waiting for the telephone to ring, waiting to hear his voice just once more. She lifted a hand and dropped it again.

He frowned. "Taylor, I know how it looks..."

She raised an eyebrow, not bothering to pretend to misunderstand his meaning. "I've come to grips with being the country cousin," she said.

His frown deepened. "What is that supposed to mean?"

"You know, the hick who falls for the city slicker and wants more than he's prepared to give."

"It wasn't like that," he said, stepping forward.

"No?" she asked, leaning back against the counter as if utterly nonchalant. In truth, it was the only thing holding her erect.

He took another step. Taylor remembered the night on her back porch, the first time they'd kissed, when he'd taken one slow step at a time in coming to her. She held her hand up in a classic "stop" signal.

He halted, his hat bouncing on his leg.

"Why are you here, Steve?" she asked coldly.

He looked angry for a moment, then uncertain. "The boys," he said finally. "Didn't Doris get ahold of you?"

If he'd said he'd come because he read it in his horoscope, she would have been no less confounded. "What?"

"They wrote me letters—"

"I know, but—"

"And in them they described working off community service at the Almost Antiques and More."

Taylor frowned. "And...?"

Steve's face was devoid of expression. "You didn't hear from Doris. Are they there now? I've already been to your place and couldn't raise anyone."

Taylor pictured him walking up her front walk, turning the doorknob of a house that was never locked and calling for them. As he'd called her every night in her dreams.

"Taylor...this is serious. Are they there now?"

"Why?"

"I'll tell you later."

I'll call you. I'm not leaving. And now, *I'll tell you later.*

"No, sir," she said, and pushed away from the counter, no longer needing that support. "This time, we play this game by *my* rules. Full disclosure. Clearly defined terms. No vague hints that you'll call me or bedtime promises about not leaving. If you have something to tell me, you tell me now."

Steve blinked at her words and Taylor realized how much she'd revealed in her angry outpouring. But she didn't care. She was tired of feeling abandoned, sick at heart she'd allowed herself to believe so thoroughly in this man that she hadn't listened to the barest modicum of reason. Not even when he'd tried warning her away.

"I think Caldrerros is the name DuFraunt was trying to say when he was...when the boys found him. They misspelled his name so many times in their letters that I finally realized that to someone who didn't speak any Spanish, the man's name could sound like Cold Dray Horse.''

Taylor's breath hitched in her chest and her fingers felt curiously numb and slow as she raised them to her temple. It made a sick kind of sense. Jose Caldrerros had never asked them for community service before, not even to paint his storefront, though everyone else on the single-block downtown district had availed themselves of the boys' sporadic beautification projects.

And she remembered someone at that impromptu party commenting on Jose's absence. And she remembered the boys' excitement at discovering a gun ''just like the one Kurt Thompson found'' at Jose's store. And recalled how many questions he'd seemed to ask the boys about the incident behind Charlie Hampton's barn.

But for all this, and for the terror that welled up in her, Taylor couldn't help one final question for Steve Kessler alone. ''And that's why you came back?''

''Of course it is,'' he said.

Taylor didn't wait for anything more. ''I see.''

''No—''

''Yes, I do,'' she said, rounding the customer counter and reaching for the wall phone. ''I'll call them and tell them to come right over.''

''Taylor—''

She held up a hand for his silence, already punching in the numbers.

''Taylor—''

Jose himself picked up the phone on the other end. She craned forward to peer at his building through Sammie Jo's dusty window.

''Jose? This is Taylor Smithton.'' For a split second, she had visions of his having gagged and bound her three sons. She swallowed heavily. ''I forgot I was supposed to take the boys to the doctor's this afternoon. Would you mind sending them over to Sammie Jo's?"

Jose said something about them sorting out items in the back but that he would send them right over. "There's nothing wrong with them, is there?" he asked.

Taylor remembered how white their faces had been the afternoon they found the nearly dead guy, and how agonized Jason's screams had been during his nightmare. And the questions he'd asked later about his father.

"Oh, no," she lied, hating the man who had brought murder back into her sons' lives. "Just a regular checkup. Before school starts." It nearly choked her to be pleasant to the man. But she didn't dare raise any suspicions.

She hung up the phone, her entire body trembling.

Steve's hands dropped to her shoulders. She shook herself free of his touch, though she felt it long after she put at least three feet and the customer counter between them.

"No," she said firmly.

"Taylor…you have this wrong. I didn't mean—"

"Oh, Steve, don't tell me what I have wrong," she said tiredly. "I was just stupid, okay? I can live with that. I've lived with tougher things than falling for a man who doesn't want me. Trust me on that one. I'll survive." She whirled to leave before he could see the tears leaping to her eyes. "Thanks for coming to tell me about the kids."

"Taylor, damn it…!"

The tinkling bells on Aunt Sammie Jo's front door drowned out the rest of his reply, but she wasn't an inch through the door before his hand encircled her upper arm and yanked her back inside.

"You don't know a damned thing about anything," he snapped, pulling her to him.

"No?"

He looked as if he literally might explode. His face was

mere inches from hers and she thought, irrelevantly, that he hadn't had much sleep since she saw him last. And she wanted to lift her hand to his brow and readjust that lock of soft brown hair that seemed to fall there just for her fingers to touch.

He'd apparently abandoned his hat on Sammie Jo's counter, for his other hand rose to take her other arm. "Don't you get it, Taylor? Nothing about this was *your* fault. I tried telling you that after we kissed that first time. I'm a *two*-time loser. I've failed at marriage *twice*. I'm exactly the kind of sap that *does* fall in love after one kiss. Why do you think I practically came unglued when the kids said that? Why do you think I argued so vehemently against the idea? I mean, I picture the whole shooting match, kids, picket fences, dogs.... You think I was going to trust my instincts this time around? What instincts? I told myself I would rather *lose* you than go through that hell again!"

It seemed as if everything cold inside her, everything that had been frozen for an entire week, softened then melted all at once. And yet, he hadn't really given her anything with his impassioned outburst. He'd only half explained.

Tears welled in her eyes, as if proof of her thawing.

"Taylor, honey," he said, "don't cry...don't you understand? I don't want to lose you."

"You can't lose what you threw away," she murmured, knowing this was true, hating the part of herself that needed to say it.

"Oh God, Taylor—"

The front door burst open again, sending the cowbells flying up to meet the wall and jangle back down again.

"Steve!"

"Cool!"

"Hey, Mom, Steve's back!"

"Is this why you called us?"

"Why are you crying, Mom?"

"Those are happy tears, doofus. Remember? In that movie?"

"Oh, yeah."

"Jose asked us a whole bunch of questions about you, Steve."

"Yeah, just a few minutes ago even. We didn't know you were back in town. We could of told him."

Taylor swiped at her eyes, having broken from Steve's grip at the first jangle of Sammie Jo's bells. She was struck by the expression on Steve's face. Acceptance, annoyance, relief and a rather exasperated well of love for her sons.

The back door opened and closed. Aunt Sammie Jo said from behind the customer counter, "I tried to head them off at the pass, but they weren't having any of it."

"We don't really have to go to the doctor's, do we?"

"Heck no, doofus. She was just tricking us about Steve."

"So, what are we going to do now, Steve?"

Steve dropped hands on two of the towheaded boys grinning up at him and brought his knee up to jostle the third. "Well, I think we're going to get the bad guy."

The three boys whooped and swamped him with a hug.

And over the cacophony, Jonah told the group at large, "I told you. It *is* just like that movie. First he gets the bad guy, then he gets the mom."

While Steve waited for Tom to show up, frustrated that he couldn't continue his discussion with Taylor—only the single most important discussion of his entire life—he filled the boys in on Jose Caldrerros's possible role in "their" case, and all three were inclined to believe it had been their perspicacity in misspelling that had given Steve the final clue to the possible identity of the killer.

To his delight, they were much less concerned about the potential danger to themselves than the fact that Jose had been both friendly to them and generous in the tasks he assigned them—and paid them for their work, unlike everyone else in town. To their payment they assigned perfidious motives.

"He was just trying to buy us off."

"Yeah, like a bribe or something."

"Or trying to make us feel debted to him, so he could ask us favors in the future."

"He's a bad guy, doofus, not like a mafioso."

"Steve, a guy can be a bad guy *and* a mafioso, can't he?"

Taylor's face was pale, Steve thought. She looked as if she hadn't slept well in days. It wasn't fear of confronting Jose Caldrerros that had robbed the color from her cheeks or added the faint shadows beneath her eyes. He knew that reason lay at his door.

He'd done this to her. Her statement, *You can't lose what you threw away,* haunted his every movement now, colored his vision.

He'd been so busy running from his own instincts that he'd caused pain to the one woman he would have moved heaven and earth to have spared. And her sons? They, thankfully, were too young to understand that hearts could be permanently bruised, that walls could be erected that had no doors. So they had simply written him, asking him to come back.

And yet, he realized, watching them, watching their mother nervously drumming her fingers on the customer counter, wasn't he being far too simplistic, discounting what he already knew about them? They had been too young to suffer the loss of a parent and had survived that particular hell. They hadn't been too young to understand what had happened, they'd been young enough to wish otherwise.

And were willing to go ahead and work toward making their dreams come true.

Steve heard a car door and straightened. But what held him perfectly rigid wasn't the sound of Tom Adams's rolling gait across the boardwalk leading to Sammie Jo's store, it was the realization that he, Steve Kessler, Texas Ranger, was the boys' dream.

And that they—and their loving, beautiful mother—were his.

Chapter 16

Steve thought it was the hardest thing he'd ever done, to walk away from Taylor and out into the oppressively hot Almost afternoon. She'd called his name just before he closed the door, but when he turned back, she'd only looked lost, a cross between hopeful and abandoned.

But she wasn't abandoned, he thought. And if he had his way, she never would feel that way again. Maybe they hadn't said all they needed to say. Maybe a lifetime wouldn't take care of everything he wanted to say to her. But she'd let him know in her anger, in her hurt, that he'd been wrong to distrust his instincts.

Everything about her was what he wanted in a woman. Everything.

You can't lose what you threw away.

He'd only lifted a finger to tell her to hold that thought, that he'd be right back to finish their discussion. To tell her that he'd never thrown anything away in his life and wasn't about to start with her.

And he was smiling as he crossed the street to confront Jose Caldrerros, the connection they'd been looking for.

Tom cleared his throat before they hit the far sidewalk.

"Nervous?" Steve asked.

Tom chuckled. "Nope. But someday you gotta tell me how you put this one together. We only stumbled on the Caldrerros angle after your Doris called to order me to be here."

"What angle?" Steve said, reaching into his jacket to release the holster strap on his gun.

"That there's a South American drug family with the same last name. We never put it together before."

Steve shot him a look. "Only just found this out, did you?"

"Yeah, well, you know how it is, right hand doesn't know what the left hand is doing. You didn't know it then? So how did you stumble across it?"

Steve grinned down at his old college roommate. "I didn't. I just knew he was involved in the fancy dudes' death. And I only found that out because Doug's kids spell as badly as you do."

"Whose kids? They looked like yours back there."

Steve resisted an urge to glance back and wave, knowing they would all be looking out the window of Sammie Jo's minimart. "Could be," he said, and had the oddest feeling he was jinxing everything by this simple, if heartfelt, admission.

Tom, who had spent some fifteen years chiding him for bad calls and worse choices, nodded and cuffed him on the arm. "About time, Ace. You've been in love with her since the first time you saw her. And I mean back in college."

"Are you going to knock on the door or do I have to?"

"You're taller. You be the target this time."

* * *

Taylor held her breath as she and her aunt and the three children pressed faces to the store's dirt-encrusted front windows and peered through the tall, slanted reversed lettering.

She watched as Steve accompanied Tom Adams across the street to Jose Caldrerros's Almost Antiques and More. While the sight of the two men, as dissimilar in height and shape as day was from night, should have struck her as humorous, the only thought she had was that she and Steve hadn't finished talking.

And on the heels of that realization came the awareness that she *never* wanted to be finished talking with Steve. His biggest crime with her had been in leaving things unsaid, unresolved. How much better that than saying things that might have ended them once and for all?

The boys had broken in before he'd been able to complete his sentence, a statement that began with *Oh God, Taylor*... What had he been about to say? What might that have resolved for her?

She wanted to wrench Sammie Jo's jangling door open to call after him that before the boys had burst in, she hadn't meant her last words to him to sound so final, so conclusive.

She'd even called his name out before he and Tom exited the store, and he'd turned. But she hadn't recanted the words, she'd only looked at his expressive eyes, the face she'd once thought capable of masking every emotion. A myriad of longings had waved across his features at that moment, robbing her of speech, stealing any and all thoughts from her mind.

"I'll be right back," he said, and then lifted a single finger in a gesture that was both a farewell and a promise.

Steve and Tom, a law enforcement equivalent of Mutt

and Jeff, strolled across the road cutting through Almost
and ducked—at least Steve did—beneath the sagging por-
tal over Almost Antiques and More. They nearly disappeared into the deep shadows of the doorway there.

"Do you think Jose will put up a fight?" Jonah asked.

"Doofus, what's he gonna do against—"

"How come they don't call in a SWAT team or something?" Josh asked.

Not taking her eyes from the shadowed porch, Taylor
said, "We don't know for certain that Jose really had
anything to do with our mystery. This will be routine
questioning only."

In dramatic contradiction to her words, a gunshot shattered the silence of the Almost heat-baked street. Two
more shots followed in quick succession. The high-
pitched ringing sound lingered after the percussion faded.

All five of the watchers, the boys, Sammie Jo and Taylor, jumped and shrank back from the window as if injured themselves.

"Jeezly crow—"

"Mo-om?"

"Oh, merciful heavens," Sammie Jo said, her hands
finding Taylor's shoulders and gripping painfully.

"He's all right," Taylor murmured, gathering her sons
to her, enfolding them in her arms as Steve had done with
her on the night of Jason's nightmare. She rocked them
back and forth, never once taking her eyes from the antique store. "Sh. He's all right."

Martha Thompson stepped out onto her front porch and
looked from the Antiques and More to Sammie Jo's minimart and back. Cactus Jack came around from the back
of the store and leaned against one of his gas pumps,
shading his eyes against the glare of the western sun.

It seemed hours before Tom Adams burst out through

the store's doorway and into the street. He held a portable cell phone to his ear and his previously immaculate white shirt was now blotched with blood.

Taylor's heart seemed to freeze in her chest.

Tom looked at the minimart for a moment with obvious disquiet, drew a deep breath and seemed to force himself to cross the street. He held up a hand at Cactus Jack but continued on toward the store.

"Wh-where's Steve?"

"He's with Jose, right, Mom?"

"Why does Agent Adams have blood on his shirt?"

The cowbells pealed an inappropriately merry announcement when Tom Adams entered the store.

Taylor looked up at him from her crouched position in front of the window. She couldn't ask, couldn't speak. She'd held her sons to comfort them only seconds before. Now they seemed to be holding her the same way.

Tom said hurriedly, "He must have known something was up. Caldrerros, I mean. Probably my car. I dunno. He opened fire before we could get out five words. The ambulance is on the way. I already called them."

"Steve's dead?" Jason squeaked, his fingers digging into Taylor's arm.

"No! No, he's not dead. I felt a heartbeat. He was wearing his Kevlar vest. Thank God." Tom felt his own, obviously vulnerable chest. "But he took it point blank. Minimum range. No range. Hell, the blast knocked him back five feet—"

"I don't think these boys need to hear every detail, young man," Sammie Jo interjected tersely. "Just cut to the chase."

"Oh, right. Well. Anyway, he was...knocked cold."

"Mo-om?"

"What about Jose?" Sammie Jo asked.

"He's down. I gotta get back over there," Tom said urgently, and left the store to run back across the highway. They all heard him tell Cactus Jack that he'd rather no one came over to the Antiques and More.

It was all he'd needed to say to have them all remaining exactly where they were, lifeless statues, immobile and frozen, watching and waiting for twenty long minutes before screaming ambulances arrived and paramedics scurried into the antique store and carried out two limp figures, one long and lean and the other short and trim.

"Mom! Mom, come quick!"

"Steve's on TV!"

"Where are you, Mom?"

"Mom!"

"Back porch!" Taylor called, trying to still her suddenly accelerated heart rate at hearing the news that Steve was on television. Being interviewed? He was *alive?*

The back door banged open and Jason spilled onto the back porch, bare feet flying, face whiter than she'd ever seen it. "You gotta come see, Mom!"

And he burst into tears.

Taylor jerked out of her rocking chair, a part of her mind noting that it rocked as violently as when Steve had pulled her up and into his embrace.

"Jason. Honey...oh, no."

"It's Steve, Mom. They're talking about him...saying he's...he's..."

Taylor felt as if every ounce of her blood sank to her suddenly leaden feet. She had to grasp the back of the wildly bouncing rocking chair for any degree of balance.

"It's on the news, Mom. Right now."

Josh called from the lighted kitchen. "Come on, you guys! It's on the news!"

Taylor was never able to remember later if it was Jason or she who crossed the back door's threshold first. But she knew she was the first into the living room. As races went, it wasn't one she particularly wanted to have won.

Jonah stood at full attention before the television set, his face rigid, his breathing labored. Josh pressed in against her side, silenced by the announcer's frightening report. Jason kicked the wall behind her and ran out of the room to slam and bang his way into the boys' bedroom.

"Is Steve okay?" Josh asked.

"Not again," Jonah muttered. "Not again. Not again."

Taylor reached for his hand. He grasped it painfully hard.

"I don't know yet. Wait…" Taylor murmured, stroking Josh's hair absently, her entire focus on the sixteen-inch color screen. *No. Not Steve.* And like Jonah, *Not again.*

"To recap the events of this afternoon, the Texas Rangers and the FBI in a cooperative effort once again joined forces in the West Texas town of Almost to roust drug smugglers from this small community. In a savage shoot-out, one of the purported drug smugglers was shot and is in critical condition at a hospital in Lubbock. Also shot in the melee was Texas Ranger Steven Kessler."

Though she'd known it, Taylor couldn't help but moan a little at hearing it repeated so starkly on the news.

The telephone started ringing.

"According to police, the injured Ranger, a ten-year veteran of the Texas Rangers and two-time awardee of the Texas Gold Star, the top honor a Ranger can achieve…"

"No…please…" Taylor whimpered, unaware she was sinking to the floor.

"Is he dead, Mom?"

"I don't…know, honey," Taylor mumbled, her eyes burning, her soul in flames.

"Contributor to various charitable organizations. His condition, at this point, remains a mystery."

Josh dropped down beside her and wrapped his arms around her numb leg.

The phone continued to ring.

"According to sources within the Texas Rangers, Kessler had just completed an investigation of the Sunrise Corporation for some three months, helping to identify key players in a large-scale child-pornography ring. That case was resolved less than twenty-four hours ago, with seven members of the Sunrise Corporation arrested for possible connections with the child-pornography ring. Kessler had been working with the FBI on the Almost case less than a month. If viewers will remember, just last spring…"

The telephone ceased ringing, but the field reporter continued her simultaneously sterile and vampirishly excited story, which seemed utterly alien to the facts as Taylor and her family had witnessed them.

"At just after 4:00 p.m. this afternoon, Jose Caldrerros, presumed to be a member of a well-known drug family operating out of Brazil, opened fire on an FBI agent and a Texas Ranger as they approached his place of business in Almost."

The scene on the screen switched to footage of the Lubbock Hospital and then a map of South America.

"Damn it, is he alive…?" Taylor whispered, unaware she was doing so, unaware she was swearing, devoid of any and all consciousness except that of needing to know about Steve.

She pictured his raised finger, the promise behind the

gesture. She remembered her last words to him. *You can't lose what you threw away.*

The telephone began to ring again. Taylor glanced toward the kitchen and frowned before looking back at the television. She was close enough to the set that she could have touched the screen, and yet it seemed far, far away, as if she were looking at it through a long pipe, a tunnel miles long.

"The fallen Ranger, noted for his active involvement with youth projects and law enforcement sponsor of the Kids versus Crime program, was transported to the Lubbock hospital in critical condition, despite the fact that informed sources say he was wearing a bullet-proof vest."

The primary announcer said they had an expert on hand to tell the viewers about the fallibility of bullet-proof vests.

A nervous man in an ill-fitting suit and bow tie came on the screen. "The idea that anything short of pure steel, and even that can be a misnomer, can stop a .357 or a .9mm bullet is really a myth. You see…"

The phone began ringing for a third time. This time Josh released her leg and pushed to his feet, stumbled into the kitchen and nabbed the phone from its perch. "What?" he demanded rudely. Then his voice altered, though Taylor couldn't hear his words. He came back in seconds.

"Who was it?" Taylor asked dully, never taking her eyes from the television set.

According to the primary announcer, while Steve had been transported to Lubbock, the FBI and fellow Rangers were moving in on Almost to secure the town and all evidence left behind after the shoot-out. So were the media crews. Live coverage would continue through the night, until the situation was resolved.

Josh had waited. "It was Aunt Sammie Jo. She's coming over."

Taylor closed her eyes, fighting the hardest war against tears that she'd ever waged and praying with all her heart and soul that Steve would survive. "Please, please…oh, just *please*."

Less than an hour after the second newscast at ten— some twenty-five people had gathered again in Taylor's snug living room. There would have been more, but most of Almost's population went to bed before the ten o'clock news, which at this time of summer was mere seconds after dark, and no one wanted to rouse them. Bad news could always wait until morning.

But those who were awake drifted to the Smithton house as softly and easily as leaves fall from trees in the colder, darker days of autumn. Some brought food, as they'd done only a week before. Some wore thin shawls over their nightclothes and shivered in her living room, unused to central air-conditioning. Some busied themselves in the kitchen, finishing up the dinner dishes and polishing and repolishing her already clean table.

Aunt Sammie Jo sat on Taylor's sofa between Mickey Sanders and Alva Lu Harrigan. Sammie Jo's Dolly Parton wig was wildly askew, and Alva Lu had pin-curled her hair with bobby pins and a thick black hair net. All three women were holding hands and staring at the television, waiting for the latest update on the young man they'd met such a short time ago.

Charlie Hampton came in the door without knocking, the way people did if children were asleep in the house or if someone had died. He didn't say a word but took up a spot behind Taylor's chair, resting his large, callused hands on her shoulders and squeezing lightly. Comfortingly.

Carolyn and Pete Jackson arrived, carrying their sleeping daughters, whom they took into the boys' room to deposit on a pallet made of extra sleeping bags and sheets. Like Charlie Hampton, Carolyn didn't say a word, only sat on the floor beside Taylor's chair and pulled a limp, chilled hand into her own.

"I told him he couldn't lose what he threw away," Taylor said, her voice breaking, admitting finally how deeply she'd plunged into a future with Steve. And horrified that those, of all words, should have been her last to him. "Just this afternoon. Right before he got shot. That's what I said to him, Carolyn."

"It's okay, Taylor," Carolyn said, squeezing her hand, chafing it, bringing warmth if not a blanket panacea.

"This is just like when Doug was killed," Martha Thompson whispered to Homer Chalmers.

Taylor looked over at Martha, afraid her words might be true, shell-shocked by the memories the night revived. Terrified of what the outcome of *this* vigil might be.

"I've already lived through this," she murmured, unaware she was probably squeezing Carolyn's hand too tightly.

"Then you can do it again," Carolyn said softly, lifting her sister-in-law's hand to blow warm breath over it.

"Can I?"

"Sure. Because you have to."

"I only knew him a few days," she said.

Carolyn pressed Taylor's hand to her face. "I fell in love with Pete the first morning he was at our place, when he didn't know whether to sit down at the kitchen table and eat his breakfast or start running for the nearest exit."

Jason came out of the bedroom, his face scrubbed of

tears but somehow looking all the more vulnerable because of the washing. His freckles stood out on his pallid face. "Is he dead yet?"

Shocked gazes ricocheted between Taylor and her "eldest" son. All that could be heard was the faint drone of the turned-down television set and, from the kitchen, the clatter of dishes being put away.

Taylor took her son's hand in hers and held it tightly. "We don't know anything more, honey."

He looked down at her, a fierce expression on his face, his eyebrows drawn to a frowning vee. "If he is okay...I don't want him coming back here."

Aunt Sammie Jo spoke up from her vigil spot on the sofa. "Jason, you don't mean that."

"Oh, yes I do!" he burst out. He yanked his hand free from his mom's. "I'm sorry we ever wrote that letter. And I wish we hadn't written him our second letters. I'm sorry he came here. I'm sorry we wanted him to kiss you so... s-so he'd be...our *dad.* You know why? 'Cause dads *die!*"

Taylor rose swiftly and enfolded her son in her arms. She led him from the room and down the hallway to her bedroom. She waited until she'd propelled him through the opened door and shut it behind them before turning him roughly to face her.

"If we hadn't wr-written him that letter, he wouldn't have come back h-here and—"

"Listen to me, Jason." She shook his shoulders a little until he looked up through panicked, tear-filled eyes. "It was wrong to write that first letter to Steve. Okay? You with me? It was full of lies and it was wrong because of that."

"I know, but—"

"But it *wasn't* wrong to want someone like Steve as a new dad. It *isn't* wrong to want somebody around to love you, to play ball with you guys, to take you out to fly a kite or just to watch TV with you on a Sunday afternoon. There's nothing wrong with wanting someone to love and who will love you back.''

Jason shuddered with a near violent spasm and thrust himself into her arms and clung to her so tightly it hurt. And yet it was the first glimmer of warmth she'd felt all night.

''He's just gotta be okay,'' he said.

Taylor wished she could pull a promise out of the hat and hand it to her son. *He will be. He'll be just fine.* But she knew, perhaps better than most, that reality often interfered with promises.

Like having to leave town for an investigation in Houston? a humbled voice inside her asked. Like not trusting twice-failed instincts?

''I want to wait up until we know for sure,'' Jason said. His voice quavered, but his chin showed a man's determination to see a terrible event through until its ending, good or bad.

Doug would have been so proud of him right then, she thought. And so would have Steve. Doug, the father of blood. Steve, the father of choice.

''We may not know tonight,'' Taylor murmured, remembering another desperate period of waiting, another dark time. She kissed her son's soft blond head.

''I don't care. I've gotta know.''

''All right. But if the other boys are sleeping, let them stay that way. Jenny and Shawna, too.''

''Nah. They're awake. They're playing cards,'' he said, then walked out of the room.

She was alone for the first time since she'd heard the news about Steve, since she'd seen the ambulance taking him out of town. She sat down on her bed, her hand trailing across the cool quilt, remembering what it had felt like to lie there with Steve, to gasp as the cold material touched her passion-heated skin.

She remembered being amazed at how far they had traveled that night, from strangers to lovers. And how abandoned she'd felt when he wouldn't look at her the next morning when he left, and that she'd felt that his silence and avoidance of her gaze had transformed them back into strangers.

And then, he'd come back. And he'd tried to explain his absence, his abrupt departure, and even understanding him, understanding what he might have been trying to tell her, she'd said, *You can't lose what you threw away.*

And she'd seen the longing on his face, the hurt in his eyes. And the hope. Dear God, she'd seen the desire for a future. The love of her sons, the ache for her.

And then she'd heard the shot that struck Steve, and the sound had reverberated down into her deepest sorrows and stirred the still-warm coals and brought a flood of unwanted memories back. But the feelings of coldness, of bleak despair she experienced now had nothing to do with the past and everything to do with the unpredictable present.

They had exchanged no commitments, had formed no ties. All she had was a living room full of caring people and the memory of a single perfect night and a few scattered, chaotic hours. All she had was nothing.

Her bedroom door opened and Aunt Sammie Jo entered. She stopped in front of the vanity mirror to straighten her wig, then joined Taylor on the bed.

"You probably don't know this story," she said without preamble. She took the hand Carolyn had tried to warm in hers. "Your mama was working in the Amarillo library right out of high school. Her family was from that neck of the woods. And your daddy…well, Barney had just been drafted and was all set to go to boot camp down in El Paso. The war was on. He knew he would be shipped out.

"I remember how he stood up so straight and tall in his new uniform. He looked every inch a man. But he was shaking in those shiny new boots. And what does that poor young ranch kid from Almost worry about just hours before he has to go off to war? That he had a library book overdue." She rolled her eyes.

"I think the book was *Thunderhead* by Mary O'Hara. He'd already had it checked out two months. He was like Carolyn's girls, horse mad. Of course, I've always liked her myself. Anyway, he could have just dropped that overdue book in the big box in the front of the library and walked away without a backward glance, but he wasn't that kind of young man."

Taylor watched the smile unfurl on Sammie Jo's face and felt some of her own tension relax. Her aunt looked suddenly years younger as she once again became Barney's kid sister, remembering her big brother's romance.

"He explained his situation to the pretty little librarian at the desk. Of course, that was your mama. That sassy little thing just up and lied to him. I don't think she ever told another lie in her whole life, but she lied right then. She lifted up a piece of paper and waved it in his face and told him it said that the government had passed a ruling that no soldier could be fined for overdue books while serving their country. And that each soldier was allowed to pick out one book from the library to take with him overseas.

"I don't know if he believed her or not. It doesn't matter. But he had the good sense to ask her what time she got off work. He took her to a cheap coffee shop and they both drank coffee and talked. And they talked some more. Until it was well past midnight and she had to go before she was locked out of her rooming house.

"But your daddy wouldn't let her go. They kissed beneath the branches of a big weeping willow tree right there in downtown Amarillo. Marry me, he told her. And she said yes. Just like that. And they loved each other every day of their lives together, Taylor. And you and Craig and Allison coming along all those years later only made things better."

Taylor's eyes had filled with tears during her aunt's gift of a story. She shook her head.

"Aren't you listening to what I'm telling you?" her aunt asked, sounding exasperated.

Taylor tried to smile and failed miserably. "Aunt Sammie Jo, I'm listening. I know what you're trying to tell me. Believe me, I know how easy it is to fall in love on one kiss. I did it with Doug, I did it with…but don't you see? Steve didn't say anything about loving me, Aunt Sammie Jo. He wouldn't even look at me the next morning." She felt a prick of self-consciousness that she'd revealed the full extent of her relationship with Steve. But she needn't have worried, not with Sammie Jo.

"He probably felt badly about having to leave Almost and go back to Houston," her aunt said reasonably, patting Taylor's hand.

"When he came back today, I told him I was just foolish, a country bumpkin who missed every signal he sent my way."

Aunt Sammie Jo smiled. "Country you are and always will be. Stupid, you are not. You're one of the most sensitive women I know…and I mean that in the good old-fashioned sense of the word, not the newfangled need-therapy kind of way. You have a knack of picking up on the merest hint of a stray emotion. So let me tell you, you wouldn't have let him kiss you if he hadn't been right there in the front seat of the car with you."

Taylor tried smiling but felt her face crumpling as her aunt's faith in her instincts sank in and she remembered what Steve had said about distrusting his own. Then, as she'd done as a child when some dreadful misfortune had occurred, she fell into her aunt Sammie Jo's warm embrace. She felt her aunt's thin arms wrap around her, holding her as tightly as she'd held Jason earlier. "Darling girl. Sh. It's okay, honey girl."

Aunt Sammie Jo rocked her slowly, gently, murmuring her name over and over while she cried. Finally she patted Taylor on the back. "Time to buck up, Taylor. You've got guests in your living room and sons cheating at cards to worry about."

Taylor felt five years old again as she straightened, brushed at her cheeks and fumbled on the nightstand for a tissue.

Her aunt waited until she'd cleared her nose before patting her knee. "Now you gotta face what Jason said out there."

"It's okay, Sammie Jo. He didn't mean it. He was just worried."

"I know that, *doofus,* but what I'm worried about is that you might be thinking along those lines yourself."

"What…?"

Sammie Jo's thin hand squeezed Taylor's leg. "I know you've had the thought you would never deal with another peacekeeper. I've heard you say it myself. Then this handsome, soft-mouthed Steve Kessler comes along and turns your whole world upside down. Then he leaves. And now, like Doug, he's been shot."

Taylor stiffened. "I know. I'm fighting it, Aunt Sammie

Jo. But I can't help feeling a little bit like Jason did a while ago. If he is okay, and if he does come back here— and both of those are pretty big *ifs* right now—how can I just relax with him, knowing that he could go out there and get killed any second? How can I put my kids through that? Again?"

Sammie Jo shifted a little to face her. She reached up and gripped Taylor's chin tightly between her bony fingers. The grip was painful and shot her straight back to her childhood.

"Now you listen to me, girlie girl. *Everybody* dies. That's the only truism we got in life. The only one. Everything else is just gravy."

"But—"

Sammie Jo's hand squeezed even tighter, then she released her. "But nothing! The moment we're born the clock starts ticking. Some go sooner than others. Like Craig. Like Doug. Like your mama and daddy. Hell, like your cousin Susie when she was just eighteen years old."

For just a moment, a stark longing leapt to Aunt Sammie Jo's face as she remembered her daughter and the long years without her.

Then she scowled. "Others, like that old buzzard Homer Chalmers, live for a hundred years and plague us every day they're alive. But the simple fact is, we're all going to go one of these days."

"Not by bullets," Taylor interjected. "Not by being a target for some psycho with a gun in his hand!"

Sammie Jo shrugged. "Piffle. I've never known you to talk such nonsense. A gun, a knife, a gruesome car accident...those are dreadful, sure, but so are heart attacks, cancers, this AIDS virus going around. What difference does the cause of death make? I'll tell you, sweetie, none at all. And worrying about it doesn't make a lick of sense. Look at *me,* honey. I know I'm going to die.''

"No, Aunt Sammie Jo—the chemo's working!"

Sammie Jo chuckled. "See, there you go again, thinking *cause* not *truth*. The breast cancer may not get me, and God willing it won't, but *something* will. A car, a heart attack or maybe Alva Lu's sponge cake.''

Her aunt patted her cheek then and stood up. "You lost a good man when you lost Doug Smithton, Taylor. You know that and I know, too. It could be this young fellow might not make it through. That'd be a real pity. But, if he pulls out, I have to tell you I like what I see in this Steve Kessler. He's been hurt some, and he's been around the block a time or two. But that's good because you've been hurt some, too, and you and him wouldn't get to first base if the teeter-totter were unbalanced. You like him. The boys adore him. They need and want a daddy. And, Taylor, honey, *you* need somebody. And more than that, I think you want *this* somebody.''

Taylor felt tears well in her eyes again.

"Besides which, Cactus and I want a fourth for bridge.''

Chapter 17

It was close to midnight when Taylor's front door crashed open, startling everyone still remaining in her living room.

Sammie Jo, who had been slumped against Alva Lu Harrigan, snoring softly, her wig again wildly askew, jumped some three inches and managed to jab a sleeping Mickey Sanders with her sharp elbow.

"Damn it, Taylor," a deep male voice thundered in the doorway, "don't you ever answer the phone?"

As one, the entire group gathered in Taylor's living room turned to see who had arrived so late. And as one, all eyes widened. Then, with the exception of Taylor herself, everyone smiled and turned warm, congratulatory looks in her direction.

She didn't see them. She only saw the man filling her doorway, filling her heart. "Steve..." she whispered, hoping she wasn't asleep and dreaming.

He smiled at her and stepped across the threshold and into the living room.

"What—"

"How—"

"Sh! It doesn't matter how he got here. He's *here*."

It seemed to Taylor that a thousand miles separated them, and yet, in some deep, inner core, she knew he would cross that chasm. One inexorable step after another.

"I thought he was shot?" Mickey said, her voice querulous from sleep.

Steve flicked her a glance. "I was. But I was wearing a vest."

"But they said on TV…"

"I know," he said. "I heard it. They also called it a melee. Jose Caldrerros just got the drop on me, that's all."

"But you were shot," Sammie Jo said. "Tom Adams said."

"Oh, yeah. Jose nailed me." Steve rubbed his chest gingerly. "Knocked me about five feet and out cold."

"You were shot in the chest and are up and walking?"

Steve shook his head. Taylor half wondered how a dream could be so realistic that she could notice such small details. "Yes and no. I was hit, but the vest blocked the actual bullet. Lucky for me he wasn't packing an AK47. The best in the world wouldn't have saved me then."

"But Tom said—"

Taylor flinched but Steve didn't bother to look in the direction of the speaker. His eyes were locked with hers. "Tom didn't know if I was badly hit or not. We've lost a goodly number of officers from bruised hearts because of the impact. So it's standard operating procedure to get a fallen officer to a hospital immediately without giving any information out to the public."

"We weren't the public," Cactus Jack said irritably.

"That little twerp on TV was right about one thing—

bullet-proof vests don't protect against everything. I was out cold until we were almost in Lubbock. I've been on every heart-monitoring device known to man since then.''

For Taylor, much of this conversation seemed surreal, as if everyone in her living room were a part of her dream and, in that strange way dreams have, were speaking separate and foreign languages. The only reality for her was that Steve was alive and taking yet another step forward. And that was the most suspect reality of all.

"Are you all right?" he asked her.

She didn't answer, afraid if she tried, the dream, the *beautiful* dream, would end and she would wake to find herself asleep in the easy chair, surrounded by other dozing supporters, and the eager news announcer would be informing them that he'd died.

"Taylor...?" he asked, his eyes locked with hers, his hat missing, his hand half-outstretched toward her.

"I thought it was like with Doug..." she whispered, linking her fingers together, afraid to reach for him, afraid to want anyone quite as much as she wanted him.

"It's not like with Doug," he said firmly. And took another step closer to her. "I'm not like Doug."

"No...I know."

"Do you want another Doug?"

"No..."

"Good."

The boys' bedroom door banged open and her sons and their cousins bounded down the hallway and spilled into the living room.

"*Steve?*"

"Hey, like, way cool!"

"Steve's back!"

"And he's, like, *alive* and *everything!*"

The children eddied around her like water around a

rock midstream, then continued onward. They fell upon Steve, hugging him, petting him, pushing him off balance. And yet he never took his eyes from hers.

"What did you say?"

"Was it you who shot Jose?"

"Is he dead?"

"We thought you were dead."

"Like Dad."

"But it's not like Dad."

Jason pulled on his sleeve, forcing him to look down at them. "Mom said it wasn't wrong to wish you were our dad. She said it wasn't wrong to want you to love us."

Something on Steve's face shifted, seemed to melt, and his eyes lifted to Taylor's. "You told them that?"

She felt a frisson of reality work its way down her arms. She nodded.

With three boys attached to his legs and arms, he still managed to take another step closer to her. "And do you believe this?" he asked.

"'Course she does," Jason said.

"Yeah, like, why would she tell Jason that if it wasn't, like, true?"

"Are you gonna kiss her again?"

"Yes," Steve said, and somehow gently freed himself from the remaining obstacles to reaching her.

Taylor held her breath, knowing she was awake now, more awake than she'd ever felt before in her life. She was both aware of all the eyes volleying between them and strangely ignorant of them. These were her friends, her family, her community. It seemed oddly fitting that they should be witness to this unusual moment, to this dramatic meeting.

Steve took the last step he needed to touch her and yet

didn't reach for her, merely waited for her to signal him, or perhaps for her to understand that he really was there, that he'd stopped distrusting his instincts.

"I tried to call you, Taylor," he said.

She didn't know if he meant during the week before or during the vigil and realized it didn't matter. She nodded, still more than half-afraid to break the spell, but aware now that she wasn't dreaming, that this was real, however perfect a dream.

"And I tried to run away from you."

Again she nodded.

"But I couldn't."

She wanted to ask him why not, perhaps needing to hear the words.

As if reading her mind, he said, "Because I love you, Taylor. I always have. Tom Adams knew it. Maybe even Doug knew it. The women I married…they looked like you, but they weren't like you at all. They weren't kind. They weren't warm. They didn't have an entire town for a family. They didn't have three great kids. You do, Taylor. You have all those things and so much more. All the things I've ever wanted in a woman. Ever wanted period."

And still he didn't touch her, didn't draw her into his arms.

Sammie Jo clapped her hands loudly in a single, sharp slap that made everyone jump and jerk their eyes in her direction. "Dang it, girl, kiss him!"

"Yeah, Mom, like, *kiss* him!"

"We forgot about that…it's like in that movie, she's gotta kiss him back."

"Oh, yeah, *that* movie."

"So are you going to kiss me?" Steve asked, his eyes shy even though he was smiling down at her.

"Yes," she said, meaning so much more. And she rose up on her toes to cup his face and press a kiss to his lips.

His smile faded and his arms wrapped around her and pulled her sharply to him. "God, Taylor, I love you so much it hurts."

She pushed that strand of hair from his brow and smiled mistily up at him. "It doesn't have to hurt, Steve. Because I love you, too."

And oblivious of the crowd happily watching them— children, aunts, uncles, friends, well-wishers all—Taylor wrapped her arms around his neck and pulled him down for a deep, telling and utterly honest kiss.

It wasn't a kiss of regret or even of longing. It was a kiss born of hope and dreams yet to come. And she knew, in his returned kiss, in the passion that flared between them, that he'd finally found what he'd most desperately wanted.

And in the silence around them, she knew their kiss, their *love* were sanctified and somehow blessed by her friends and family, by the town, and augmented by the hopes and dreams of everyone watching them.

* * * * *

Be sure to watch for the next book in the
ALMOST, TEXAS *series, coming soon from*
Silhouette Intimate Moments.

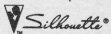

SHARON SALA

Continues the twelve-book
series—36 HOURS—
in October 1997
with Book Four

FOR HER EYES ONLY

The storm was over. The mayor was dead. Jessica Hanson
had an aching head...and sinister visions of murder.
And only one man was willing to take her seriously—
Detective Stone Richardson. He knew that unlocking
Jessica's secrets would put him in danger, but the rugged
cop had never expected to fall for her, too. Danger he could
handle. But love...?

For Stone and Jessica and *all* the residents of Grand Springs,
Colorado, the storm-induced blackout was just the beginning
of 36 Hours that changed *everything!* You won't want to miss a
single book.

Look us up on-line at: http://www.romance.net   36HRS4

Share in the joy of yuletide romance with brand-new
stories by two of the genre's most beloved writers

DIANA PALMER

and

JOAN JOHNSTON

in

LONE STAR CHRISTMAS

Diana Palmer and Joan Johnston share their favorite
Christmas anecdotes and personal stories in this
special hardbound edition.

Diana Palmer delivers an irresistible spin-off of her
LONG, TALL TEXANS series and Joan Johnston crafts an
unforgettable new chapter to **HAWK'S WAY** in this wonderful
keepsake edition celebrating the holiday season. So
perfect for gift giving, you'll want one for yourself...and
one to give to a special friend!

Available in November at your favorite retail outlet!

Only from

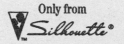

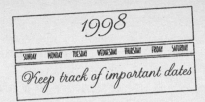

1998

| SUNDAY | MONDAY | TUESDAY | WEDNESDAY | THURSDAY | FRIDAY | SATURDAY |

Keep track of important dates

Three beautiful and colorful calendars that celebrate some of the most popular trends in America today.

Look for:

Just Babies—a 16 month calendar that features a full year of absolutely adorable babies!

1998 CALENDAR
Just Babies
16 months of adorable bundles of joy!

Hometown Quilts 1998 Calendar
A 16 month quilting extravaganza!

Hometown Quilts—a 16 month calendar featuring quilted art squares, plus a short history on twelve different quilt patterns.

Inspirations—a 16 month calendar with inspiring pictures and quotations.

Inspirations
A 16 month calendar that will lift your spirits and gladden your heart

Steeple Hill™

HARLEQUIN®

Value priced at $9.99 U.S./$11.99 CAN., these calendars make a perfect gift!

Available in retail outlets in August 1997. CAL98

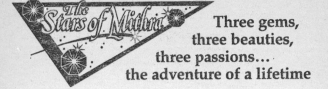